PELE'S TEARS

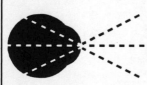

This Large Print Book carries the
Seal of Approval of N.A.V.H.

PELE'S TEARS

SHARON K. GARNER

THORNDIKE PRESS
A part of Gale, Cengage Learning

GALE
CENGAGE Learning·

Detroit • New York • San Francisco • New Haven, Conn • Waterville, Maine • London

GALE
CENGAGE Learning®

LIBRARY OF CONGRESS CATALOGING-IN-PUBLICATION DATA

Garner, Sharon K.
   Pele's tears / by Sharon K. Garner.
      p. cm. — (Thorndike Press large print clean reads)
   ISBN-13: 978-1-4104-4362-5 (hardcover)
   ISBN-10: 1-4104-4362-0 (hardcover)
   1. Women glass artists—Fiction. 2. Floriculturists—Fiction. 3. Gems—Fiction. 4. Kauai (Hawaii)—Fiction. 5. Large type books. I. Title.
   PS3557.A71669P45 2011b
   813'.54—dc23   2011035060

Published in 2011 by arrangement with Tekno Books.

Printed in the United States of America
1 2 3 4 5 6 7 15 14 13 12 11

To strong women and dear friends:

May we know them; may we be them; may we raise them.

Donna S.
Doris G.
Dorothy B.
Jeanne A. and the members of the Clue-finders mystery readers' group
Kriss K.
Laura M. E.
Pearl G. (in memory)
Peggy B. (in memory)
Rose Anne S.
Sherron S.
Shirley S.
Susan P.
Vivien K.

Long may we rave!

And to the cats who have owned me: writing partners, heart mates, and dear companions always.

CHAPTER 1

"Where's Lani and who the devil are you?" Dante Kahoa's unmistakable voice floated up from the open front door at the foot of the stairs.

Lani twitched when she heard it. It was her second shock in as many minutes, making her eyes widen and her fingers tighten on the paper she held out in front of her with two fingers of her left hand. Two minutes ago she had been peacefully packing stained glass projects in her cottage's loft. Then she opened an envelope and found this, and now Dante was downstairs.

She tore her horrified gaze away from the paper. Holding it in that way was a useless attempt to distance herself from the pain generated by the words printed on the heavy paper in a fancy font and in blood red ink. She'd found this one, her second, a moment ago in last week's stack of mail she had carried up to the loft at some point and forgot-

7

ten. The words were printed larger this time. Two words had been added. This one read "Pele's Tears — or him." And printed drops of blood dripped down the page. Her tormentor was getting creative.

Downstairs, her Australian friend Aidan responded in a good-natured way. "She's somewhere about the place, and the name's Aidan. No need to ask who you are, mate. Lani told me all about you."

She felt a little jab of satisfaction that Aidan was holding his own. The ringing strikes of his special hammer against a chisel on her flagstones had ceased just before she'd opened the envelope. She had promised him a beer, which was the reason he was out front now, taking a break and standing squarely in the sights of a blast from her past. She had a suspicious nature where Dante, her childhood friend, was concerned. Was his presence here at this moment merely a coincidence?

She glanced at the note again and common sense kicked in. It was laughable to even think that Dante might have sent it. Notes would be too subtle for him. No, there could be only one reason he was in Maine: to haul her *'ōkole* back to Lehua. Well, he could try.

She dropped the note, resisting the urge

to kick it away, squared her shoulders, stood tall, and started down the wide-tread stairs on unsteady legs, still clutching a soft buffing cloth in her right hand. For a moment, she felt ready to take on Dante and the future.

As she descended below the floor level of the loft, her former partner in juvenile crime was revealed to her from scuffed *paniolo* boots, up a long, muscled body that appeared to go on forever, to a venerable black Stetson. His cowboy look was new to her and it suited him. When she backtracked to his Hawaiian-sky blue eyes and their warm, appreciative stare locked in first on her bare legs then points north, she swayed under the impact and abruptly sat down. Any stair step would do.

Dante Kahoa, tall, broad-shouldered, and with presence to spare, could easily be a member of the old *ali'i,* Hawaiian royalty. She had believed it when she was twelve, and she still believed it looking at him now.

"*Aloha,* Dante. I thought I recognized the voice, or maybe it was just the attitude." A catch in her voice ruined her shot at nonchalance.

He draped himself bonelessly against the frame of her front door, bisecting the remaining small amount of space with one long arm and one long-fingered hand resting against the opposite side of the opening, effectively keeping Aidan behind him and barred from entering.

"You know them better than anyone, Lani," he said in that slow, deep, resonant baritone that gave his words power and still gave her chills.

Dante had sprung that voice, clear and firm, on her one day when he was thirteen; there had been no breaking or warbling for him, unlike his poor brother. And that new, intensely male voice had rocked her adolescent world many times.

Now the sound of his voice regressed her to a rapid, embarrassing succession of too personal memories: She had been fourteen and had set a rendezvous with a local bad boy in Lehua's flower prep shed. She was ten seconds away from turning Noa Takei loose on her bra hooks when Dante and Noa's brothers walked in on them, in a kind of intervention for Noa. She was collateral damage, in that Dante did his own intervention on her at the same time, away from the others.

She gulped before diving in to drown the memories. "So what brings you to Maine?"

He produced a momentary sneer that would have put Elvis to shame. "You sent for me, so you can skip the innocent part." The words were packed in ice.

She stilled. She had sent for him? *I sent for him?* Had he received a note and, just as she had suspected him a minute ago, he had automatically suspected her? Her brain would tie itself into knots, along with her tongue, if she kept up this convoluted train of thought or tried to voice it. Distract by attack, that was the thing to do in any situation involving Dante.

"If you think I sent for you, then you've been drinking too much 'ōkolehao, all by yourself at Lehua," she said, but her bravado was a little wobbly.

The corners of his wide mouth lifted in a cockeyed grin. "Wondering about my love life already? What makes you think I'm alone at Lehua? And I haven't touched *ti* liquor since you and . . . since you got dog sick on it when we were kids." Pain took a swift journey through his eyes, wiping away the grin.

Her breath hitched. She knew the name that belonged in that pause; she saw the face that should be at Dante's side right now. Dom. Dante's gentle twin brother had joined her in trying 'ōkolehao for the first time one night in one of the high fields. He had also shared her misery and had thrown up beside her. With any memory of Dom came the guilty belief that Pele's Tears, with her help, had cheated Dominic Kahoa out of his life and had cost Dante his brother.

Dante apparently read her thoughts, nothing new there, and had decided to take the conversation where he wanted it to go. His expression changed and she braced herself. One of his pronouncements was coming, however much she didn't want to hear it.

His voice, though pitched low, rang out in her small entryway. "You know why I'm here. It's time to get past whatever is keeping you away from Lehua. It's time to get your *'ōkole* back home, Noelani Beecham."

In reaction, she shot to her feet and her fingers clenched within the cloth's soft folds, reminding her that it was there. She lobbed it across the short distance separating them. It smacked Dante in the middle of his broad chest. He scarcely blinked. Together, they watched gravity peel her embarrassingly ineffectual missile of choice off his shirt, in slow motion, and deposit it at his feet.

"Go home, Dante. I didn't send for you in any way, shape, or form. And I think it would be better for everyone at Lehua, especially you, if my *'ōkole* stays right here."

Ignoring the storm warnings gathering on

his features, she deliberately studied his battered Stetson, crisp, sedate plaid sport shirt, black jeans halfway into the broken-in stage, and his hard-worn, sensible leather boots that mocked both dudes and urban cowboys.

At first, he stood quietly beneath her cool examination, but he soon retaliated with a sharper scrutiny of her that brought heat to her cheeks. She steeled herself for the fierce battle heading straight for her quiet life. Just as she drew breath, he flanked her.

Disarming as anything, Dante's lips curved into his familiar, welcoming, gentle smile that meant home to her and made her blink at the little boy peering out from the man's tawny, even-featured face.

"*Aloha,* Lani," he said softly.

And the years instantly fell away, along with her ability to breathe, hauling her back to her first visit to Kauai. She was running stark naked between the fraternal Kahoa twins, four years old to their five, on Lehua's tiny beach, while Rosemary Kahoa, their grandmother and her godmother, looked on. From that moment, Dante had fascinated her as brown-eyed Dominic never could, and she was forever bound in some mysterious way to *this* brother with the Italian name and the Hawaiian sky in his eyes.

When she was older, and having come to better know the bearer of the name, she had looked it up in a baby name book, deciding that Dante, "enduring," had been his parents' blessing as well as his given name.

And Dante wouldn't let her abandon Lehua. The image of the man he'd become, standing before her now, blurred when her eyes filled with sudden tears.

"Damn you, Dante," she whispered.

She was dimly aware that she launched herself toward him off the stairs. He caught her against his broad chest, as smooth and hard as *pāhoehoe* lava beneath his shirt. With his arms around her, and hers around his neck, she breathed in the familiar scent of him, his aftershave layered with . . . Dante. He effortlessly lifted her off her feet and rocked her from side to side.

"Nice catch," she murmured after allowing herself a minute to wallow in safe and warm and don't go there.

She slid down the front of his body onto her feet, an unexpectedly aware journey on her part. She returned his smile, dragged herself away from the memories, and took a step back from the biggest one. A lone coherent thought waded out of her emotion-clogged brain: She couldn't go back to Lehua — yet it was becoming unbearable for her to stay away any longer.

"*Aloha* to you too, Dante."

Aidan watched them from the doorway then edged past, giving them an assessing look out of the corner of his eye.

She felt guilt, regret, and sympathy in equal measures. Her friend had offered his stonemason skills at cost to replace the damaged flagstones in her hallway, a condition of her cottage's sale. And he had run smack into this. Up until a few minutes ago, she and Aidan had been heading for something more than friendship. That attraction and its potential had crashed and burned the moment she'd seen Dante in her doorway.

When she caught Aidan's eye, she mentally shook herself. "Where are my manners? Aidan, this is Dante Kahoa."

"We've introduced ourselves, more or less," Dante replied.

"Yes, I heard." Her voice tightened. "Aidan, you'll have to excuse Dante. Where he comes from, he's *kahuna, ali'i,* and all-around dictator wrapped up in one overbearing package. He sometimes forgets himself when he's out in the real world."

"It's the same place you come from, Lani. And you already told Aidan all about me."

15

Self-confidence rolled off Dante in waves. The result was that she wanted to slap him stupid. She longed to kick him as well, remembering just in time that her feet were bare and his boots were sturdy. A palpable force in the air made her glance from one male to the other. The two men hadn't taken their eyes off each other. Understanding came quickly. They had squared off, each silently taking the other's measure.

"Look at you," she said in amazement, "like a pair of dogs sizing up each other, standing stiff-legged in my hall."

"There's no harm in that, as long as we don't lift our legs against the woodwork." Dante grimaced more than grinned and held out a hand to Aidan, who took it with a matching expression. "It's nothing personal, Aidan, just that Lani and I have important business to discuss. The clock's ticking on a legal matter."

"No worries. I've work to do," Aidan replied and continued down the hall, leaving her to her own devices — or, rather, to Dante's.

She had seen Dante in action many times before, in a watered-down, young adult version, so she was familiar with the mixture of exasperation and awe bubbling inside her now. Rosemary, Dante's *tūtū,* grandmother, on one of her visits to Maine had tried to prepare her for this day, warning her that Dante had refined his skills. She'd said her grandson had grown into the kind of man that honest men liked and trusted, without knowing how or why it happened. She'd also said he had matured into the kind of man that women of all ages wanted — women who had no doubts at all about what, exactly, they wanted him for.

Dismayed at Dante's use of the words "legal matter," which gave him leverage, disconcerted at how slickly the full-strength, mature Dante had neutralized the other male present and suddenly conscious of her disheveled appearance when Dante, while waiting for her answering move, again let his gaze trail down over her, she mentally put up her hands and surrendered.

"I concede the first round," she responded, glaring at him. "Come into the kitchen where I can kill you in peace. Besides, I owe Aidan a beer."

Having dressed early that morning for a long, lonely, hot day of packing up her workshop, she wore khaki shorts that bared quite a length of her legs and a cropped red cotton tee that flashed a modest stretch of midriff below her full bust. Somewhere along that day's obstacle course, she'd

17

kicked off her "slippahs," leather sandals in this case rather than flip-flops.

Her curly, wavy hair, which Dante and Dom had told her years ago was the light chestnut color of a *hapa* wood tiki, was haphazardly pinned to the top of her head with a pair of chopsticks, a trick Rosemary had tried to teach her — and which she apparently hadn't yet mastered. The chopsticks waged a valiant but unsuccessful campaign to keep her hair from curling onto her cheeks and neck.

Aware of all these things that put her at a distinct disadvantage against the neat, clean, well-groomed, well-covered man behind her, she keenly felt Dante's head-to-toe appraisal from behind as he followed her down the flagstone hall to the kitchen. By the time they'd traveled the short distance, irritation as well as self-consciousness warmed her cheeks.

She closed the kitchen door behind them then leaned against it. "Know this, Dante. You'll have to drug me, get me drunk, or knock me out and carry me onto a plane to get me to go with you to Lehua."

Had he forgotten that it had taken Rosemary's death to get her back there for even a few hours three months earlier?

"Know this, Lani. I promise you that any

and all of those things can be arranged." He stood beside her scrubbed pine farmhouse table and swiped his hat off his head, every line of his body shouting tension. "Look, you sent for me, forced me to come to Maine to get you, and I'm ready to reverse the favor. You *are* coming home with me."

She spied a healing gash high on his forehead, sidetracking her thoughts. "So what happened to you? Father, brother, husband, or one of each?"

He touched the three butterfly bandages holding together the edges of the wound at his hairline. "Innocent of all charges. It was a temple dog, actually. I heard a sound out in the garden and went out to see what it was, without turning on the lights. Somebody had moved one of Tutu's garden statues right out into the middle of the path. I laid myself out like a *kālua* pig in my own garden."

In the old days, she would have laughed at the thought of Dante laid out like the pig in the pit at a *lū'au.* Now she got chicken skin, the Hawaiian version of goose bumps, all over her body when she thought of the possible connection between the threatening note lying on the floor above their heads and an object moved out into a Hawaiian garden path where Dante would approach it at speed in the dark.

"I stand corrected this time, but the mental picture alone is worth a thousand words," she replied soberly. Maybe she would tease him more about it later. Right now, she was still surprised he'd shared the embarrassing story with her. "I know! It was probably someone else you kept accusing of sending for you. I did *not* send for you. *How* did I send for you?"

He scowled, resembling more than ever a tiki god. "Two words on a plain sheet of paper. No return address but a Portland, Maine, postmark on the envelope."

She wasn't fast enough to swallow her gasp. So Dante had received a note and had been set up for an accident. Her first note had been only two words.

Better make sure.

Her throat was so dry now that she nearly croaked the words. "I don't live in Portland. And these two words were 'Come fetch'?"

He watched her through narrowed eyes. "That's how I interpreted them. It's time for you to come home anyway. Are you afraid the Aussie will get lonely? Bring him along if he's that good."

His words and insinuating tone, and the immediate heat in her cheeks, swept everything else from her mind. She gaped in open-mouthed surprise and shock but recovered quickly.

"Back off the big brother role, Dante. You have no right to play it. It's none of your business now who I choose to . . . do whatever with." Her voice skittered to a halt while she made flapping motions with one hand. "I swear you're part sheep dog where I'm concerned."

"Maybe. I herded you away from trouble often enough."

"I'm familiar with that thought process. You tried it all, did it all, so I didn't have to."

Her skin temperature ratcheted up several more degrees under the weight of his knowing look, which was quickly followed by a darkening frown. He sailed the Stetson onto the table.

When he started toward the door she was blocking, and Aidan on the other side, she took a step forward to meet him, pulling open the door behind her. At the same time, and without conscious thought, she reached out and placed her right thumb in the middle of Dante's chest, on his breastbone.

In their younger days, the trick had worked with both brothers, somehow making them unable to move forward. She had gloried in this tiny bit of physical power she had over

21

them. She suspected that Dante humored her now when he stopped advancing, although he showed great interest in her action.

After staring at her rogue thumb then looking up into his face, she said loudly, "Aidan, Dante is wondering about *my* love life now. He wants to know if we're lovers."

Dante's face briefly went slack with surprise and shock before a grudging smile tugged up the corners of his full, sculpted lips.

Out of sight, Aidan continued pounding, but a grin played in his voice when he answered. "The thought has crossed my mind once or twice, mate. Any chance of that cold one, luv?"

"I'm getting it," she answered, bumping the door closed with one hip that was well trained in *hula*.

She gave Dante a flat-palm pat where her thumb had been and what she hoped was a smug look as she swung away toward the refrigerator to pluck a longneck bottle off the top. They stayed nice and warm up there, just the way Aidan liked his "cold ones."

CHAPTER 2

"Cheers, luv," Aidan said, flashing a grin at her and a neutral look Dante's way, before she again closed the door between the two men.

Dante jerked a chair away from the table and folded his long body down onto it. "*I* stand corrected this time. When was the last time you checked your mail? If you didn't send that note to me, then maybe you got one too. Mine came last week."

She dropped into the chair nearest her before she spoke. "Actually, I've gotten two, at last count. Why didn't you call me about yours?"

"For the same reason you didn't call me about yours. I thought you'd sent it. After that, I was busy getting things in order so I could leave the farm and come here to sort you out — and trip over a stupid garden statue in the meantime. We have fields of anthuriums coming on to harvest, you know." Accusation spiced every word.

"Well, I didn't send it. And if I moved something so you'd fall over it, I'd want you to know it was me. And you also know I always have a lot more to say than two words."

"How well I know it. With you back at Lehua, there goes the peace and quiet."

"I'll check this week's mail," she muttered through clenched teeth. "I stopped home delivery two weeks ago. I picked up a pile last week, carried it up to the loft then forgot about it until a little while ago. That note, the second, is upstairs. I picked up another batch today."

The neat pile of mail lay forgotten and unopened beneath some newspapers on a narrow table in the hall. During her hurried mail run earlier that day, she'd scarcely looked at the haul. Now she carried the stack to the kitchen, sat down, and scooted the pile toward Dante. She watched his long fingers walk through the business-size envelopes, ignoring the rest, until he paused, picked out one, and flipped it across the table to her.

She pulled back, not wanting to touch it. Pain emanated from that long, white envelope with the Lihue, Kauai, postmark, along with something confusing, nasty, unnerving, and very possibly evil.

"Open it," Dante said softly.

"You open it. I already opened one today. That's my limit."

"I'm here with you this time, and it won't bite."

When she was with Dante, she often found she was able to do things she couldn't or wouldn't do on her own, whether she wanted to or not. With fingers that trembled, she picked up the envelope and sliced it open with the letter opener she kept on the kitchen table.

Inside was the familiar heavy paper folded into thirds. The two damning words were printed on it in their fancy font in blood red. There were no added words or printed blood drops this week. Dante reached over and plucked the paper from her nerveless fingers, making her jump. He threw it down after he read it. Neither of them said the two words aloud, eyeing each other instead.

Pele's Tears, Kahoa style, weren't the small, tear-shaped pieces of lava usually associated with that name. The Kahoa's Pele's Tears were something quite different indeed. A hidden trio of egg-size gems, in fact. And that's exactly what Rosemary always said, egg size.

She finally spoke. "This is number three. I

burned the first one. Last week's, up in the loft, has a dash and the words 'or him' added after the, um, first two words. I opened it moments before you showed up with a broken head."

She paused, again unsure. "So help me, if you're playing games, Dante. *'Iole* sounds much too pretty to mean 'rat,' but an *'iole* by any other name . . ." She gulped softly.

"I've been called worse. By you, no less. But I don't play games like this, Lani. You know that. And I've tried hard never to lie to you, and I wouldn't start with something like this. I didn't send this or the others." He exhaled on a heavy sigh.

"Although you've practiced judicious withholding of information on me, sneaky and subtle certainly aren't your style. And you don't have a cruel streak. But if we didn't send the notes to each other, then who sent them to us?" *Who else might know about Pele's Tears?* she added silently, with a shudder.

"Maybe someone Tutu talked to during her family research."

"And who, specifically, might that be? Because that eliminates probably only half the population of the state of Hawaii." Still shaken, she pushed herself away from the table, going to the sink to fill the electric

26

kettle and switch it on. "Coffee?"

"I thought you'd never pick up that pot." When she turned his way, he gently slapped one hand palm down on the tabletop, apparently coming to a decision. "Side trip. Look, Lani, I see the Sold sign out front, and I heard in town that you sold to raise cash. This has to be the perfect time to come home." He indicated the note on the table. "We'll sort this out there."

Nobody in town actually knew why she was raising cash. It was just in case, in a weak moment, she might decide to ship her worldly goods, and her sorry self, halfway around the world to Hawaii. Home.

"Then the note alone didn't give you this sudden need to see me back at Lehua?" she probed, making her hands stop grouping up kitchen things to pack. Or to sell. Or to send . . . where?

"It prodded me, especially when I thought you'd sent it. But the main reason I need to see you at Lehua is Lehua's legal and financial bottom lines. You own half of everything now because Tutu wanted us to share it. Your half comes with responsibility because mine sure did. I'm willing to share."

Dante's grandmother, who had left them equal parts of Lehua Flower Farm on

Kauai, had been both godmother and a second mother to her, bringing her to Lehua every summer then taking her in at age twelve when her parents died on a notorious, twisting two-lane California highway.

Her voice grew thick with memories. "In another month or so you'll own all of it anyway if I default on the residency clause."

"You think so? But you're not going to default." His gaze sharpened. "So you actually read some of that ocean of paperwork the legal eagles generated? I'm glad."

"Some, as you said. I don't want or deserve anything from you or Lehua. Since Dom . . ." Her voice choked to a halt. "Surely you don't think I belong there."

She remained where she was, turning her back toward him to stare out the big double window above the sink. It looked out on what had been her land, between two hills, to the Atlantic Ocean. The view usually calmed her.

Dante gave a little snort of disbelief. "You belong there as much as I do. You're an orchid in a sunflower patch anywhere but Lehua. It's in your blood. Your soul is in Lehua. Like my blood and my soul. I'll never own all of it because half will always be yours, whether you want it or not. Don't ask me how or why, but you belonged to

28

Lehua from the moment you set foot on the place. We all saw that."

He was right. She hadn't felt at home, or even comfortable, in her own skin since she'd left Lehua. And now was a good time, with most of her stained glass projects that weren't contracted going into storage until she decided what she wanted to do with them — and herself.

"I'll consider it because of what I owe you and Rosemary, but I won't be bullied. It's my decision."

Yeah, right. Now that Dante is applying pressure, I'll be a diamond by the time he's finished with me.

She busied herself again by setting out mugs and the cookie jar. "It's the height of the tourist season around here, you know, and I sold the furniture from the guest room. You'll have to make do with an inflatable mattress. How long are you staying?"

"I'm needed at Lehua, the half owner who gives a damn about the place." He paused. "It's not just Lehua that needs you, Lani. I need you. I admit it. So come home and lord that over me. But help me. Please. I thought we'd head back the day after tomorrow."

She turned to him, her arms opening to encompass everything around them. "Are you serious? I couldn't possibly be ready to go anywhere by the day after tomorrow." Her hands ended up on her hips. "And if you 'need' me at Lehua then why haven't you come to Maine to harass me and bully me into it before now? Or you could have just visited any of the times Rosemary came over."

He apparently found her salt and pepper shakers riveting. "I kept in touch. I was busy on the farm."

"Occasional postcards at first that said, 'Hi, Lani. How are you? Gotta go do this or that,' fill in the blank there, until you stopped sending them entirely. That's keeping in touch? And since when do you need an invitation to do anything you want to do?"

His blue gaze slammed into hers. "I don't. But the last time I checked, the Pacific was an equal opportunity ocean. Planes and ships still go both ways. It's a feature. And you can write, can't you? And e-mail?"

She turned away from its intensity. "I know, I know. I'm as guilty as you are for not staying in touch. But you know why I can't go back to Lehua."

Her mind drifted toward brighter memories of Lehua where, thanks to Rosemary, she now had a place to live and work at her craft, along with a steady income — but only if she returned there to do said living and working. She admitted silently, again, that she yearned to go home to the place she loved more than any other.

By the time she finished wallowing in memories, Dante had made the coffee and nearly emptied the cookie jar. She wasn't surprised that he'd figured out how to operate the French coffee press. He'd always been a quick study and a good problem-solver.

"Hungry, as usual?"

"Always." He looked at what was left of his snack. "Kona coffee. Macadamia nut cookies, my favorite. You're wearing red, my favorite color. Are you sure you didn't expect me?"

"Nobody could ever prepare for you, Dante."

"True. What smells so good?"

She pinned him with a look before she went into the small pantry off the kitchen to fill a colander with the last of her potatoes and carrots. "You're in luck. I'm using up the last of my fresh food today and cooking a pot roast." She glanced at him before turning away to peel potatoes. "I was amazed at what Rosemary did, you know. I don't want or deserve half of Lehua. I'm

31

not of Kahoa blood."

"But you're of Kahoa spirit. And you have a few drops of Kahoa blood, along with lots of Hawaiian blood from your mom. Maybe not as good as Kahoa . . ." he added softly.

She couldn't help the tiny laugh that choked through unshed tears. "Well, maybe a pint of mongrel Hawaiian."

"Tutu knew where you belonged," he said softly from behind her.

She'd forgotten how quickly and quietly he could move. She froze for a second before continuing her peeling with a firm grip on the paring knife. She felt the heat of him, standing close yet not touching her. He deliberately blew on the back of her neck, his warm breath tickling and making the curls dance that had come to rest there.

She hunched a shoulder against it. "Stop."

"You moved as far away from Hawaii as you could go, but Tutu knew." His voice changed, becoming flat. "You should have come back to the house after the funeral. That was some *lū'au*."

"I just couldn't bear it," she said on a gulp, the words forcing past the lump in her throat. "And I can't go back now!" The words burst from her, their edges ragged.

"Oh, yes, you can. And you will. For your sake and mine and Lehua's," he said, his

32

voice rough.

"I'll give you my half when the three months are up," she told the potato she held. "I'll sign off."

"Ah, now we come to the part of the legal stuff you didn't read, apparently. You can easily default on residency, and soon, but you can't give your share to me. So I can't allow you to do the first, and it's legally impossible for you to do the second."

She frowned at the potato. "What do you mean?"

"I mean I'd have to buy you out, which I can't afford to do, so your half goes on the market if you default on residency. There's a survivor's clause too, just to make things interesting. The only way either of us can get all of Lehua right now is to kill the other one. And that prospect is looking less and less extreme, I can tell you," he added, a desperate note in his voice.

Shocked, she swung around to face him, the mangled potato in one hand and her ancient paring knife in the other. She had underestimated exactly how close he really was.

His eyes on the knife, or her chest, she wasn't sure which, he said, "Resort developers are panting in the wings, Lani, waiting for you to do nothing. And you can come home. There are no ghosts at Lehua."

She looked at him with puzzlement and wonder. "I don't understand. Why don't you hate me because of Dom? I hate myself because of Dom."

"I know and I want you to stop. Now. I was angry that he died, that a part of me was gone from my life. But I wasn't angry with you. And I came to believe very quickly that Dom died because it was his time, or through his own carelessness, or bad luck, or Fate, or however you choose to look at it or believe it. We were stupid, thrill-seeking kids, all of us."

She studied a button on his shirt and held her breath for a moment against the sudden pain. "But he was showing off for me. And I encouraged him, and you, to look for Pele's Tears in caves on the *pali* face."

There. One of them had finally said the words out loud. Blinking back tears, she skewered the potato on the knife then, with one vicious downward stroke, ending in a hollow *thunk,* she sunk the knife tip into the wooden cutting board on the countertop beside her.

CHAPTER 3

Dante stared at the quivering knife. "I'm glad you used a potato instead of me to get that out of your system. I wasn't sure there for a minute, what with the survivor clause and all."

"Don't mess with me, Dante," she told him in a choked voice that was half tears and half laughter. "I'm not in the mood for it."

His breath escaped on a hiss. "Fine. Just don't say those two words again. Please." His voice had gone quiet, and he turned around to lean against the sink beside her, turning his back on the impaled potato.

"No ghosts, huh?" she asked, skepticism heavy in the words.

Shoulders touching in companionable misery, they studied the white piece of paper on her kitchen table on the other side of the room.

"Maybe two." He sighed. "But they're

35

both still gentle and friendly and we know them."

She gasped with pain, remembering Dom and Rosemary. "And love them." Then she turned her head to study his profile. "You didn't send me those notes, Dante Kahoa?"

He turned his head to meet her gaze. "I did not, Noelani Beecham. And you didn't send mine?"

The truth was there in his eyes, just as it must be in hers. "Stir up something that's painful for you too? I couldn't do that to either of us." Fear of stirring up painful memories for him was another reason she had stayed away, but she didn't say it aloud. "Whoever sent the notes knows the story of . . . them. And if that person also knows about Dom then it's cruel as well. And what's the point? We don't know where they are."

He gave a harsh laugh. "They aren't anywhere. They don't even exist. I just hoped the note meant you were ready to come home, but you wanted me to force you into it, like jumping off our rock."

She shivered in response. She had never been able to jump off that porpoise-shaped rock into the Pacific far below until Dante threatened to take her into a dive with him. And he would have done it too, so she finally did it herself. Once. Once had satisfied him and had given her a feeling of satisfaction and a sense of accomplishment. But once was enough.

He shifted. His arm now touched hers from shoulder to elbow. "Listen to me. My being here is no clever ploy to get you to come home just so I can keep Lehua. I need your help." He pronounced each word clearly. "We're at a crossroads there, and I need someone to sink or swim with me. We've had a couple of bad years. I'm in the middle of converting part of the farm, and diversifying the rest. I need your help, your input, your support, and your mind, such as it is."

She jabbed him in the side with her elbow, but two words piqued her interest, which had probably been his plan. "Converting what and diversifying how?"

His eyes and face closed the shutters, not to conceal but to maintain her level of curiosity. "I'll tell you when we get there." And he would, or in his own good time, whichever came first.

"I'm so confused, and these notes just add to it. I don't know what to do." She cringed. She sounded like she was twelve again.

"Then I'll tell you what *we're* going to do. We're going home together, where we both

37

belong. But we're going to talk ourselves through Dom's death first. Tonight. Clear the air. Every detail. Cleansing by fire. That's what's keeping you away from Lehua, isn't it? In order to set in motion the going home part, I'll have to go out later to arrange some things. I'd like to clean up and change clothes first."

She recognized his standard diversion ploy and let him get away with it only because that "cleansing by fire" line of his had glued her feet to the kitchen floor. "The bathroom is across the hall. There are plenty of clean towels," she said in a monotone.

She heard the two men talking out in the hall, then Aidan's laugh when Dante said something she couldn't catch. By listening to Dante's determined footsteps move through the cottage, she knew where he went, knew when he retrieved the bag he'd dropped in the hall, knew when he went into the bathroom, then quietly closed the door.

He leaned against the bathroom door, taking long, deep breaths. It was all about remembering. He had forgotten a lot about Lani, like how she had kept him off balance at the end of their time together at Lehua. And why. He'd almost lost it a couple of times today, especially when he saw the Australian acting like a homeowner. A surfer? In Maine, yet. Who knew?

But it was when Lani came down those stairs that the way she affected him came slamming back. And she had grown. In all the right places. What a beautiful, graceful woman she had become, something he hadn't really taken in at Tutu's funeral. His palms had immediately become so slick with sweat that he almost slid out of the doorway. That *wahine* had legs up to her *'ōkole.* The best legs on Kauai and in Maine, he'd bet.

And if he wasn't mistaken, and he was seldom wrong about things like this, she wore a red lace bra under that short red T-shirt. He especially liked to see a woman's skin showing through lace, especially red lace. Or black. In fact, now that he thought about it, he might have developed his tastes through his early exposure to Lani's collection of colorful lingerie. He remembered coming upon rainbows of bras hanging on doorknobs when he ventured, invited or not, into her room in the big house at Lehua. Maybe this bra had been meant for the surfer, but he didn't mind reaping the tantalizing glimpses of her skin's permanently tanned tones through it. Not at all.

And she still looked like she floated instead of walked. If he couldn't see her feet at the end of those long, long legs, he'd think she had wheels. He wondered if she could still do *hula* that brought men to tears, and sometimes to their knees at the same time, but for different reasons. Thinking about her last performance with her *hula hālau,* her *hula* group, still made him lightheaded.

Side trips, Kahoa. Focus.

When he had finally remembered the surfer standing behind him and that note he thought she'd sent, wondering again how she could do that to him, it made him *huhū* all over again. That was good because when he was angry, then at least, he could focus.

He was pleased that she couldn't pretend she wasn't tense, that his being there didn't affect her, especially when she threw that cloth at him. Good thing he knew her well enough to keep her off balance too. It sure leveled the playing field.

Man, she felt like home in his arms. And he knew it was all right when he saw her and the surfer together. They might have been heading in that direction, but it wouldn't happen now.

It had gut punched him when she said she hadn't sent the note and that she had received more than one. He was glad she hadn't written it, but who did? Who had the guts to do this? He could take being threatened, or even set up for a little accident, but the slime ball better leave Lani alone. At the thought of someone hurting her, his insides turned to water and he clenched and unclenched his fists at his sides. This was not good.

Every time Dom's name came up or she thought about Dom, he'd watched her pull away into her hurting place. He had to get her to talk to him about Dom and to come home with him. He needed her, in ways he could only imagine. So he'd pulled tonight's Hawaiian intervention thing out of his *'ōkole*.

He had to get out of there for a while. He needed to call in some favors, make some plans, line up some help, take care of some details, and he had to keep Lani out of his head while he did them.

And how was he going to follow through on this cleansing by fire thing tonight without killing both of them inside or ruining their lifelong friendship?

Mindlessly, Lani finished preparing the last of her vegetables and put them around the beef roast and seasoned broth in the covered pan she'd taken from the oven. She had

41

intended to invite Aidan to share this meal with her.

Just then Aidan opened the kitchen door partway to say he had finished the job and was leaving. She probably looked the way she felt at that moment, like every hair was standing upright on her head. She became aware of his athletic, surfer's body beside her as she cleared her work area. Aidan smelled of sunshine and the sea.

"You okay, luv? You looked as if you'd been pole-axed when you first saw him."

Dante had put his large *paniolo* boots squarely into the part of her life that Aidan had been about to fill. Before Dante's arrival, she and Aidan had been well on the way to a love affair that would never happen now. She had been the one holding back, as usual, and now her concentration had been thoroughly hijacked.

"Very attractive, I'm sure. Dante has that effect on people sometimes."

"You recovered in fine form," he added with a grin. "In his arms in less than five minutes. Good on him."

She shook her head, her cheeks warming. "It's not like that with Dante and me, but I folded like a house of cards, didn't I? He wants to talk me through things to get me to go back to Lehua."

She had confided in the friendly, sexy, slightly older Australian about her life at Lehua. She had also confided in him about Dom's accident and her lingering guilt and self-anger about it, leaving out the reason they had been on the cliffs. She still wasn't sure how or why the confession had happened, other than he was there, she needed to talk, and it was easy to confide in him.

"I think you should go back to Hawaii with him." When she looked accusingly at him, he held up one broad hand, scarred from working with stone and sharp hand tools made of metal. "You've already left here anyway, in your head. Set yourself up somewhere near the *kahuna* but on your own. Work things through in your mind. I'm heading home soon, by way of Hawaii and some surfing. I'll look in on you. Maybe pick up some work in the flower fields."

"You'd be welcome, Aidan, but I'm not sure I can or should go back there." When he didn't answer, she stopped wiping and shining a section of granite countertop to glance at him.

"You're a terrible liar, luv, especially to yourself. You're aching to go back. If I can see it, so can he. Best to give in gracefully." He flexed his shoulders on the next words. "I can hang about here for a bit longer if

43

you like and make myself look busy. Be on the premises, should the need arise."

She chuckled in response. "I told you. It's my mind Dante's messing with, not my body."

"Then it's only a matter of time. Look, we're not fools, you and I. You slipped away from me out there in that hall, and there wasn't a bloody thing either of us could do about it. See you in Hawaii, luv."

She stared after him. With that enigmatic parting shot, along with her check for the work and a light kiss on her forehead, he was gone, his good-byes said that easily to what might have been between them. *Men!*

She resumed shining the same section of countertop, vigorously now, and pondering Aidan's last observation until its subject entered the room.

Dante now wore his boots with tan chinos and a vintage aloha shirt patterned with flowers that matched the color of his eyes. He moved within a halo of scent made up of soap and the light, botanical, spicy after-shave he'd had specially made for himself since he was a teenager.

That act, so totally out of character for the Dante she had known then, resulted in this pleasant, fiercely male scent that had defined him — and masculinity — for her since that time. He'd always smelled manly to her after that, even when he was being a jerk or he was dirty and sweaty from working in the fields. Dante and his aftershave had become, for her whole life, the joint standard by which she judged other men and how they smelled. So far, not one had measured up.

Shocked to admit that to herself, she threw down the busy cloth in disgust but continued to wind the air between them like a hound, unable to stop herself. She ended up staring at the drops of water glistening in his thick, dark hair.

She'd never gotten to know Dante as an adult male. He'd been an impressive specimen at seventeen when Dom died. Tutu had shipped Dante off to the Big Island as soon as he graduated a few weeks later, to a *paniolo* family friend, to work off his guilt, sorrow, and angst on cattle and in hard labor before college at the University of Hawaii at Manoa on Oahu.

Rosemary had thrown herself into her own work, and Lani had buried herself in her studies, working hard to get college credits in high school and graduating with honors. She'd left for college on the mainland as soon the ink was dry on her diploma, secretly vowing never to return.

45

"What are you thinking about?" he asked when she continued to silently stare, through him at that point.

"About . . . after it happened."

"Those were dark days."

"And you were the only light. You were the strong one. You kept Rosemary and me sane."

Pain, like a restless animal, shifted in his eyes. "I could have used a little light myself. But you and Tutu kept me sane by needing me." He held up his hands in a defensive gesture, telling her to leave it alone. "Let me help you with the meal. I can still set a table."

He demonstrated that skill while she packed up more kitchen items and they talked. They ate at the big old table in the kitchen. During their meal, she kept up a steady stream of conversation on neutral, nonvolatile subjects. And she knew she wasn't fooling him because he met her babbling with a half smile on his face that she itched to smack aside so hard that it came to rest beneath his right ear.

Later, she heard the hiss of the inflatable mattress from down the hall while she loaded the dishwasher and tidied the kitchen, carefully avoiding prolonged, mindless sessions with a cloth and the counter-top.

She pulled sheets, a light blanket, a pillow, and a pillowcase from a packing box outside the bathroom and took them to the guest room, stopping short when she found Dante bouncing on the mattress on the floor like the boy she'd seen in his face earlier.

"This is comfortable," he said, surprise in the words.

"I know it is." She threw him the fitted sheet. "I used it for a while until I could afford bedroom furniture. I'll help you with it."

In a quick move, he rolled off the opposite side onto his knees on the floor. He proved himself adept at this household chore as well.

"You remember how to set the table and make up a bed. Rosemary domesticated both of us in the end."

"Not only Tutu. I learned a lot from the *paniolos* on the Big Island. They refined my skills. I had to change all the beds in the bunkhouse at first and help the cook. And those men taught me how to take care of myself in all ways, from sewing on buttons to defending myself to the fine points of making love, and which women to do it with. So tell me what *you* do around here in the evenings."

She closed her gaping mouth and turned off the video bytes playing in her head, x-rated this go-round, of the time she'd glimpsed Dante making love with one of the flower field girls in the flower prep shed. It had looked pretty exciting to her at the time, never mind the fine points he learned later. She'd been eager to try it, hence the Noa incident.

"I work. I read," she said hoarsely. "I take in a movie in town or rent one. I watch TV. I sit out back. There's a little patio out there. I teach a stained glass artistry class now and then." She made a point of concentrating on his hands while he finished making up the bed.

"Maybe you can teach a course locally, if you have time. Kauai Community College can probably help you set it up. Mei goes there."

She swiped the name out of the air like it was a butterfly and her brain was a net. "Who's Mei?"

"You'll find out when you get there." Their busy work was done, and he told her quietly, "Your dinner filibuster was effective for the short-term but I meant what I said. I made some calls and I have business to tend to now, but we're having a serious talk when I

48

get back."

Her stomach bungee jumped to her feet then retracted up into her throat. "I get to choose the subject."

"There's only one subject tonight. And don't go to sleep because I'll wake you, no matter the time. We finish this tonight." They were still on the floor, him sitting back on his heels, his fingers splayed on thighs she knew to be rock hard. "I can't buy you out, and you don't want to saddle me and Lehua with some ruthless, hotshot developer or corporation for a partner, do you? I'll help you get used to the idea of Lehua as home again," he ended, his voice rough with tension. "I'll try to be in at a decent hour."

An emotion welled up inside her, and she didn't want to call it by name. "One of the calls you made? You always were a fast worker. I'll lock up if she keeps you out too late."

One corner of his mouth pulled up in a half smile. "Just can't help wondering about my love life, can you? Unfortunately, it's all business tonight. And if you lock up, I'll kick in the front door, a door you no longer own I'd like to point out. You know I will."

She had no doubts he'd do it, so she silently said every Hawaiian swear word she could remember then stalked off to her little patio out back.

CHAPTER 4

Dante shouted good-bye and drove away in his rented pickup.

"I'll bet it's red. Dante's trucks are always red. Anyway, it sounds red," she muttered to the night.

She changed into jeans and a regular-length cotton T-shirt then went to the loft to take up where she'd left off with her packing. The first thing she did was pick up and lay aside the note to show Dante later.

Her stained glass workshop and the projects living there didn't hold their usual allure for her that night. She had trouble concentrating as she packed up more projects because she dreaded what was coming later. Before today, she had decided that anything that wasn't under contract could go into storage until she was set up somewhere, maybe even Australia. Now she could save herself money, and the time she would have spent fooling herself, and ship the whole workshop contents straight to Lehua.

She remembered that Kauai had been on her mind long before she'd heard Dante's voice that day. The warm cottage loft had reminded her of the soft heat of the Lehua valley. The overhead fans, silently and efficiently moving the air, had taken the place of the Hawaiian trade winds in her roomy stained glass workshop. She'd even caught the scent of flowers that grew in Lehua's fields.

Common sense had prevailed, telling her that Maine, most of the east coast in fact, was in the throes of a summer hot spell, and the scent was simply an old tropical-scented candle collapsing into an oily lump in the loft's unusual heat. So, unsuspecting of the Hawaiian whirlwind about to descend upon her, she had plodded forward with the day's tasks.

Nine weeks before, when she returned from Lehua after Rosemary's funeral, she had focused her concentration on her work and the sale of the cottage. She'd choreographed her brief visit so that she arrived immediately before the service began and left immediately after it ended, in a car that waited to whisk her away to the airport. She had been thankful to return to the mental and physical activity of her Maine existence, after yet another catastrophic loss in her life.

A flurry of letters from Rosemary's lawyers had followed her back to Maine. Rosemary's stained glass workshop, in a separate cottage at Lehua, was now hers, along with half the big house and half the valley, which included Lehua Flower Farm, if she returned there to live and work. She'd been given paradise, but at a heartrending price. What had Rosemary been thinking, arranging things that way? Dante surely should have inherited everything outright.

She again mentally shook herself away from Lehua. *I can't control my dreams at night, but surely when I'm awake my thoughts ought to be more manageable.*

She went downstairs to close up, except for locking the front door. She knew Dante to be as good as his word. He would break it down. She left a light glowing for him, the *pikake* stained glass accent lamp she'd designed and crafted, which sat on the narrow entrance hall table. She had made the lamp as a gift for Rosemary but hadn't the courage, as Rosemary's apprentice, to present such a gift to the master. But it was good. Very good. Rosemary had told her so when she noticed it during her last visit.

Looking at it now, Lani could almost smell the scent of Lehua's jasmine emanating from it.

She had become known for designs like this one, lush and tropical or Hawaiian in theme. If she lived and worked in Hawaii, the source of her inspiration, her designs would bring the price, the clientele, and the attention she needed for her work. She clutched at any good, sane reason to return there, any her mind could lay claim to.

She left her bedroom door wide open, not sure if Dante would try the knob before he applied a boot to see if she had defied him and gone to bed. She climbed the stairs to the loft again, this time to quietly sit in the moonlit window seat and put her thoughts in order for the coming ordeal. Dante was right, damn him. She had to find some peace, somehow, about Dom and Lehua.

She had briefly seen a counselor who held private sessions once a week in the church office in town. She had quit after the woman advised her to discuss her feelings about Dom's death with Dante, who was key, she'd said, to Lani forgiving herself and moving on. And Rosemary, who had loved her deeply, had tried unsuccessfully to relieve her of the burden of guilt she carried over Dom's death. If Rosemary had failed and the counselor had failed, how could Dante possibly help her tonight, in her own loft, five thousand miles away from where they had lived it?

When she had come face to face with him at the foot of her stairs that afternoon, a part of her recognized him as a walking, talking chance for her to go home. She suspected he was right about a lot of other things he'd told her that day, like she didn't belong here, for starters. How could she deny it when she heard Lehua's call every waking moment, as surely as she'd recognized Dante's voice? Like a child, she just wanted him to make it right again, tonight, to make it all like it used to be, an impossible task since there were only two of them left.

She started out of a doze when Dante returned to the cottage, listening as his footsteps on the flagstones below made a beeline for the foot of the stairs. She held her breath. Maybe he'd had a few drinks on his journeys tonight and would put off this madness until daylight.

Then she swore softly when he quietly called her name and started up the stairs. He'd always had an uncanny sense of both her physical location and her state of mind. So be it. In a cold sweat, she stared out into the moonlight that bathed the landscape, the window seat, and most of the loft.

He stopped on the last step to look around. "Nice work space. Not as good as you'll have in Tutu's cottage, though."

She made a little noise as she pivoted around to put her feet on the floor and look around the loft, shaking her head under the burden of a sudden realization. She was scarcely able to keep her voice level when she spoke. "I'm seeing for the first time, because you're here, that this is my version of Rosemary's workshop. I wonder if she saw it."

"So what? She wouldn't have cared. She would have considered it a compliment."

A skylight and a bay window mimicked the glass walls of Rosemary's workroom at Lehua. They filled her workroom and office with Maine's clear light by day, and starlight and moonlight by night. She had turned the resulting deep window niche into a seat with a thick, soft cushion and lots of pillows. It was her favorite place in the whole cottage.

He stepped up into the loft, slowly came to her, and sat down on the opposite end of the cushion. "This is a perfect place to make love," he said softly, grinning.

Dante always brought her to anger or laughter in short order, so her shocked laugh was no surprise to her. "I guess it is. And to think I've only used it to read, sketch, and think." He knocked her smile into the Atlantic with his next words.

"So instead of making love here, this beautiful place is where you wallow in undeserved guilt," he said carefully, watching her.

"Oh, I can do that anywhere." She felt cornered and her anger soared. She shot to her feet. "There's nothing like cutting to the chase, Kahoa. Okay, here I am. Fix me. Say now what you couldn't say then that will erase from my mind the picture and . . . sounds . . . of Dom falling. I dare you to find the words. And it's all tied up with Lehua, so how can I —"

"You can't erase it." His words cut across hers. "I can vouch for that. I see and hear the same things you do every time I close my eyes, if I let myself. But I know you can stop running from it."

"Really. And just how do I do that?"

"Every time your mind goes there, take it somewhere else, make yourself see good memories instead, a happy memory of Dom. Look, we witnessed it together. This talk of ours won't make all this go away, but it will make it *over.*"

The noise she made was equal parts sob

and laughter. "Funny you should say that. A counselor advised me to share my feelings with the other witness." She scrubbed her palms up and down the front of her denim-clad thighs, wiping away perspiration. "Her words, not mine. You're so much more than 'the other witness.' So who did you talk to, Dante, to reach this point?"

His full, sensuous mouth arranged itself in a thin line. "You. I talked to your picture. Didn't you hear me? And don't you dare tell anyone. What we say in Maine stays in Maine. Agreed?"

She nodded, not finding a mental picture of Dante talking to her picture funny at all. She wished she'd thought of it herself and had talked to *his* picture.

"This is going to hurt both of us, but that can't be helped. And that counselor was right. I came five thousand miles to listen, Lani. The *kahuna* is in."

She didn't say anything while she collected her thoughts, pacing in front of the window seat, feeling as if she were about to step off a — *Oh, don't go there. Just say what you feel. No matter how stupid it sounds.*

"I feel that I betrayed you and Rosemary that day, as well as Dom, everyone I loved and who loved me." She paused on a choked laugh. "How can so much pain sound so lame?"

He leaned forward, his voice intense. "Betrayed how? It was a rock-climbing accident. He lost his footing. It could have been you or me. How is that betrayal?"

"We were up there because of me," she told him fiercely. "After everything the three of you had done for me, I led you and Dom to those cliffs."

"We voted to go, unless you had a gun that I don't remember. And don't belittle or forget what you brought to our lives, Lani. You were the light of Tutu's life. And to Dom and me you were the third side of a triangle with us. I have the tattoo to prove it."

She was immediately distracted, doubting he had meant that to happen. "You got a tattoo? When you wouldn't let me get one?" She quickly scanned the parts of him where skin showed then maliciously added, "Yours doesn't show either."

He got to his feet. "What? Noelani Beecham, did you . . . ?"

"What if I did?"

"Really? Where?" Then he stopped and they studied each other. "How can we think about tattoos at a time like this?" he asked, a dumbfounded look on his face. "It's like

Dom . . ."

"It's like Dom is here. He would have taken the conversation there. But we can't. We shouldn't. You're fixing me, remember?"

"You show me yours, and I'll show you mine. Sorry. Side trip. Go on."

"I've kind of lost the moment. I guess the bottom line is that I'm the one who pushed to find . . . the gems. And Dom died because of it."

He shook his head in disbelief. "Tutu chased that dream all her life. Each of us wanted to be the one to find them for her, if they existed. We agreed, all of us, to climb the cliffs and look for caves on the face. We were all caught up in the sense of adventure and excitement."

She stepped up to him, suddenly calm, and held his gaze. "But I suggested caves and cliffs," she whispered miserably. "I'm the one who secretly read Rosemary's journal and decided where to look. I feel responsible."

"Don't." Pain chased sadness across his face. "And you aren't responsible. What about me? I was the oldest. I could have stopped it. One word from me and none of us would have been on that cliff face."

"You were older than Dom by ten minutes. And we would have argued with you,

60

outvoted you. Remember, we voted? It wasn't your fault!"

She swayed as she crashed into the wall of her own words, their meaning sinking into her pain and guilt and sending out ripples of understanding and self-forgiveness. But, as usual, Dante was there before her, with a hand on her arm to steady her.

"You mean just like it wasn't your fault?" he whispered. "And it wasn't Tutu's fault, though she felt she had failed the three of us by not protecting us somehow. And when Dom died before my eyes, I had to be strong. I couldn't let anyone see me cry. Then I was sent away to deal with my guilt." His words were harsh, his voice strained.

Shock and realization hit her with a one-two punch. She raised her hand to briefly cup his cheek with her palm.

"You too? Oh, Dante, I'm so sorry. When Rosemary sent you away, I thought it was to keep you safe from me because I'd already killed one brother, one grandson."

"No. No, she never thought that," he repeated fiercely.

"Maybe she thought we'd turn our guilt on each other, blame each other, destroy each other."

His smile had no power behind it. "Or take comfort in each other's arms. Remember how aware of each other we were at that time, what was starting between us?"

"I haven't forgotten. If only we had told her that we needed each other to get through it. Why didn't I tell her? Why didn't you tell her? Because we both felt guilty, that's why. I see that now. Can you ever forgive me for abandoning you?"

He gathered her close in a fierce hug and she felt him tremble. "Let's forgive ourselves for abandoning each other, and just let it go. But you have to come home now, where you belong, and help me save Lehua. You and I, we're *'ohana,* Lani. Family. And we're all the *'ohana* that Lehua has left."

Held against his solid, warm body, she felt safe again for the second time that day, and after many years of being in free fall. A flurry of memories washed over her in those moments, scenes of her life those years on Kauai: Rosemary, Dom, and Dante's presence around her like a protective wall when her parents died; coming safely to a familiar, loving home at Lehua after their double funeral; the comfort of her bed in her old room under the eaves at the top of the big house; their loving influence on her shattered life; even the warm Hawaiian sun showed up, shining down upon her head as she remembered working beside them in the flower fields.

Then the fact that half their number was gone thrust itself to the front of her mind. Dante was the only family she had left. He cradled her head against his shoulder when she began to sob.

"There's still two of us," he whispered, reading her thoughts. "Two of us still belong to Lehua." He held her, patted her, and kissed her hair, rocking both of them gently, until she grew quiet.

She hiccupped against his damp shirt and said, "Can you stay for a few days to help me pack up? I think it's time I get my *'ōkole* back home, to Lehua."

CHAPTER 5

She watched Dante transform overnight into a man trying to outrun a lit fuse or, in this case, to stay ahead of a woman he feared might change her mind. That would be her. He threatened her with kidnapping and all manner of horrific Hawaiian curses if she backed out on him, and, thankfully, he didn't leave her time or energy to think. He could have saved himself the trouble. Once she had made up her mind, she was committed to her decision. Or resigned to it; she wasn't sure which.

In return, she didn't examine too closely his methods for securing air freight trucks for her stained glass projects, equipment, and supplies; clumps of townspeople and kids to help load those trucks; or the bewildered presence of the cottage's middle-aged female watercolorist buyer who showed up on his arm to meekly purchase everything Lani agreed to leave behind, even the unseen contents of vaguely labeled boxes sealed with tape.

In the end, Lani didn't know whether to be proud, ashamed, or simply amazed that it took only forty-eight hours of applied Dante to sort through and pack up this temporary life of hers and ship it off to her real one five thousand miles away.

A few days later, she woke up just after dawn, with a headache and fully clothed, in her old bed under the eaves of the big house at Lehua. They had been late getting in yesterday, and the rest of the day and evening had disappeared into an impromptu gathering and welcome home *lū'au* for her in Lihue, Kauai's county seat. The truth was that she knew it really hadn't been impromptu, as *lū'aus* cannot be if they include *kālua* pig; the result was that she drank more than she should have, on purpose, to soften her first reactions to Lehua. And Dante had let her.

She suspected that had been his plan, and since she couldn't remember how she got to Lehua, it must have worked. Other than the headache, she didn't feel hungover. Apparently she had fallen into her old bed, or been placed in it, and had remained there until that moment. She saw no damage except that her purple bra, one satin-and-lace strap and a bit of lacy cup, was peeking out of her matching purple-flowered tank top and blouse, now twisted around her torso.

Finally, a neuron nudged loose a memory and she remembered a chicken, of the rooster persuasion, waking her at the crack of dawn and at regular intervals after that. Another sound, the deep purr of a powerful motorcycle, had also interfered with her attempt to sleep-delay the inevitable. She quietly plotted turning one into fried chicken and the other into spare parts while she stared at the dried-up *leis* hanging everywhere. Her room was just as she'd left it, including the teenage-style furniture and outdated beefcake wall art.

Gag! How long do I have to live with this?

But first things first. She sat up cautiously on the edge of the bed, thinking she should probably stand up soon to test-drive her not-hungover feeling. When that went well, she risked a shower in her tiny bathroom with the slanted ceiling that nestled under the eaves of the large, hybrid plantation-style and New England saltbox-style house. Rosemary had put in the bathroom especially for her when she came there to live.

She mentally steeled herself for her journey down the stairs and through the big house, prepared to repel bittersweet memories like a Jedi knight wielding a light saber. That was shot down before it had a chance to fly because, after making her way carefully down the attic steps, she opened the door at the bottom only to run into two young men, strangers to her, outside the door of Dom's old room.

The first, looking like something out of a travel brochure for Hawaiian vacations, with sun-streaked hair, tanned muscles and all, said with a slow smile, "You must be Lani. Dante told us you were coming home."

This kid should be wearing low-slung swimming briefs and have a surfboard tucked under his beefy arm, she mused, instead of hiking boots, shorts, and a graphic, in every sense of the word, T-shirt.

She closed her mouth with a snap when his words sunk in. "He did, did he? And you are?"

The Hawaiian-ad surf god ran a hand through his perfect hair and poked his tiny Oriental friend. "I'm Puno and this is Kenji. We're in the apprenticeship program for organic farmers."

Feeling really intelligent, she parroted, "Apprenticeship program for organic farmers?"

"Yeah. We're farm apprentices, and Dante is our host farmer." He named their group.

That made her a host farmer too, she guessed. She'd read about the small, privately run and funded program similar to one run by the state. Farm apprentices got some food and tent space for around five hours of work a day, weekdays. The emphasis being on tent space, not house space. She'd even read that some apprentices relied on catchment systems for their water, and solar energy for electricity. Those other apprentices must have been made of sterner stuff than these.

She was still digesting this information and her newfound status, and imagining what she would do to Dante for not telling her all this, when bedroom doors the whole length of the hall began to open and close like a hotel fire drill. There were a few girls and women, but mostly guys, one in the geezer range, in same-sex duos.

After introductions, more explanations, and a mass exodus by the farm apprentices to the area where their tents would be located after today, Lani tottered downstairs without a memory in sight. She pointed herself toward the kitchen, which was in the saltbox, lean-to style extension at the back, and was making good headway. Then, a girl,

68

wearing the briefest of floral bikini tops and a see-through pareau draped over the matching bottom and around her shapely hips and graceful legs, wished her *aloha,* with a surprised look on her face, and glided into the room that housed Lehua's office. Dante hadn't been kidding. He wasn't alone at Lehua.

Lani followed the vision, stopping in the office doorway. "You'll never make me believe you're an apprentice farmer."

The girl answered her with a sweet smile. "I'm Mei, Dante's secretary."

Uh-huh. Dante had mentioned that name. In the spirit of one-upmanship, she replied, "I'm Noelani Beecham, Dante's business partner."

The girl rose gracefully to her feet behind the desk. "I'm sorry, I should have known. But I didn't recognize you. I thought you were an, um, overnight visitor." She remained standing but blushed becomingly.

Now why would this girl think she should recognize someone who had left Lehua a long time ago. "A private female guest of Dante's, you mean?"

The girl nodded, with the same smile. "Sorry. It seldom happens. That's why I was surprised."

The fact that it happened at all was

enough to make her want to move into the cottage that very day. "And are you Dante's *private* secretary or Lehua's secretary?"

"Oh. Oh, I'm Lehua's secretary. Your secretary too. I don't date older men. I'm just a family friend, sort of. And please don't think I dress like this for work. I was surfing and I'm in early. I just wanted to check the telephone messages before I take a quick shower and change in the bathroom beside the office. Dante lets me use it, but I'm not allowed to leave any bras or things lying around. He's very strict about that."

"I'll bet he is." Lani grinned, imagining the look on Dante's face if he'd heard himself described as an older man.

The girl continued. "I'm a student at the community college. Shaka is my grand-father. I live with him."

Lani recognized her then. Little Mei had been, well, little, when Lani had left Lehua.

After that encounter, she made a deal with herself and stopped all thought processes about Dante and his staff or, rather, their staff and their workers. She ate toast, spooned out the sweet, juicy flesh of half a fresh papaya, and drank two cups of Kona coffee before she ventured outside.

Her trip to Rosemary's cottage and work-shop, through the fragrant, lush, venerable garden behind the big house, was relatively painless. The sight and scent of plumeria and *pikake,* Rosemary's favorite flower and Lani's mother's favorite jasmine, respectively, triggered occasional twinges. They let her know that old hurts and healing memories surrounded her here, and would make themselves felt when she came upon them.

The key was in the lock, although she couldn't remember this door ever being locked. She took it out and stepped inside. The closed-up, abandoned feeling of the place hit her in her chest. She immediately slid aside the glass doors in all four walls to open up the downstairs to the surrounding *lānai,* the deep, covered porch that went the whole way around the building. The trade winds would have right of way here again, as they had in Rosemary's time. Rosemary had created this small living and working space without true walls, at least on the lower level, for that very reason. Lani let the heavy, carved front door stand open too.

The upper floor, which housed the large workroom and studio, a storage area, and a tiny full bathroom, was supported by heavy wooden ceiling beams and strategically placed carved ironwood pillars.

She took a quick look around upstairs but found herself going back to Rosemary's

71

front door again and again to hover uncertainly. Correction. Her front door. Her cottage and workshop. She found herself there yet again, still not sure why. While she pondered this mysterious need, she was startled by a movement above her head. An uninvited, four-footed intruder was quietly keeping her company. The cat must have slipped in while she was checking out things upstairs. The premises were, after all, once again open to all comers, four-footed and two-footed alike, except that stupid rooster.

She was still watching the cat when, in a *déjà vu* moment, Dante suddenly filled the open doorway space in front of her. And she knew down to the very core of her being that he was what she'd been waiting for. She needed Dante's blessing, his presence, his permission, right now, before she could take ownership of her place here, in this cottage, and assume her share of Lehua from the grandmother who had given him a secure and loving childhood, and from the brother who had shared a short life with him here, beginning in the womb.

And she wasn't surprised when Dante, somehow knowing this, gave her all those things without saying a word, bringing a kind of peace into her and into the space around them. He disguised it by simply reaching out and laying his palm lightly on the top of her head, and he ended it by gently tugging on a loose curl.

She broke the emotional silence first. "Now I'm truly home, and it's good to be here. You were right, Dante." Then she added, to lighten the mood, "And, as much as I hate to feed your ego, I have to say I love the cowboy look on you."

He took her cue and drew himself up to his full, impressive six feet three inches. "These clothes are still comfortable and practical, but the only things I wrangle these days are flowers, greens, fruit, and coffee plants."

That brought her up short and again drove the intruder from her mind. "Coffee plants? And what else?"

"Salad greens and tropical fruit. They're all ways we're diversifying. We'll still be half flowers, with the other half in fruits and greens for local restaurants, and eventually we'll have our own coffees. I renamed the shop Beans and Blossoms."

She bristled. "You could have said! You could have consulted! And another thing you forgot to mention is the merry band of farmers who have been sleeping in the big house."

He appeared maddeningly unruffled. "Ah,

but only until they finish their tent platforms today. They're no trouble. They cook at their campsite."

"And I met Lehua's secretary."

"Mei is a good kid. She just got in with the wrong crowd in Kalele, and Shaka panicked."

"That's no kid, Kahoa. And who runs the wrong crowd in Kalele these days?"

"Still the Takei brothers, pretty much."

"Ah, but those Takei boys have wonderful smiles. And I have an in with them, don't forget."

"Right. Your old friend Noa, who's now a librarian."

"I know, I know. Rosemary told me." Lani's head pounded as she tried to take it all in. "Okay, what else haven't you told me, like who was the idiot on the motorcycle this morning? And I want the name of that stupid rooster and where he lives."

"Cranky after your late night? The idiot on the motorcycle would be me. I bought a vintage Harley and had someone help me fix it up. I use it to get around the farm. And the stupid rooster is ours, more or less, although we don't allow him any followers. He's wild but he continues to hang out here, despite no sex. His name is The Colonel."

74

She scowled and massaged her temples. "A good Southern name and he'll make good Southern fried chicken. He's mine."

"You'll get used to him. You settling in okay?"

Only Dante would trowel on an overload of information then ask that question of a slightly hungover woman surrounded by boxes and packing crates. How had they gotten here so quickly? She successfully beat back her exasperation and the momentary urge to shove him so that he fell backward over the nearest crate.

"It'll take time to unpack all this stuff, but I was home from the minute I woke up a while ago in my old room in the big house."

He nodded once, his understanding complete and immediate. "I'm glad because it's your house too, you know."

"Ah. We should talk about that arrangement. We're both adults now, with adult lives."

She wasn't eager to discuss it, but her meeting with Mei and the others in the big house had made her consider moving into the cottage sooner rather than later, if only to avoid the embarrassment of running into one of Dante's overnighters or of overhearing the sound effects of a visit. The opposite side of the coin, of course, was what Dante's reaction might be if she showed up with an overnighter of her own. Her stomach twisted at her mind's film clips of any of those scenarios.

He simply shrugged, but he wasn't getting off that easily, even if she was too cowardly at the moment to discuss her moving over here.

"So why didn't you mention tropical fruits, salad greens, and coffee plants earlier, and apprentice farmers and secretaries?"

"Because this changeover isn't cheap, quick, or easy —"

"Unlike some of your old girlfriends," she tossed in.

He bared his even white teeth in an unconvincing smile. "Nice one. I barely felt the blade. As I was saying, I was afraid I'd scare you, or you'd turn even more mulish at the prospect of coming back if I told you all this stuff up front."

"Excuse me? Did you just say 'mulish'? In reference to me?"

"Well, then, I was afraid you'd go all stubborn on me. Side trip, Beecham. Focus, please. The apprentices are very nearly unpaid help. Everything will be organically grown, so they're in at the startup, literally planting the changeover fields for us. Coffee will come soon enough. It takes years for a first crop of coffee beans, even in Hawaii. Just be thankful that I know when to ask for help. Oh, and have you seen Aumoe?"

She glared at him, refusing to be side-tracked. "Now that I'm here, don't expect me to be a silent partner, Dante. I want to know what's going on, all of it. I expect to have some input on any other changes you're thinking of making. Not to be contrary, or as you so cleverly put it, silver-tongued devil that you are, mulish, but to bring in another viewpoint."

"Silent has never been a word I've associated with you." He held up both hands at her look. "I mean, I agree and I'm counting on you. Now, have you seen Aumoe?"

Her Hawaiian was still a little rusty so it took some mental sorting to find the right word — and see the light. "*Aumoe.* Midnight! I remember now. Rosemary told me about him." With a smile, she pointed to the stained glass window above their heads.

Her uninvited guest was one big cat. He was as black as his namesake, midnight, and on a moonless night to boot. Lehua's resident cat watched them with vivid green, tilted eyes. Rosemary had told her that Dante declared that the cat's eyes were the color and shape of Lani's. Aumoe was doing his watching from the three-inch lip that surrounded a circular stained glass window above the front door. There was a lot of overhang, both a front and back leg.

Dante, looking puzzled, must not have understood her gesture because he hadn't yet moved. So she reached out, took his hand, and pulled him farther into the room with her. His warm, callused hand closed around hers, sending heat radiating up her arm. The scent of clean clothes and something fresh and green, mixed with his familiar aftershave, wafted to her as he turned, looking upward to follow her pointing finger. From his precarious perch, Aumoe gave a *chirrup* of greeting.

"Someday I'm going to find out how he gets up there," Dante said, throwing a dark look at the big cat.

Lani's attention wavered toward Rosemary's window, which was new to her. Rosemary had used round, polished glass cabochons to depict a yellow sun, a clear moon, and one pale blue star, representing the heavens within a medium-blue glass sky. The star was at the very top of the window with the sun and moon angled below it in the middle sky.

Beneath the sky, in an almost geometric pattern of straight lines, the earth was represented in root beer ripple glass, the fields in shades of smooth emerald glass, and Kauai's rivers in light hues of blue ripple glass. She knew this last was a touch of artistic license on Rosemary's part, because Kauai's red dirt is heavily suspended in her rivers. The Waimea pours into the blue Pacific like blood.

The *pali,* cliffs, in the foreground repeated the warm brown ripple glass in a variety of shades and irregular shapes. In this window, Rosemary had neatly depicted Lehua's relationship with the land and its long history of growing things. But the style of the window was very different from her godmother's usual botanical designs. And something about it made her uneasy. She looked forward to studying it more closely.

Dante's little sound of impatience brought her back to the present. "*Pupule.* Crazy animal. And how does he get down?"

"I was about to discuss the ups and downs, no pun intended, of the situation with him when you got here. Mostly how to get him down."

A decorative stepstool sat nearby, outside the tiny kitchen. She dragged it beneath the window for Dante, all the help he needed with his height. Not knowing how the cat might react to her, she would have been reluctant to try it herself.

He stepped up on it. "Just cooperate with me, cat, and neither of us will shed blood." He gently lifted Aumoe off the window's narrow curved lip, draped the huge, shiny-coated feline over his left shoulder, and stepped down.

"I think someone slipped you a black panther," she blurted, amazement thick in her voice as she met Aumoe face to face. "How much does he weigh?"

"Fifteen pounds with his shoes on. I brought him onto the place as a kitten, but he adopted Tutu. He hasn't been over here since she died. He must have known you'd be here today."

She didn't question his reasoning or his straightforward manner of conveying it. Lani loved cats and never questioned their special gifts. Stroking Aumoe's head, her thoughts turned again to her beloved god-mother.

"Dante, the day of the funeral is a blur." She hesitated at his sudden stillness. "I can't remember what I said to you that day, but I'm sorry we lost Rosemary. She was a true Hawaiian lady in every sense of the word. I owe her and Dom and you more than I ever imagined, more than I can ever repay, and I miss her presence in my life down to the depths of my soul."

She knew that Dante's relationship with his grandmother had been loving and unique. Rosemary never married after a post–World War II love affair at age sixteen, which resulted in her only child, a son named Kimo, who married late in life and was the twins' father. Rosemary had raised Dante and Dominic from age three when their parents died, besides taking in Lani, her goddaughter, when Lani was twelve and the boys thirteen.

Fate had been harsh to Rosemary's and their parents' generations long before it made a destructive foray into their own. But Rosemary's capacity for love had stretched even to Lani's mother, a distant relation, whose name had also been Noelani, but who had never been nicknamed Lani.

Now, she was aware of Dante's blue eyes, a gift from his Italian mother, checking out the depths of her aforementioned soul, all the while contrasting warmly with the tanned gold of his skin, a gift from his Hawaiian father.

"*Mahalo,* Lani. You told me that day, but you looked and sounded like a zombie — then you were gone."

She bowed her head in shame. "I'm sorry. I was still being selfish and wrapped myself in my own pain and memories and misery."

"It was a comfort to me to see you there at all. I know it was rough on you. Tutu would be glad you're home to stay, you know. Glad her goddaughter lives at Lehua again."

"She knew what was best for me, as usual."

In the short silence that hung between them, he scratched behind the cat's big ears. "Aumoe misses her too. Do you mind him being around? Because he'll take advantage of the open doors and make himself at home, just like now."

"I don't mind. Both of you are welcome over here anytime. And I'm thankful for the opportunities I've been given at Lehua, past and present," she added softly. "Would you like something to drink?"

She reached out to stroke Aumoe's sleek, silky dark head, and her fingers briefly came under the hard warmth of Dante's palm.

"I'll take a rain check on that. I have to run to Kalele to see if the hardware store has a part we need. I want you to take three days to get settled, seeing as how you're hip-deep in packing crates. Then I'm asking for help. We need your organizational skills to get us through this, and Beans and Blossoms needs your artist's eye and woman's touch right now. We can't lose our momentum there. If you'll start by sorting that out, I can spend more time with Shaka and our handpicked crews, learning aspects of our new business and nurturing the new plants.

"And I was serious about anthuriums coming on, and all the equipment has to be in running order. Nothing has changed, Lani. All hands still turn out for major harvest days. You okay with that?" He watched her closely, waiting for her reaction.

Thoughts of helping harvest Lehua's flowers again, seeing the farm's retail shop again, and perhaps playing a part in making it all succeed gave her a rush of joy and anticipation. She had loved her clerk job at the shop when she lived with Rosemary.

"I'm rusty, but I'm in. And when you have a minute, I want to show you something up in the workroom. A lovely old trunk I've never seen before. The key is in the lock but it won't turn. I'd like to move it to the storage room, but it's too heavy to slide. I'm afraid I'll ruin the wood floor."

Wariness joined a lingering sadness in the depths of his sapphire eyes. "I wondered what happened to that," he said grimly. "Tutu knew I'd have burned it because of one thing I'm sure is inside it. That's why it's in the trunk she left you and not in the one she left me."

Shock raced through her at his words, followed by the realization that she already knew what that one thing must be. "The Pele's Tears journal," she whispered, then clapped a hand over her mouth as she heard the words. The anonymous notes and the threat they had received slammed into her and shattered her peace.

At her words, a momentary spasm crossed his face. "I'll be back in an hour or so. I can pick up takeout. We'll have to come to some arrangement about the grocery shopping and cooking. Helen still comes in to do the laundry and clean for us. She could probably be tempted into shopping and cooking, if we play our cards right."

Lani remembered Helen, a master *lei* maker of Philippine heritage. "How is she?"

"Did Tutu tell you that Helen and Shaka hooked up after you left?" At Lani's amazed, slow shake of her head, he continued. "Well, they did. Big time. Helen has some silver threads in her dark hair, but devils still dance in her eyes, and Shaka is still crazy about her."

"Good for her. Good for them."

When she was younger, she naively thought Shaka and Rosemary, working the farm together all those years, should share more than friendship in their lives, despite a ten-year age difference between them, and Shaka being "hooked up" elsewhere at the time and Rosemary still in love with her "beloved." Years had brought understanding. She now understood the special friendship and working relationship they'd shared and hoped that she and Dante might mimic it. She was afraid, however, that their friendship might catch fire. Again.

"Tutu wanted you to have the cottage, the workshop, and everything in both. I respect that. I'll open the trunk and move it for you after we eat. I just don't want to know or talk about anything that's in that trunk."

"But what about the notes? We have to —"

He turned, interrupting her. "Forget about the notes for now. We're probably victims of a poison pen, a weak mind, someone who couldn't help themselves. I'm just glad you're home, Lani. It'll be good to have you around again. We can bounce ideas and problems off each other."

She hoped he was right, but she had the uneasy feeling that his explanation for the notes was too simple, what he wanted it to be, not what it was. Someone had gone to a lot of trouble, sending the notes from places that were five thousand miles apart.

She watched Dante walk away, his easy, one-two boneless saunter failing to hide the tension in his well-muscled body. He carried more on those broad shoulders than a sturdy cat, yet unwavering determination marked every step. It affirmed her confidence in him that she and Lehua were in capable hands.

Adding tropical fruits, greens, and coffee beans to Lehua's flower business had surely been Dante's ideas and planning, and he would've had to convince Rosemary of their soundness. With her sudden death, he had shouldered the burden alone. Until now. He deserved her support and help. If they failed the challenge of diversifying and converting the farm, they would have to hear out the developers who waited just out of sight, like scavengers.

As if acknowledging the daunting tasks that lay ahead of them, Aumoe watched her, eyes half closed, until man and cat turned the corner of the big house.

CHAPTER 6

Lani sighed and started for the stairs, determined to finish her list of things to do this first day back, which included making the tiny galley kitchen usable and stocking the bathroom in the studio above it. But a framed picture on an end table sidetracked her. Her breath caught when she saw the four people in the photograph.

Rosemary had been tiny compared to them. Dante towered over his grandmother, while she and Dom were each just a head taller. With age, Rosemary had worn her coarse silver hair layered to follow the curve of her head. While she had appeared to be physically strong and robust, she was fine-boned, like a bird, with a light, almost musical voice.

After Lani put down the photo, she still didn't make it all the way to the top of the stairs. She stopped halfway up, looking over her shoulder toward the empty doorway.

Dante had been the strong one, the enduring one, the serious one of the fraternal Kahoa twins. Dominic's brief life had been full of joy and fun and smiles. Everybody liked Dom. Not only had he been ten minutes younger and many inches shorter than Dante, he'd had a stocky build. And, while Dante had watched life from the sidelines, Dom had met the world head on and welcomed it. Long before Dom's death, however, Dante had not only charged out of his shell, he'd taken time to stomp on it.

The brothers had befriended her on her first childhood visit to her godmother, treating her more like a younger sister than a visitor, the third side of a triangle, as Dante had put it. Subsequent visits only strengthened their bonds of friendship. In Maine, Dante had mentioned a tattoo in reference to the triangle analogy. She had already mentally added that to her list of things to ask him about. For sure.

Dante had already begun to change when she'd come to Lehua to live for five years. The three of them had still seen each other comfortably, yet differently. Then, in her teen years, she'd felt a tension that hadn't been there before. She could put a name to it now. Sexual awareness had briefly reared its head between her and Dante. Dante had been her first crush, or her first love; she could never decide which.

And here she was again, this time living with Dante without Rosemary and Dom to dilute the heady mix. Their attraction to each other, honed when they were teens, was still there because she still felt its slight pull every time he came near her, like he was north to her compass. It would be better for them and Lehua if she turned the storage room upstairs into a bedroom and moved into the cottage. They didn't need distractions right now. She mentally added that topic to her list of things to discuss with Dante.

She ran up the remaining stairs, vigorously rubbing her upper arms against the chill that suddenly touched her, a frisson of fear and anticipation that gave her chicken skin. Pausing at the top, she stared into the huge workroom, all other thoughts fleeing. After a quick peek earlier, followed by a dart into its shadowy depths when she spied the lovely trunk, she had avoided thinking about how she might make the studio her own. She decided in that moment to think of this workspace as being the gift it was, from Rosemary, with a condition. She would always have Rosemary's silent, loving presence observing and counseling her as she worked. And that was fine with her.

She wiped her damp palms on her green cotton shorts. In a moment she'd have to open herself to experience the workshop fully for the first time without Rosemary's beloved physical presence, a presence that had kept her world from spinning out of control when her parents died. She steeled herself, drew a deep breath, stepped inside, and turned the control that worked the sunshades on the tall windows and on the skylights in the ceiling.

She went still, her hand still on the lever. Maybe it was Rosemary Kahoa's spirit, or maybe it was simply Hawaiian sunlight, but as the blinds retracted downward, a blaze of glory and *aloha* filled the room to greet her. Light, like a living thing, poured in through the wide floor-to-ceiling windows that made up two of the high walls, one for the displays on its surface, one for work lighting.

To call the display window on the right a mere window was sacrilege, although it had started life as a plain window. Now it was a work of art, covered in a collage of stained glass panels. She was drawn to that side of the room.

The colors and patterns of the flora and fauna of Hawaii, the theme of most of Rosemary's work, nearly overwhelmed

90

Lani's senses. Then there was the quality of the light itself. Gloriously colored rays penetrated her eyes, nose, ears, and beyond, deep inside her. She stood within the indoor rainbow and breathed in its essence and hues.

The panels, marching up the glass window, were Rosemary's practice panels. Nearly every stained glass window she'd ever done, for churches, homes, and government buildings, had come to life first as a downsized practice panel. Rosemary had mounted her favorites, with a buffer of airspace between the panels and the glass, over one of the workshop windows when she built the cottage. Other panels had been sold to or given to the clients, depending on how easy they were to work with or on the depths of goodness Rosemary sensed within them.

Unable to stop herself, Lani carried out a ritual she had performed from the time she was a little girl, every time she entered this room alone. She stepped forward, deep into the colored light, immersing herself in it, and held out her hands, palms up, testing its presence, lifting her face to it. She expected it to have weight that she might feel on her skin, like rain. She sucked in a gulp of air, unaware that she had been holding her breath. Rosemary's blessing of light, added to Dante's silent blessing of touch earlier, left her breathless and humble and, finally, possessor of the workshop and cottage.

A noise behind her made her turn around. Dante stood in the doorway with his boots in his hands, watching her, his lips parted.

Her hands dropped to her sides. "How long have you been standing there?"

He dropped the boots outside the door. "Long enough. Relax. I knew early on about that weird little thing you do when you come in here alone. I just haven't seen it in a while. And it's still weird, Beecham."

"You watched me do this when I was little?" She gave him the stink eye, Hawaiian dirty looks.

"You did it in front of us the very first time. After that, Dom and I studied you when you visited. You were a rare and exotic little thing."

"Does this mean the whole island knows?"

"No, just me and you. And Dom. Maybe Tutu knew, although we didn't tell her."

"I feel violated."

"Really? I didn't feel a thing. Usually, when I violate someone, I feel a tingle, at least."

"You and Dom were barefoot in those

days." She shifted her glare to where his boots lay.

"It's all wooden floors up here. I was being considerate."

"Right. Considerate. Did your mouths hang open every time you two watched me?"

"Probably. You should see yourself standing in that swath of colored light. You have the whole Hawaiian goddess thing going on." He held up a plastic tube with a pointed tip. "Liquid graphite," he said.

Her mind went utterly blank when he leapfrogged the subject. "For what?"

"The trunk lock." He paused, his face and voice growing somber. "I'm doing this under protest. Understood?"

"Understood. And I'm grateful. Thanks for helping me out." She sketched a mock salute.

He frowned, picked up the trunk without breaking a sweat, and carried it into the storage room, putting it down where she directed, against a wall.

The lovely humpbacked captain's trunk was a new addition since she'd last been in Rosemary's workshop many years ago. She walked over to it, leaning down to take another look at the rusted lock mechanism and the small, delicately ornate key sticking out of the lock. The key still wouldn't budge.

"Go get some of those paper towels you liberated from the big house. You can leave the toilet tissue."

She did as he asked, wondering how he knew her bathroom and tiny galley kitchen contained stolen goods.

When she returned, he got down on his knees in front of the trunk, clutching the strip of three paper towels. He tore off one to wipe his fingers later then smoothed out the remaining two on the floor beneath the lock.

She knelt at a right angle to him, smiling to herself. Despite the first impression told by his venerable hat, which upon closer examination was clean and well brushed, and his broken-in, yet clean and shiny boots, Dante was the neatest man she'd ever known, cleaning up after himself as he went on any job.

He inserted the nozzle as far as he could into the lock's opening and squeezed, working loose and removing the key first. He repeated the steps then sat back, not quite relaxed, on his heels. "We have to give it a minute to soak into the rust in the mechanism."

He grinned unexpectedly, and she blinked as a duet of dimples dove into his cheeks. She kept forgetting about those, although

94

she was sure every female in the valley had no trouble remembering them very well, especially if repeatedly exposed to them. They were fingertip deep and on both sides. *So unfair.* She had one, a shallow little thing.

Those dimples also made her realize how physically close to each other they were, her bare knees brushing his denim-encased hard left thigh. He didn't move away and neither did she, although a voice in her head told her she should do so. It quieted when she reminded it that this was Dante, whom she'd known longer than any other living person in her life. She relaxed fully back onto her heels with a quiet breath.

In his Hawaiian-sky eyes, she tracked the moment he registered her closeness and his awareness of it. His eyes followed her pale pink bra strap as it slid in slow motion down her upper left arm from beneath her hot pink tank top. The warm knowing was gone as quickly as it had flared when she hiked up the strap into place after he looked away. But before he looked away, she had time to explore the brandy-colored icicle shapes around his black pupils, feathering out into the heavenly blue of his irises. She'd forgotten the brown icicles as well.

If he wouldn't break the heavy silence that now rested between them then she would.

"I thought you were going to Kalele?"

"Shaka is staying a few days with his daughter Mary, Mei's mom, in Lihue to take care of some family business. I called him, and he said he could easily get the part in Lihue and bring it back with him. I remembered that the graphite was in the corner cupboard in the big house kitchen."

Heat from his body warmed her in the cool room as he applied more graphite to the trunk's lock. She studied his face while he worked, his clean-shaven square jaw and planed cheeks, then moved on to the width of his shoulders, and the breadth of his chest beneath his denim work shirt. Dante was powerfully built, like the Hawaiian *ali'i* she'd imagined him to be when she was younger.

Unbidden, a memory crept in, that of the soft, wet warmth of his full, beautifully sculpted lips moving against hers. She'd been sixteen when it happened. Right after that kiss, Dom died, Dante graduated alone from high school, and Rosemary sent him off to work on a ranch on the Big Island.

She cleared her throat to clear the memory, putting friendly but businesslike tones into her voice. "Thanks again for doing this for me."

He shot her a quick sideways look. "Anytime you have something that needs to be fixed or heavy work that needs to be done, just ask Shaka or me. If we can't do it, we'll see that it gets done."

She nodded. "I don't have much patience with unpacking, so I tend to do it in spurts. Two hours in the cottage, one hour at the house. Thanks for the three days. That'll be just about right to give me manageable mayhem over here and to put all my stuff away in the right places in that time capsule of a room of mine."

"It's pretty bad, isn't it? If you just lose the posters and the old *leis,* then we can switch out some of your old furniture with pieces from the other bedrooms until you can afford to get some new stuff. I'll help you paint when things calm down."

"Sounds like a plan. And I agree. Later, after I settle in. I'd planned on pulling down the posters and stuff today anyway." She hesitated, wanting to get the words right.

"I promise to pull my weight at Lehua, Dante, but I also need to establish myself in Hawaii as a stained glass artist as soon as possible so I don't lose what little momentum I have. You and the farm will come first, though. You won't have to face things alone anymore."

"*Mahalo.* That's good to hear." A frown,

97

then a look of discomfort, briefly crossed his face. "Did Tutu tell you about the gallery that opened in Kalele? Maybe Melika, the owner, will show some of your stuff. I need to check in with her about some things of Tutu's she still has there. Maybe we can go in together."

"Sounds good. So what else is new around here?"

"Not much besides our apprentice farmers, a different, uptight ornithologist studying honeycreepers on our *pali,* and lots of new plants. That little shack in the middle of Kalele still has the best shave ice on the island."

She suddenly craved the cool treat of her childhood. "My mouth is watering. Another thing to add to my list of stuff I want to do. Yesterday, if not sooner." A brief, comfortable silence fell between them, but she again felt compelled to break it.

"You'll have to teach me, Dante. I don't know anything about growing coffee beans or tropical fruits or greens."

"Don't worry about any of that right now, and don't push yourself too hard over the next couple of days. You should get your driver's license changed over, though, and we already did the change of address thing before we left Maine. I notified the lawyers.

Those are all important things because of the residency requirement."

"I never allowed my driver's license to expire here." She shrugged at his surprised look. "I just couldn't do it."

"Really? I guess we're good then. If you do something about the shop and help out with the flower side of the business for now, I'll teach you the things you need to know when you need to know them. That would be after I learn them myself."

"Nothing new there."

He smiled. "The shop will eventually carry Lehua coffee beans, grown right here, but they'll be roasted elsewhere until we see how it goes."

"What made you choose fruits, greens, and coffee beans for Lehua?"

"They're fast growers and quick money. We have a nice market right here in the islands, so we don't have to think about the exporting hassle, coming up against California and other fruit-producing states and countries that guard their markets fiercely. Hawaiian-grown coffee already has an international market and reputation, and the altitude and soil on some of our valley's slopes are perfect for coffee trees. Simple."

She watched him completely relax back on his heels now as she had done earlier.

"Simple? My mind boggles when I think about what you've taken on."

"Well, realistic then. I hope you have some great ideas to throw into the pot." He stopped and looked around them. "I almost moved into this cottage, you know," he suddenly confided. "When I came home from the ranch, I wanted a place of my own. But Tutu needed a place of her own more. Very independent, my grandmother."

"I remember that part of her personality very well."

"We worked it out," he continued, "and I enjoyed staying in the big house with her, but she wanted a debate every time she needed help with anything, even changing a light bulb that was out of her reach. I had to sweet talk her into it."

Lani had heard from the island girls before she left Lehua that Dante was very good at sweet talk. She had to wonder what the outcome would be if he ever, seriously, decided to try it on her.

Rosemary had told her that when he returned to Kauai from Hawaii, he became notorious for flitting from girl to girl like a butterfly among Lehua's blossoms, never becoming serious about any of them.

"And it's a good thing I was around," he continued, unaware of her wandering thoughts. "She had *pilikia* over here just before she died. Someone turned over this place pretty thoroughly."

Pilikia. Trouble. That was easy to remember. "Here? In the cottage?"

"Nothing was taken and no damage was done, except the mess."

If she had antennae, they'd be spinning like rotors. "Like someone was looking for something in particular, you mean? Did you find out who did it?"

He studied her for a long moment, frowning, and she knew he was exercising his ability to read her mind. "It was probably just kids. There's a crop of them at loose ends in Kalele. Hell-raising is my guess, so rein in that imagination of yours."

He was probably right. Kids. The word brought a flood of memories. "Rosemary took me on at a rough age, for her and for me."

"We were all at a rough age when you moved in. Two teenagers, both boys, and a girl on the threshold." He shook his head. "I don't know how she managed, with the farm and her work and everything."

"I do. She surrounded herself with good, reliable people. And don't you remember? She had a knack for disciplining us without saying a word, simply emanating disappoint-

101

ment in sad waves. We'd have done anything to keep her from being disappointed in us."

She and Dante and Dom had been shaped by the love of the same woman, a woman who corrected with a look, loved with a touch, inspired with a word. Had Rosemary passed on those abilities to them? Not so much.

But those aspects of Rosemary's parenting had made them responsible and mature beyond their years. They had worked hard in the fields, in the shop, in the studio, even in the kitchen, taking turns concocting meals when the schedule demanded it. And they knew how to strip a bed and do laundry. Luckily, the three of them always got along, except minor skirmishes when Dante or Dom teased her, and their teenage rebellions had been minor — or secret.

She nodded toward the trunk, her hands unsteady from the memories. "Hasn't that stuff soaked in enough?" Her voice wobbled there.

He studied her a second too long. The key turned smoothly in the lock this time.

He got to his feet, without lifting the trunk lid, gathering up the paper towels from the floor and wiping his hands on the one he'd saved. "I'm starving. I'm going to Kalele anyway, for food."

"Wait." She rose gracefully to her feet, unable to let him go without broaching the subject. "Have you considered, when you put everything together, that Rosemary's break-in, our notes, and your little accident just might be connected?"

He went very still. "I try very hard not to consider anything that doesn't immediately concern diversifying this place. You're home, and that's what's important to me and Lehua. I don't want to think about or know about notes or anything else until somebody forces me to think about them or know about them. And don't go off on the Lani Beecham version of *Hawaii Five-0* over this."

She stopped to consider this. "Hmm. I had a crush on Jack Lord, and that was from reruns. Can't you think of anyone Rosemary might have told your family story about the gems?"

He closed his eyes for a moment. "Besides you? And sometimes you scare me."

"Not helpful, Danno. The notes —"

"Let trouble come to us, Lani." Exasperation lay heavy in his voice. "Tutu talked to lots of people in her research. How can we possibly know how much she told them? Or maybe a developer is just trying to stir up trouble."

"You see developers behind every plumeria tree. How many developers know or care about Pele's Tears?" She caught herself but not in time to stop the two words he hated. "Sorry. And can't you see that trouble is here already? I know I'm definitely troubled, and that includes the feeling that this isn't over." She shivered. "Now feed me. Chinese, please. We'll put our heads together over takeout."

"No, we will not put out heads together about that. Leave it be, Lani."

He leaned the tiniest bit toward her to reinforce his words, but she stepped up to him, her bare toes very nearly touching his socks, challenging him with a look. Then, suddenly, she was ashamed of herself. They were allies in many things now, important things, and he didn't need this from her.

She dropped her gaze to his shirt pocket. "All right. This round goes to you. At least we can wait for *pilikia* together."

Her tumbled thoughts about Pele's Tears and their tormentor fled when the material around the pocket expanded and tightened as he flexed his wide shoulders.

"Deal," he said, then stepped away from her, turned, and left her alone with the trunk.

He also left her alone with a naked truth she didn't want to acknowledge. Single men who looked like Dante Kahoa were usually milking the bachelor scene for all it was worth. He'd have no problems there, even if he didn't bring his conquests home very often to the big house at Lehua.

Stupid dimples anyway!

CHAPTER 7

Lani dragged her attention back to the trunk, lifting the heavy lid after she was sure Lehua's resident rock star had left the building. A cloud of sweet, spicy cedar scent, mixed with melancholy, engulfed her. On top were baby clothes, hers, with her school records, awards, and school papers layered beneath them.

Below were the same layers of her mother's and father's lives. She recognized a small, handmade quilt in the *maile* vine pattern, crafted by her grandmother, her mother's half-Hawaiian mother. It was carefully wrapped in tissue paper, with more of the paper in the folds to prevent sharp creases. Rosemary had shown the quilt to her many times, promising it would be hers when the time was right. She lifted it out now, planning to gently drape it over a chair, or to somehow display it where she could see it every day.

Even if he hadn't told her, Lani would have known instinctively that Dante had found a trunk, maybe two, much like this one somewhere in the big house, depicting his and Dom's childhoods.

This was Rosemary's way. Lani was aware that in the antique roll-top desk downstairs she would find the deed and the paperwork for the cottage, neatly arranged in one clearly labeled manila envelope, a paper trail of this dwelling's life. And here, in *her* trunk, Rosemary had lovingly gathered the essence of a lifetime of love between a godmother and a tiny girl named Noelani. The things Rosemary had given Lani to hold close told her that Rosemary had loved her the way she had loved her work, her life and her place in it, her boys, her home, and her long-dead beloved, with deep, abiding, all-encompassing *aloha.*

As Lani dashed tears from her eyes, she realized that she had come to the end of her treasures. Not dwelling on what wasn't there, she simply felt limp and ready for a nap, until the light shifted and, like gifts, there were her godmother's familiar sketchbooks and project notebooks lined up across the trunk's shadowy bottom.

Each sketchbook contained drawings that had birthed Rosemary's stained glass windows and panels. Lani leafed through the yellowed paper and spent delightful minutes matching drawings in the books with the practice panels marching up the window in the workroom. Sinking cross-legged onto the floor in front of the trunk, she fanned out the books around her, realizing what she'd been given.

The project books were the core of Rosemary Kahoa's life as a stained glass artist, giving details of her projects' executions and anecdotes about the clients who had commissioned them. What a treasure-trove. She had longed to write a history of Rosemary's stained glass work, but Rosemary had always gently refused when she mentioned it. Finally, she'd given her permission by gifting Lani with the primary sources to do it.

After that creative high, the low set in, and disappointment clawed at her. She had not found the Pele's Tears journal. Maybe after Dom's death, Rosemary, in the throes of guilt and mourning, had destroyed the record of her methodical search for the Kahoa family treasure. Dante had made it clear to each of them at the time that he never wanted to hear those words again, and he had made known to Lani several times recently that his feelings hadn't changed.

Perhaps Rosemary had honored his wishes in that way.

She rose to her knees to replace the items she wanted to store in the trunk. As she lowered an armful to the bottom, she spied something else, a familiar shape that made her freeze. Face down, and blending into the shadows of a dark corner, lay a rather lumpy old leather-bound journal, with a silver pen attached by a worn silken cord. She flipped it over with one shaking finger. It was Rosemary's Pele's Tears journal. Her sickening jolt of recognition turned to a cringe at the unbidden memory of her illicit venture into its pages, and the tragic consequence. She gingerly lifted it out, afraid to open it again. What if she somehow hurt Dante this time just by looking upon the words?

But Rosemary had given permission this time for Lani to read her private words. Maybe that would make a difference. Rosemary had put the journal in *her* trunk, the believer's trunk, wanting her to read it. That meant it belonged to her now. With both horrid fascination and a sharp longing, Lani made herself comfortable, her back against the trunk, and prepared to hear Rosemary Kahoa's lilting voice in her head once more, praying that after her new, permission-granted foray into the journal Dante wouldn't die.

She opened it at the green slip of paper that said "Start Here." Tears blurred Lani's vision at seeing her full name written in the familiar, flowing script.

My sweet Noelani,

If you're reading this, then I've moved on to be with my beloved, and you're in possession of your treasure trunk. As I write this, I haven't yet told you about the trunk.

This journal, my keiki, *my darling child, as you already know, chronicles my search for Pele's Tears.*

My search almost ended with Dominic's death, but I decided to continue it in his memory. You joined me in my belief that the elusive trio of gems is real. The boys humored me, I think, with Dominic believing a bit more than Dante ever did.

So, out of respect for Dante's feelings and wishes, and your uncanny way of making him see sense, I will confirm to you and you alone that we were right to believe. The fabulous egg-size trio of gems exists. How do I know this? Because I found them, of course! I'll share with you later the decision I made concerning them.

Then it will be your choice, yours and Dante's, whether or not you search them out, if only to see them, or to sell them. You have my blessing either way.

Lani paused, gasping, her eyes tripping over the words as she reread them. Rosemary had found Pele's Tears? They were real?

As you know, I researched both my family and its legend, and searched for the gems my whole life. I continued my quest quietly after you left and Dante returned. And, as was my habit, I kept a low profile, to avoid attracting the attention of those who might dig on the grounds or break into the house looking for treasure.

Lani swiped sudden perspiration from her upper lip, remembering the incident here at the cottage. "See!" she said aloud to the absent Dante.

The word echoed off the walls of the storage room, reminding her she was alone and that someone had been in the cottage at least once without permission. She fought to bring her rampaging imagination to heel, with little success.

Surely there must be a connection between the break-in, the notes, and Dante's arranged accident in the garden? Someone else knew Rosemary had found Pele's Tears, someone she had confided in. That's what the notes were about. Her confidant was betraying her and wanted the gems for himself. But who would Rosemary have trusted that much? She turned back to the journal, hoping for answers.

I avoided telling the three of you the story of Pele's Tears until your ages were in the double digits. There wasn't a traditional age to expose young family members to the story, so I waited. Dominic's death proved to me that I didn't wait long enough, or that I should have taken youthful enthusiasm, lack of fear, and feelings of immortality into closer consideration. In other words, I should have watched all of you more carefully after I told you. For that, I will never forgive myself.

The details of the Pele's Tears story are written out in the first part of this journal, and you already know our family's quiet legend of the gems and my search for them. I think, when you read it again, you'll agree that the glory of the story is lost in translation to paper. Much better to "talk story" about them, the way we did a few times, the four of us. Those are bittersweet memories now.

I'll refresh your memory briefly, or maybe it's just because I love to tell this story, like I'm hearing it again for the first time from my father.

Our family has a history of mixing our blood with haole *blood. It started when James Talbot-Kahoa, a New England sea captain, came to these islands and married my many-greats grandmother.*

Just a little side trip here, as Dante would say: I would have joyfully carried on the tradition had my beloved lived. I did, however, have my Kimo, our only child. Kimo, late in life, married the lovely and volatile Inez, the twins' Italian mother. The family habit continued in your remote branch of the family when your mother, a distant relation, met your father in college on the mainland and fell in love.

But back to the good captain. Captain Talbot-Kahoa sailed clipper ships from San Francisco to the Orient and the South Seas. He adopted Hawaiian ways and myths wholeheartedly, even taking the Kahoa name. I don't know where or how he acquired the gems. I found no bill of sale or other transfer of ownership anywhere. When James came upon, bought, or stole the trio of egg-size stones, he named them by adapting them to the old Hawaiian love story chant of Pele and Lohi'au, thus Pele's Tears.

My father, a stained glass artist in his own right in a family of various artisans, was enamored of the story, and he passed his enthusiasm on to me. His interest waned at its very peak when my mother died. When I began my search, I visited every panel and window or other work of art this family had created and which still exists, just in case. I examined any bits and pieces of glass left from other times, with no success.

I found no spurt of money injected into the family coffers at any point that would mark the sale of the gems, which led me to believe they hadn't been found, separated, cut into smaller gemstones, or disposed of. I was right.

Pele's Tears exist, my keiki. The glorious trio shines and lives again in the light because I gave them back to the light. You'll find them through the light, but away from family and loved ones, as did Captain Talbot-Kahoa and, possibly, as my father did. That's all I'll tell you, but I've left two things that might help you, if you choose to ponder them. They're in a silk pouch in

114

the back of this journal, in a little pocket I made with paper and glue.

Lani used her thumb to hold the back cover upright while she let the weight of the journal's pages fall away from it. No wonder the journal felt and looked lumpy. She pulled out the peacock-blue silk pouch and dumped the contents into her left hand. A piece of heavy parchment covered with spidery, pale, handwritten words was wrapped around the ugliest gold pendant she'd ever seen.

It was strung on a sturdy gold chain. Part of the large, roughly circular pendant was in a puffed, quilted pattern of gold, and the jagged bottom edge looked like someone had taken a bite out of it. Its only redeeming feature was a few round, smooth olivine cabochons set within the top one-third of the gold.

On the paper, which she'd have to study more closely and very privately, she caught the words "glowing eyes." Stunned, Lani gaped at her discoveries for a full minute before turning back to the journal itself.

I hope my decision atones for any past sins of the family because the gods surely called for atonement from the Kahoas for some reason. Dominic's death was proof of that, for me at least. I believe my father may also have found them but left them where they were to protect me, in case they were the cause of my mother's death. Our family was never prolific, and our history is littered with early deaths. I fear that might be the price we have had to pay for the manner in which the gems came into our possession.

So, if Rosemary found them and hid them again, that meant she was afraid for Dante too. Chills climbed Lani's spine as the next passage confirmed it.

And so I assign to you and Dante, the last of his and your family lines, the task of letting them pass into history — or not. I suspect you might choose to look for them, reclaim them, and sell them to help Lehua. I don't know how you'll convince Dante to help you, but you must. I don't want you to search alone, as I did, but you must watch over him if he helps you. I fear the curse might be strong in his blood. While you are farther removed from the direct Kahoa bloodline, you should be very careful as well.

When you convince him, I'm hoping the special bond you two have always shared is strong enough to overcome any linger-

ing evil attached to our families and the gems. If you choose to search for Pele's Tears, and if you find them, it will be your decision what you do with them. As I have said, you have my blessing on your choice, whatever it might be.

Now I'm weary, and this story is yours, my keiki, *to do with what you will. If you choose to search with Dante, I hope your journey won't be as long or as difficult as mine.*

And if you decide to write that book about my life's work, you have what you need, my sketchbooks and projects books, in your treasure trunk. As you know, the financial paperwork for each project is downstairs in the filing cabinet.

If you search and find Pele's Tears' place of peace, I hope you might want to write their story as well, to exorcise them from your lives and move them into the pages of Hawaiiana.

Remember, you'll find them through light. I was very careful about that.

Lani glanced away from the page, unseeing, thinking of the things Rosemary had just told her. Pele's Tears shine and live again in the light? Rosemary gave them back to the light? Find them through light? Find their place of peace? She had no idea what or where Rosemary meant, or what the two disparate objects she'd found might point to. Maybe that was her godmother's intention. It certainly wasn't much to go on if she chose to search for them. Who was she kidding? Of course she was going to search for them, with or without Dante. She went back to the journal's final page.

My primary sources, or photocopies of those sources, are stored in the lid of your treasure trunk. The liner pulls down. Real cloak-and-dagger stuff!

Consign their story to the annals of the Kahoa family, or start your own search for Pele's Tears, with Dante's help. Whichever you choose, don't forget to live your life while you journey.

Don't mourn me, my dear. Play the World War II big band records and CDs I've left for you downstairs, and imagine me young again and dancing with the one and only love of my life. That's what my heaven will be, dancing again in his arms.

Aloha, *my sweet Noelani.*

Lani pulled in a deep breath on a sob, not realizing her breathing had been fast and shallow. Briefly, she wondered if Rosemary's mind had been clear when she wrote this part of the journal. Ashamed, she quickly shoved the thought away. Her godmother had been the most sensible, down-to-earth person she'd ever known, right up until her heart gave up the fight.

Gentle but headstrong, white-haired and artistic Rosemary Kahoa had been a treasure hunter to the end — and had found Pele's Tears! *Good for you, Rosemary!*

It was too much to take in. And how could she tell Dante? Should she tell Dante at all, or should she just search on her own, despite Rosemary's wishes? And what about the note writer? Who was the other person who knew all this?

With hands that shook, she tugged at the edges of the flat trunk-lid liner. It pulled down in one stiff piece. Beneath it, under the trunk's "hump," books and papers, held up by straps, filled the space. She hastily shoved the liner back into place, slammed the lid, and sat back on her heels.

Finding out that Pele's Tears existed was like finding out that Hawaii's legendary race of small people, *Menehunes,* and the Easter Bunny and Santa Claus were real. It was a lot to get her mind around. She decided to hold Rosemary's revelations close to her heart for a few days until she settled into the rhythm of life at Lehua again. Meanwhile, she would study Rosemary's clues when the time was right — and she would study Dante when the opportunities presented themselves — hoping he'd give her an opening, a sign, that he could hear this bombshell without disowning her or strangling her.

CHAPTER 8

Lani put everything back into the trunk
except the sketchbooks, the project notebooks, her quilt, and the journal, then
closed the lid gently this time, locked it,
and took the key out of the lock. She wiped
the key with a tissue and fed it onto the
pendant's long, sturdy gold chain, put it
around her neck, and dropped the cluster
beneath the neck of her tank top. Later, she
would hide them in her room in the big
house.

In a subdued mood, she worked in the
workshop for the next hour, unpacking her
own things and packing up items she didn't
want, didn't need, or couldn't use. She'd
taken Rosemary's musical advice. Downstairs, her godmother's big band CDs
played one after the other. On her many
trips to the lower floor, she found herself
walking around the young, in-love, imagi-
nary couple dancing there.

Her stomach rumbling, she looked out one of the storage room windows yet again to finally see Dante's 4X4 lava-red pickup truck pull up to the big house, with its deep *lānais,* red-tiled roof, and saltbox-style second story and lean-to kitchen at the back, and then continue around the house to the cottage.

She was halfway down the stairs when his knock and *"Aloha!"* sounded. Instead of striding in, he paused on the mat outside the open door. She knew Dante usually ignored the Hawaiian custom of removing footwear before entering a home, saying *paniolo* boots were exempt, but she got the impression that he swiped his venerable Stetson from his head simply to cover his hesitation. She watched his thick, soft, irrepressible dark waves spring toward freedom.

Stopping on the bottom step to study him, she said in disbelief, "Don't tell me you're waiting for me to invite you in?" Suddenly feeling the burden of her new knowledge about Pele's Tears, she sat down on the step behind her.

"I'm just trying to respect your privacy, and I hope you'll respect mine."

Despite her discomfort, her words filtered through a grin as she tossed off her favorite childhood challenge to him. "You'll never make it back to the truck with my food, Kahoa. Get over yourself and get in here. I'm starving."

When they were kids, it had always been "You'll never do this or that, Kahoa — or Beecham."

"What took you so long?" She took one of the carrier bags from him. "And what about our privacy and the sleepover crew I met in the hall this morning? It was like a fire drill in a bordello."

He grinned. "You speak from experience, do you?"

"Nope. Too particular. You're not going shy on me in our advancing years?"

"It was a temporary glitch. I have to get used to you on my turf all over again." He paused to shoot her a look. "We have this history together, but we need to respect each other's adult space at the same time now."

"When you stomp on our history, my space, or my privacy, I'll let you know. And I invite you to do the same to me. How's that for simple and fair and decided?" She opened the bag, stuck her nose inside, and inhaled deeply.

One step had brought him into the cottage's Hawaiian parlor, the equivalent of a

123

living room on the mainland. The area had been Rosemary's reception area for clients.

"Kitchen, parlor, or *lānai?*" she asked.

"The kitchen. The heart of the home."

Her steps slowed as she silently recalled meals, snacks, family conferences, and homework around the granite island in the big house kitchen. It had been Rosemary's loving presence that had bound them together there.

"Rosemary made us the heart of her home and her life, in the big house kitchen."

"I know. Where do you think I learned it?" he said quietly, holding her gaze. "Are you okay? You're awfully pale. You weren't when I left."

She nearly choked. "I'm fine. Something I found in my trunk just knocked me a little bit sideways."

He didn't ask.

They settled down to eat at the inlaid wood table that folded down flat against the wall, transforming into a piece of artwork when not in use. She opened the bags one by one and set the Chinese takeout boxes between them. Because she was out of practice, she declined chopsticks. He used his with dexterity.

"Show off," she said while they passed the containers back and forth, neither of them needing plates.

The table was small and her knee brushed his. She moved it, but as soon as she relaxed, back it went, resting lightly against his. Without missing a bite, he hiked back his chair and rearranged his long legs until one of her knees was trapped between his.

She avoided looking at him then pointed the conversation in practical directions. They discussed shopping and meals and agreed to ask Helen for a few more hours a week. A trip to the bank would be necessary to open a household checking account they could both use. If Helen declined or couldn't help sometimes, they hashed out a schedule of sorts. Lani would shop for staples; Dante would pick up any special or bulk items she ordered or had put aside at the grocery store in Kalele. Shopping wants and needs were to be posted on the refrigerator by Thursday evening. They would be on their own for breakfast and lunch, although Lani would add quick, appropriate choices for those meals to the shopping list. If Helen failed them, each would be responsible for dinner one weeknight per week, leaving two nights per week for leftovers and one night for individual take-out, eating out with friends, or finishing off what was left. Weekends were date nights.

Find your own, both food and dates.

During their discussion, she didn't broach the subject of her moving into the cottage and tried to avoid even a stray thought about Pele's Tears.

"What would you like to drink?" She got up to set out glasses. "I made some iced teas."

"Then I guess I'll have iced tea."

"Good choice." She smiled and opened wide the door of the small refrigerator. In a ta-da gesture, she indicated a row of three small pitchers inside. "Name your poison."

With his gaze locked on the selection, he wiped his full lips on a paper napkin. "You keep up this tea thing while I'm planting coffee trees, and I'll have to run you off the place," he said softly. "Pick one, the more exotic the better."

She poured two glasses of a green tea flavored with lotus flowers then sat down again. They ate for a while in silence. She wondered what his reaction would be if she just got it over with and blurted out her new knowledge.

To keep from doing so, she instead blurted out the next thing to come into her head. "So tell me about Aumoe. How did you get him?"

He smiled. Dante carried a very nice line

126

of dimpled smiles. "I was on my way home late one night —"

"Or early one morning. Of course you were."

"— minding my own business," he continued doggedly, ignoring her comment, "and certainly not looking for a pet. But there he was, sitting alone on the outskirts of Kalele, looking for all the world like he was waiting for someone. Apparently it was me.

"When I stopped, just to see if he was hurt, he climbed my jeans then my shirt. He was in my face, meowing like crazy. I would swear he was saying, 'Where have you been? I've been waiting right here for you.' "

Lani's heart went out to the black cat and this basically kind but reluctant-to-let-it-show man sitting across from her who had stopped and given a defenseless kitten a safe, loving home. "Poor thing. Someone must have abandoned him."

"I guess so. He curled up on the seat beside me, and he's been at Lehua ever since. He never goes farther away from the house than the cottage."

Glancing up from her food, she looked pointedly at his ring finger. "Now tell me about this love life of yours that you keep accusing me of being interested in. Some people might think you're dying to tell me all about it, which is why you keep bringing it up. That group would include me, by the way."

"I don't keep bringing it up, you do." He raised his head and caught her in his blue-laser gaze. "I will if you will."

"Oh. It's a deal then," she said brightly, "because I haven't got one that I've noticed. I've apparently misplaced it. Or maybe it hasn't caught up with me yet. Things were shaping up nicely with Aidan, though, until you made your pilgrimage to Maine."

"In all the excitement, I've misplaced my love life too. What a coincidence."

"Not fair!" But she conceded gracefully. "Aidan is stopping here on his way home, hoping for work of some kind. So we'll have a chance to take up where we left off."

"Really." With an accompanying thunderous frown, he deftly changed the subject. "So in two days' time I can put you to work on farm and shop business?"

She nodded. "Thanks again for giving me the time. The unpacking is going well enough that I can easily be in your hair around the place in a couple of days." She added in a disgruntled tone, "Why am I so nervous about that?"

"I have no idea since my hair and my nerves are familiar stomping grounds for you. Seriously, you're probably nervous because little Lani Beecham is all grown up now and owns half the valley to boot. You'll relate to the people you knew here differently now, just as they'll relate differently to you. We'll all get used to it."

She blinked, instantly believing him. It would be all right, given time. "I don't remember you being this astute."

He snorted. "And I'll bet there's probably a lot about me you'd like to forget."

"Not really. It's more fun to remember every tiny detail. My time with you and Dom and Rosemary was magical."

He stood up, putting the leftovers into a bag. "Reheats. My night." He flashed a wide grin. "I'm glad you're home, Lani."

"Same here. I know that bad memories will still happen but I can handle them better here at Lehua, thanks to our cleansing-by-fire talk in Maine."

"It helped me too, you know." And he was gone.

Exhausted, she went to bed early that night, her fit of nervousness subsiding. She would look in on the shop whenever. She would study Rosemary's clues whenever. She would unpack more of her stuff whenever. Her last thought as she drifted off was how much she had missed this place and how lonely she had been on the mainland with nothing of Lehua around her except memories.

Unpacking took up most of her time over the next two days. On her fourth morning home, The Colonel went off with the sun. She realized by then that he and Aumoe apparently had reached an agreement. Each pretended the other wasn't there: cannot be seen, cannot be heard. It saved embarrassment on both sides.

As soon as she was dressed in black shorts and a yellow T-shirt, Lani's thoughts drew her, coffee in hand, across the garden to the circular window above the cottage door. It hadn't been there when she left eight years ago. Sometime in those years, Rosemary had found Pele's Tears and never let on. And Dante had told her this was one of the last projects Rosemary had done. Was this window another clue? And if it was, why hadn't Rosemary mentioned it in the journal? Did it somehow represent a particular place on the farm?

She analyzed the window as sunlight poured through the jewel-toned glass. She'd have to recheck Rosemary's journal just to be sure of the wording, but this creation certainly lived in the light.

If she applied the Pele's Tears story to the

window, then the clear cabochon moon in the sky could be the diamond in the family story, which represented Pele's tears of pure joy at her love for Lohi'au, a young, handsome chief Pele met at a *hula* festival on Kauai. The goddess took the form of a beautiful young woman so she could join the dancing. Having human desires, Pele fell in love with him.

The smaller blue glass cabochon, depicting the biggest star in the heavens, fit the middle part of the story, a sapphire, Pele's tears of sadness when she had to leave her young lover on Kauai and return to the Big Island.

The window's sun was deep yellow, almost orange, like a setting sun. No stone in that color range played a part in the family story. She had always imagined the reputed Pele's Tears ruby to be blood red, since it symbolized Pele's tears of anger when she discovered her lover's feelings for her sister, which led Pele to kill him. Rosemary hadn't used red in this window.

There was only one way to rid herself of her niggling doubts. She'd have to climb up there, not one of her favorite things since that day on the *pali* when Dom died. The decorative stepstool Dante had used to retrieve Aumoe from the ledge wouldn't

131

bring her level with the window where she needed to be, so she set down her coffee mug and went outside where she found a small utility ladder behind the cottage. She carried it inside to the front door.

Aumoe, suspecting she had designs on his sunny, curved window ledge, strolled in to watch her every move. She jiggled the ladder, checking that it was fully open and braced properly on the floor. With legs quivering, she mentally grasped her courage in both hands and climbed upward, a step at a time, to the three-step ladder's very top, where she stood clutching the ledge. She kept her gaze on the window until she was up close and personal with the sky in the circular stained glass piece.

The sun, moon, and star certainly looked like innocent glass cabochons set into the panel. She peered at them closely, her nose almost touching the glass, her eyes very nearly crossing. *Nah.* To use the gems in this window was simply too obvious.

"What are you doing up there?" Dante's voice came from somewhere around the backs of her knees.

She loved Dante's voice, but she had discovered over time that if she heard it in any combination of sudden, loud, or angry, it was like the voice of God delivering a

132

message of biblical proportions. The results were unpredictable. Like now.

Her knees buckled without a fight as she simultaneously jumped, screamed, and let go of the ledge. She lost her balance and folded backward right off the ladder, kind of like sitting down in midair. She waited for impact with the tile floor, and the crunching pain that must surely follow, but something slowed her fall then cushioned her landing, something solid yet squishy.

Dazed, but happily safe at floor level, she sat quite still, making little squeaking sounds of shock before looking to her left and down. She was sitting on Dante, right where his diaphragm would be, and he was making little huffing sounds in counter time to her shocked little squeaks. He must have plucked her out of midair, bless him, and her momentum took him down with her.

Despite signs of his distress, like his Hawaiian-sky blue eyes bulging and his tanned face turning putty-colored, she was too shocked and amazed to move.

Finally, in a rasping voice she'd never heard from him before, he croaked, "You can get off me now, unless you're planning to hatch me."

Apparently, that was all she needed. She swore in Hawaiian, trying some new words,

133

as she rolled off him onto her knees then to her feet and extended her hand to help him get up. His pained grin told her she hadn't gotten the words right. She'd have to listen more closely when he went on a swearing binge.

What would she tell him she'd been doing up there? If he suspected it had anything to do with Pele's Tears, she'd have to sit on this *huhū,* angry, Hawaiian again. She stopped as a new thought leapfrogged into her mind. Under the right circumstances, and with everyone breathing properly, she wouldn't have minded being in this situation at all.

"I'm so sorry, but you scared me to death. Are you okay?"

He sat up, retrieving his hat. "I'll let you know."

He finally took her outstretched hand, unfolding off the floor in one smooth movement then pulling her close to him, eye to eye. "Are you okay, *pōpoki* eyes?"

"Other than a heart attack, my cat eyes and I are fine."

"What were you doing up there?"

She stepped back and looked away. "I was looking at Rosemary's window. Studying it. It's like nothing she ever did before."

"Uh-huh. And did this looking and studying have anything to do with that trunk upstairs?"

This was typical of him. While she worried herself down to her last nerve about this subject coming up between them, let alone how to break the momentous but disturbing news to him, he brought up the subject himself. Irritating, that's what he was.

"Maybe. I thought you didn't want to know?"

"I don't. Forget I asked."

She saw her opportunity slipping away. "But you don't understand. Rosemary —"

His forefinger against her lips stopped her words. It rested there in tantalizing stillness. "I don't want or need to know. Just don't do anything stupid, like climb ladders or cliffs. We went down the stupid and gullible road together once before." He finally took his finger away, slowly, with a little side-to-side caress.

She closed her eyes in a combination of memory and awareness that his words and that lingering finger had brought. When she opened them again, she was looking at his lips, sculpted and sensuous and tempting as sin. She sought something less dangerous to look at, discovering that his assessing stare wasn't it.

"Is that boy bullying you already?" Shaka's beloved, familiar voice broke their staring match.

"Just keeping me in line, that's all."

She turned away from Dante and toward the man who had been the closest thing to a father figure she had known since her own father's death. Shaka was the only person, other than Dante, that she'd briefly sought out after the funeral.

Slim, wiry, and falling short of her own five feet eight height by at least two inches, Shaka studied her through deep brown eyes and years of unconditional love. He opened his sun-toughened arms, and she ran into them.

"Little Noelani," he said softly. "Sorry I couldn't stay longer at your welcome home *lū'au* up Lihue way. You was feelin' no pain."

"That was the objective."

"I was doing some stuff for Mary. You remember Mary, my daughter, Mei's mother?"

Lani felt a gap where several fingers of his left hand should be resting against her back. Shaka had lost most of his index, middle, and ring fingers in a farming accident at Lehua when he was a teenager, leaving the full thumb and little finger in a perpetual shaka sign. Hence his nickname.

136

Despite the meaning of his nickname, Shaka didn't "hang loose" often. He took life seriously and was proud of his job as Lehua's inventor, troubleshooter, and foreman.

"I remember Mary, and I've met Mei, all grown up. How are you, Shaka?"

She looked at him closely in the light, concerned, seeing things she had been in no shape to notice in Lihue. But she'd swear his dried *lau hala*-tone skin sported more wrinkles since the funeral, and his fuzzy dark hair was even more grizzled with white.

"Getting too old and feeling too old to wait much longer for you to come home, Lani."

She swallowed the lump in her throat. "Well, I'm home now, Shaka, for good. Dante tells me it's time for me to earn my keep around here." Avoiding Dante's suspicious stare, she asked, "May I hitch a ride with you to the shop? I can get in some exercise by jogging home after I look around."

On the mat on the *lānai* outside the front door, she shoved her feet into her running shoes that sat beside her "slippahs," taking her socks along with her to put on in the truck.

Dante handed her a set of shop keys. "I

137

was bringing these to you. You might need them. Have fun."

With a wave of her hand and a feeling of relief, she was glad to leave Dante, his stubbornness, his tempting mouth, and his all-seeing gaze behind for a while.

CHAPTER 9

She and Shaka caught up with each other's
lives while they rode to the mouth of the
valley in his decrepit, rusted pickup truck.
He'd refused Dante's old one at trade-in
time, declaring this one was "mo bettah."

"What's this I hear about you and Helen
Hiroki?" she asked in what she hoped was a
teasing tone.

"That *wahine* the best thing that could
happen to this old man."

"I'm glad. For both of you. When I saw
Mei on my first morning home, we didn't
recognize each other."

"That Mei, she's a wild one," he told her,
shaking his head. "She worry me and her
mother to death. You see this hair? Mei the
reason it look like this. She got into some
trouble in Lihue. Dante told me to bring
her here. When she got into trouble in
Kalele, he gave her a job, put her to work.
She live with Helen and me. She settle

139

down some, but we still worry about her."

They passed Shaka's house, halfway between the big house and the shop. He rented from Dante, from them, really. It gave her pause when she realized that she and Dante now owned every inch of Lehua Valley.

Lehua's newly refurbished Beans and Blossoms, the wholesale end of Lehua's flower farm and soon-to-be coffee bean business, sat near where their private dirt road met the end of the paved county road. Shaka swung the old pickup into the shop's enlarged, graveled parking area. The new, larger lot was a real improvement.

In the old days, Rosemary had appointed her as assistant manager when Lani organized the other kids who worked with her at the shop into an efficient team. She had been in charge of scheduling, and it had been a sore point between her and Dante.

"Can't stay, Lani. The boss and I installing a conveyor belt in the packing shed today."

Lani felt her smile begin. "Dante just thinks he's the boss. Even though he's thought that from the time he could walk, we all know you're the real boss of Lehua. And let me guess. The conveyor belt is your idea and design?" When he nodded, she continued. "I don't know what we'd do without you, Shaka. Thanks for the lift." She planted a resounding kiss on his leathery cheek.

She turned and stared at the newly expanded cement block building, then walked around it after Shaka drove away. Dante had doubled its size. A mural artist, someone local, she hoped, had done a great job of painting its outside walls with scenes of fruit and flower fields, crops that grow in Hawaii. The whole building was a traffic-stopping, jaw-dropping work of art. They also now had a tall lighted tracking sign that stood above the roofline, which shouted, over and over again, "Welcome home, Lani," in red against black. Dante. So sure of her return that he'd probably put it on the sign before he left for Maine.

The shop was scheduled to open in another hour, according to the hours posted on the door. She used her new key to let herself and her memories inside.

A short, snaky line of shiny new shopping carts greeted her on the other side of the glass double doors. Beyond the carts, on both sides of the first wide, well-lit aisle, were two new, large lighted glass coolers. Tall and short containers of Lehua's finest blooms lined the stepped shelves inside them. As in the past, anything they didn't grow themselves, they bought from other local growers. Surrounded on both sides by protea, anthuriums, hibiscus, orchids, bird of paradise, ginger, and *leis* of all descriptions, Lani felt she was in the company of old friends.

She blinked when she saw a rare *maile lau li'i mokihana* rope *lei* among the *leis.* The small-leaved *maile lau li'i,* the most fragrant of the *maile* vines, and the light green *mokihana* berries, which looked like small, rounded dice, grew only on Kauai.

"Has to be a special order," she said to herself.

Looking down, she noted that the floor was a little dirty. Other than that, everything looked neat. Mats at the entrance would help with the dirt-tracking problem.

She continued her inspection, moving toward the checkout area between the sparsely filled aisles of wire shelves. Dante was right. The place needed attention. Fast. The racks she passed had a few varieties of bagged coffee strung out like islands across a sea of wire. Better, fuller displays and several lines of coffee, tea, and flower-arranging accessories were definitely called for. Local crafts would be a big draw and would sell well too. Maybe they could take crafts on a consignment basis.

And they needed to advertise, featuring specials and maybe a flower club. They could print up punch cards for that. When a customer bought, say, nine stems, plants, *leis,* or bouquets, they'd get the tenth free.

Lani patted her shorts pockets, looking for something to write on, then spied a small notebook and pen at one checkout. She began making notes. A bell over the entrance door would alert the clerks to someone entering, and observation mirrors in each corner would allow them to see what people were doing once they were inside. From her earlier experiences of working here, she knew that the clerks talked when things were slow, sitting on the bagging area of the checkouts, resting their feet on the shelf beneath. Stools at each of the checkouts would solve that problem.

She also noted that the updated checkouts were now at right angles to the shelves. The clerks should be able to look straight back the aisles from the checkouts. She examined how the aisle displays were fixed to the floor. It would be easier to move the displays than to move the checkouts.

Also, it was too quiet, and she didn't see any speakers around the ceiling. People didn't like to shop without light sound to cover their comments and discussions with friends about their purchases, and music would also mask any personal conversations the clerks were having. Soft Hawaiian background music and chants would solve both problems.

She grunted with satisfaction to see that Dante had added a second restroom, one marked *Kāne,* the other *Wahine,* each with two stalls.

With the new space, inside and out, new product lines, and larger bathrooms, they'd have to put out the word that Lehua's Beans and Blossoms could now accommodate tourist vans or one bus, if arrangements were made ahead of time. Maybe they were already doing that; she'd have to ask. But they'd have to make it worth the trip, get more stock in here, like now.

She made yet another note. She'd have quite a report for Dante tonight. A lot of it would be praise for him and what he'd accomplished so far.

Her gaze fell on the little control panel and keyboard for the tracking sign outside. Since reading Rosemary's journal, and failing to find the right words or the right time to tell Dante what she'd found out, she had felt a sense of urgency about their Pele's Tears tormentor. If she did what she was thinking of doing, she would not only trigger Dante's anger, but precipitate the need for her to tell him what she'd read in the journal. Soon. Maybe even tonight if he came this way and saw the sign.

But maybe a well-worded new message would curb the relentlessness she sensed in this person and stop future deliveries of cryptic notes or arranged accidents until they could sort themselves out. She knew that she, personally, was reeling from the activities of the past three days and the prospect of a major harvest in the near future. So much for taking it slow and settling into Lehua's rhythm.

The sign system was intuitive. She easily typed in the new message, previewed it, and sent it through before she could change her mind. Beans and Blossoms' lighted tracking sign now read, "Coming soon: Pele's Tears." She'd think of something later to fulfill the implied promise to shop customers.

The two clerks arrived fifteen minutes before opening time. That was good. Maile was a dark-haired beauty, and Kalana, the shorter of the two sixteen-year-olds, was equally beautiful but rounder and more voluptuous. Lani had no problem imagining Dante's enjoyment at interviewing these two.

The girls wanted all the summer hours she could give them right away, before school started, and all the hours she could manage for them on weekends and after school. While she was at it, she lined up their circle of friends, who would work for pizza, to set up a stereo system and reorient the display aisles. She also shamelessly picked their brains for family contacts in the tourist industry so she could set up tour stops at Beans and Blossoms, and asked for the names of anyone they knew who did Hawaiian crafts and might like to fill some of their shelves with consignment items.

As soon as she had a chance to consult with Dante and go over her impressive shopping list with him, she'd have a session on the computer, ordering new lines, floor mats, and anything else she hadn't thought of, from businesses in Kauai or the other islands, if possible.

She quietly observed the girls for a while. Maile and Kalana were good clerks. They had the basics down. Dante had probably enjoyed teaching them those as well.

Her time in the shop meant the day was slipping away from her, and she had work to do on stained glass projects that were contracted works in progress. Once finished, those projects would go back the way they

146

had come, but from Hawaii to the mainland this go-round, giving them a certain cachet that she hoped would build her reputation as a stained glass artist of Hawaiian heritage and inspiration.

She took the rare *maile* vine and *mokihana* berry rope *lei* out of a cooler, inhaling its mixture of spicy and anise scents. It carried a red Special Order tag that was blank, so she took it to the checkout to ask the girls about it.

She had plans for this wonderful *lei,* this adornment of stature that was usually worn to special social gatherings, or given to honored visitors or graduates or the bride and groom at weddings. It would be put to special use today.

She was starting a tab for herself and one for Dante, each labeled Personal Use, when the girls told her the *lei* was for her and that Dante had ordered them not to sell it. She froze with its weight resting across her left forearm.

Maneuvering the *lei* so she could accept the price tag one of the girls was handing to her, she turned over the tag and saw her name written there. Beneath it was Helen Hiroki's signature. Shaka's Helen, a master *lei*-maker, had made these special *leis* in Lani's time here at the shop, gathering the

147

maile lau li'i vine and *mokihana* berries herself up in the mountains.

She saw Dante's hand in this too, so sure she would come home with him that he had probably commissioned this *lei* for her before he came to Maine. Why didn't she just ask Dante where she should go and what she should do, instead of wasting time believing she had some control over her life? Damn the man, and the fact he knew her well enough to know she'd want this very *lei* right about now as a remembrance offering.

She would be glad of the opportunity to jog off her frustration on her way back to the house after her detour. With the rope *lei* hanging around her neck and down both sides of her body, she started toward the overlook, knowing she would soon hear the sound of waves and feel the bittersweet tang of memories.

Their road from the valley came to a Y beyond the shop, and the end of the paved county road was a few yards off to the right, in Kalele's direction. She took the left-hand dirt track, moving between Private Property signs after she reached the turnaround. A path to the right wandered around outcrops of lava rock until it ended at a wall of green. The overlook was on the other side of a thick windbreak of Australian casuarina trees and Hawaiian native shrubs, at the top of a small *pali* that overlooked the end of Lehua's beach.

She pushed through the thick plants. It had been from the overlook that Dante had scattered Dom's ashes, and probably Rosemary's, into the trade winds and the Pacific below. The trade winds were usually strong here, but this was one of those late summer days when Hawaii was without her trade winds.

Rosemary had taken the overlook in hand during their childhoods, for safety reasons. A small semicircle of stone terrace and a thigh-high wall now reinforced the cliff edge, providing an excellent overlook and a quiet, peaceful, private place, with the sounds of wind and waves for company.

In the very center was a stone platform with a smooth, polished lava stone top edged in teak. It was big enough to use as a table, as a meditation platform, or, she always added to herself, as a sacrificial altar should the need arise. And she spoke from experience. She had been the perpetual virginal sacrifice when Dante and Dom felt in touch with their Hawaiian side and needed a pretend victim.

From the platform's surface, the ocean

view was visible over the low wall. She had periodically used the platform to watch for Hawaii's green flash, a fleeting splash of emerald that appears momentarily on the horizon just at sunset or sunrise. Because of the overlook's orientation, it had to be sunrise, but she hadn't seen the flash before she left the island. Dante had despaired of her. She had always blinked or looked away or fallen asleep at the wrong moment. He had smugly told her earlier that he still saw it almost every time he looked for it, when the conditions were right.

Rosemary had also brought Dante, Dom, or her here when life got rough. For her that had been after her parents' deaths; when her first experiment with the opposite sex, Noa Takei in the flower prep shed, ended badly with the infamous Dante-Takei brothers intervention; and when Dom died. She was sure Rosemary had reason to bring Dante here much more often than either her or Dom through the years. She still didn't know half of what Dante had done, but Rosemary's talks at the overlook must have worked because, as far as she knew, he didn't have a police record.

As she watched the sea, she shifted her weight from one foot to the other. High places still made her nervous. But she wanted to do this properly, for the loved ones she'd lost. So she moved to the far right side of the wall. She sat down on its flat top and swung her legs around and over, facing the sea, taking on faith that below her dangling feet, a small, sloping outcrop of lava rock still shielded her timid view from the blue and turquoise sea that flung itself with foaming abandon against the rocks below.

A sudden, unexpected flower-scented wind ran its fingers through her hair and ballooned out her yellow T-shirt. She recited aloud, through tears, an ancient Hawaiian prayer she had been forced to memorize in school and had never forgotten. Her parents, Dom, and Rosemary would have that prayer today as well as the *lei.* She leaned forward a little, took the *lei* from around her neck, kissed it four times, one for each, and then flung the fragrant green rope out into the cooperative wind, like a Hawaiian fisherman casting a fishing net.

"I remember, Mom and Dad. I remember, Dom and Rosemary," she choked out, tears blurring her vision and voice. "I'm so thankful that all of you were part of my life. *Mahalo.*"

She gripped the edge of the wall, breathless, as she watched as the *lei* sailed far beyond the surf then was gently lowered to the surface of the Pacific when the wind suddenly died as quickly as it had sprung up.

She curled forward over her legs, covered her face with her hands, and settled in for a good cry. Caught up in the moment, and with crashing waves as background noise, she didn't sense anyone near — until hands rested on her back.

"Pele's Tears — or you," a husky voice rasped near her left ear.

Her center of gravity was off, and she jerked away from what she sensed was a strange and unfriendly touch. The result was that she half jumped and half fell forward off the wall like a hundredweight sack of rice, and with just about as much grace.

Her arms windmilled like she was swimming in midair. And what was probably her last breath came out in a long, rather useless scream. Meanwhile, she was treated to visual bytes of blue sky, bluer sea, black rocks, and white foam. Her sound effects ended when she smacked into the outcrop of crumbling lava rock. But her trip wasn't over. Her momentum sent her into a roll on the downward sloping outcrop, continuing the out-of-control, hellish journey.

In slow motion, she slid over the edge. At

the last second she flung herself sideways and clawed at the plants growing in the new soil on the outcrop's deteriorating, slanting surface. Each hand found a hold while the rest of her body danced with death above the rocks, sand, foam, and waves below her.

Her impact with the lava rock left her gasping for air, so she didn't have enough breath to scream again. And, since there were no horrified cries or offers of help coming from above, she kind of guessed she was on her own.

She had one option, since letting go really wasn't an option. She had to haul herself up onto the outcrop. Then she'd think about catching her breath, screaming for help, babying her right upper arm that felt wet and warm, and clinging like an 'opihi, a limpet, until Dante missed her and came looking.

She could do this. She was in fairly good physical shape because of her morning runs, and because wrestling heavy glass panels and windows around her studio had given her upper-body strength. The outcrop held her away from the cliff face, though, so she didn't have the luxury of footholds any-where.

She studied the lava rock above her right hand for a new handhold, thanking the

Hawaiian gods that this old lava no longer had the smooth surface of *pāhoehoe* lava. It took all her courage to let go when she spied one, snaking her right hand upward to close on that higher handhold. Then she did the same with her left hand, alternating until she could lift one leg over the edge of the outcrop and pull herself, panting, onto the small, rough, uphill space.

If she stood, she might get dizzy, so she rolled herself into a ball, daring to look up at the overlook's wall, out of reach above her. She wondered if the person had even checked to see if she had saved herself. He certainly wasn't making any effort to help her. At that point she was simply grateful that no unfriendly face peered over to watch her struggles, a face whose owner might pelt her with rocks until she fell.

Safe for now, she opted to think rather than panic. There had been no push. What happened had happened because of her re-action. So, did someone just want to scare her, and was he as surprised as she was at the result? The scaring part had worked really, really well. Did the person then run away, afraid of what he had done? Still dazed, she tried to remember the words he had whispered in her ear.

An hour or more passed as she did her

thinking, huddled on the outcrop, shaking with fear, reaction, and pain, occasionally trying to work up the courage to call out for help, but afraid the person who had been there earlier might answer her, knowing she was still alive. If it was all the same to him, she'd rather have Dante rescue her.

It was funny how all the prayers she'd ever learned came back to her, word perfect. Then, like a benediction among those prayers, which were muttered in both Hawaiian and English for good measure, she heard Dante's voice call her name.

CHAPTER 10

She answered Dante's shouts, telling him precisely where she was in a surprisingly calm voice. His face, showing disbelief and fear, soon appeared over the wall's edge.

His eyes widened. "Lani? What? Are you okay?"

Now that Dante was there, it was okay to panic. Just a little. Her voice caught on a sob. "Well, of course I'm not okay! Get me off here, Kahoa. Now!"

"Calm down and hang on. I have a rope in the truck."

"No! Don't you dare leave me alone."

"Look, I need the rope and the truck's up at the road. I know you used to call me a Neanderthal all the time, but my arms really aren't long enough to do this. If they were, I wouldn't need the rope." He looked calm, yet his voice shook.

Okay, one point to him. "Stop trying to make me laugh and listen up." She locked in on his still-amazed stare, willing him to understand what she was saying. "Watch your back, Dante. Make sure you're alone up there. Now please, please hurry up," she whispered.

His mouth thinned into a straight line, and he gave a tiny nod of understanding, slowly turning his head from one side to the other, looking along the wall. He disappeared. She heard him moving around then he reappeared after a moment.

"We're okay. Sit tight. I have to get that rope." He waited for her nod then disappeared again, his boots smacking the terrace as he ran.

She knew real fear then. This was the part in the horror movie where the ledge would give way, just as she was on the verge of being rescued. Or what if the person who caused this was still hidden nearby? What if he hurt Dante? She cowered as far away from the edge as she could manage, which was really hard to do on such a small surface.

"I'll come down to you."

She screamed at the unexpected sound of his voice and saw him jerk in reaction.

"No! No, don't," she gasped. "It might not support both of us. I scraped my right arm, but I think I can manage."

A well-tied *paniolo* noose slithered down onto the lava rock beside her.

He had pulled on leather gloves. "Put that over your head, then under your arms and tighten it."

She had the rope in place before he finished speaking. Now, if the outcrop gave way, Dante could save her, no matter what the script said.

"I'll brace my feet on the wall and pull on the rope. You can help by finding footholds, holding on to the rope to steady you, and walking up the face."

She studied the thin, suddenly flimsy-looking rope, then looked up at what appeared to be a long, long distance to the top. "Tell me this is going to work, Dante. Tell me I won't fall." She knew she sounded like the frightened sixteen-year-old she had been when Dom died, and her words were bringing back bad memories for both of them.

She heard Dante swallow before he answered in a gruff voice. "Have a little faith, why don't you? I won't let you fall. I did this hundreds of times on the ranch. You'd be amazed where cattle end up sometimes, *hūpō* animals."

"Well, thanks for that endearing analogy, comparing my situation to a stupid cow's!"

His grin told her his words had been a ploy to make her angry. If she was angry, she'd be less scared. Disgusted with herself for being so easy, she gingerly stood while he took up the slack in the rope until it was taut. She put one foot against the rock face, hesitantly leaned back into the noose, and closed her eyes.

"I'm ready."

"Eyes open and looking up would be good here."

So she opened her eyes and involuntarily took a giant step up the cliff face when he pulled on the rope. She contributed more useless screaming at that point. Gripping the rope as if her life depended on it, which it did, she discovered she wasn't good at this. Dante's sheer strength and skill pulled her to safety.

She arrived at the top breathless, bruised, scraped, dirty, scared witless — and thankful she hadn't wet her pants. She abruptly sat down on the wall's flat top, her back to the sea, while Dante loosened the rope and removed it from her shaking body.

"Want to tell me how you ended up down there?" he asked softly, glancing around them. "Anybody who can *hula* like you isn't clumsy. And what did you mean when you said . . . ?"

"I'll tell you in the t-truck."

He flipped up the torn sleeve of her yellow T-shirt and looked at her arm. Then his eyes grew hard as his gaze became even more restless. "Can you walk? Do you need a doctor or a hospital for your arm?"

"Yes, no, and no. Just get me out of here. Please."

She suddenly felt warm and floaty. Her arm no longer hurt, and numbness stole through her, settling in her brain. She'd concentrate on Dante and what he was doing. That's what she'd do.

Watching her watching him, Dante quickly coiled the rope onto the ground, tied it off, put his arm through the center, and shrugged the coil over his head so that it hung around his neck and under one arm. She expected him to offer her his free hand.

She gasped when he swept her up into his arms with flattering ease and carried her off toward his truck. Trembling and silent after an initial little whimper, she wrapped her arms around his neck like a strangling tropical vine, shoved her face against the skin beneath his ear, and breathed in the safe, sane scent of Dante.

When she was comfortable in the truck's passenger seat, with his red bandanna handkerchief tied around her arm, he climbed in his side. He turned the key in the ignition like he was wringing its neck, closed the windows using two buttons, hit the auto-lock for the doors, started the AC, and turned sideways in the driver's seat to face her.

"Now what happened back there?" His tone brooked no argument.

"I'm n-not sure."

"Take slow, deep breaths and think it through for me, one step at a time." His tone had gentled. "What did you do when you got to the overlook?"

She sucked in a full breath. "I sat down on top of the wall, facing the sea, the part of it that's above the outcrop, to throw the rope *lei,* the one you had ready for me at the shop, over the edge. In remembrance of my parents, Dom, and Rosemary. I recited a Hawaiian prayer and threw the *lei* over. After that, I kind of hunched over my knees, crying." She paused, returning to short, shallow breaths when she relived what happened next.

Her words picked up momentum. "S-Someone rested his hands flat on my back and whispered something in my ear. It freaked me out." She looked at him in horrified embarrassment. "In fact, I think I lost my balance and fell off the wall! How lame is that? And don't you dare tell anyone." That little flash of anger made her dizzy. "He didn't try to help me after I fell. I was down there a long time before you came." Her voice definitely wobbled there.

He had peeled off the gloves, and the knuckles of his left hand turned white where he gripped the steering wheel. His blue eyes glittered. "Tell me more about how this guy touched you. You know what I mean."

"No, no. Nothing like that. I just knew it wasn't a friendly touch."

He went very still, his sleek brows lowering, and his voice became quiet and dangerous. "What did he say?"

Dante's temper was the stuff of legend around Lehua. When they were younger, she sometimes pushed him to the brink then backpedaled by making him laugh. This wasn't one of those times. She was glad his anger wasn't directed at her.

She took a few seconds to think, hoping he'd calm down. She felt her eyes grow round when she heard in her head part of what the voice had said. "It was something about Pele's Tears!"

His voice lacked any inflection when he spoke. "And you're sure you didn't just really piss off Maile and Kalana at the shop with that sign?"

162

The words were enough to make her close her eyes and count to ten. She only made it to three, however. "If you're trying to re-assure me or distract me with humor," she said carefully, "it's not working. I'll do something you'll regret in another minute, Kahoa."

He held up both hands, palms out, in mock surrender. "Are you sure he said those words? I mean, you were upset. The wind here sometimes —"

"I know all about the wind here, thank you very much. And the wind didn't talk to me! I may have been *hūpō* enough, like one of your cows, to fall off the wall, but I wasn't blown off the wall because there's very little wind right now, as you well know." Her voice was rising and she clawed it down into the range of human hearing. "I felt hands, Dante, warm hands. But I can't remember exactly what he said. It'll come to me. Give me time to process this."

His face briefly took on a gray tint beneath his tan skin tones. "Damn," he said before one fist smacked the steering wheel.

"And we have to talk about Pele's Tears, just like we had to talk about Dom's death. Really. Trust me on this. There's something you don't know that you really need to know."

He looked away, running his left palm around the leather cover on the steering wheel. "There's a lot about that fairy tale I don't want to know, especially right now."

"Rosemary left me her journal to read for a reason." She paused before throwing out a hint of what was to come. "Pele's Tears is no fairy tale, Dante."

He studied her, discomfort and wariness in his eyes, then he sighed. "Stop right there or I'll think you're imagining things and haul your 'ōkole to the closest ER. Let's go back to the house. We need to tend to that scrape on your arm. And we'll talk. I promise."

She nodded her agreement because her teeth were beginning to chatter in reaction. Huddled on the bucket seat next to him, she wrapped her arms around herself and shook.

He got them home in record time, and she insisted on walking into the big house without help. But in the kitchen, he stepped in front of her, put his hands on her waist, and lifted her up onto the edge of the cool granite island. This brought her to his eye level. His face blurred when tears filled her eyes. This was where Rosemary had tended their injuries when they were kids.

A vacuum cleaner roared somewhere upstairs.

"Maybe we can get this cleaned up before Helen sees it."

Helen had agreed to take on more hours to shop and cook meals for freezing and reheating, at least until they got themselves sorted out.

He took off his Stetson and dropped it onto the island. Released from its confines, his thick, dark hair went even more wavy, if that was possible.

"I need to get at that arm," he said, gathering a first-aid kit and a bowl of warm, soapy water.

"This T-shirt is probably ruined even if I soak it to get the blood out. I could just cut off the sleeves, I guess." Not thinking, she raised her arms into the air and simply pulled it off over her head, planning to cover up with it.

He apparently turned at the same moment because when she could see again, he stood looking at her with his hands full, having stopped so suddenly that the water continued to slosh over the edge of the bowl.

"I had a slow-motion moment just then. Yellow today. Really? Do you own stock in a lingerie company or something?"

She adjusted the T-shirt over her yellow

lace bra, even though her bras weren't see-through and showed less than a bikini top would reveal. "What do you mean? And you'd better clean that up."

"Well, in Maine that first day your bra was red. The night you came home to Lehua and I put you to bed, it was purple. The day I opened your trunk for you, it was pink. Today it's yellow. Do you always . . . ?"

"With matching bikini panties underneath. Always lace. And they always match the top I'm wearing that day. I love the colors. And, no, I don't own stock in lingerie. Why are we discussing my underwear?"

He set down his supplies, grabbed some paper towels, dropped them into the water on the floor, and stomped on them. "Sorry. Side trip. I, um, like lace."

"I remember. You used to sneak into my room and look at my bras hanging on the bathroom doorknob. I like lace too. Lace and I go way back."

"They were draped over every doorknob in the room, and on drawer pulls and bed knobs. And I deny that I sneaked. It was more like planned reconnaissance. Or maybe research."

"Sneaked, reconnaissance, or research by any other name, Kahoa."

Then, with a surprisingly gentle touch and

warm hands, he used what was left of the warm, soapy water to clean the deep scrape on her upper right arm. After that he poured hydrogen peroxide over it, patted it dry with a clean towel, and applied an antibiotic salve.

Lani gritted her teeth beneath his tender ministrations, letting him think it was because it hurt. Maybe it was because of their lace discussion but, to her dismay, Dante's touch was sending wave after wave of heat over her skin. If he knew that, she'd have to kill him to get rid of his I'm-the-man cocky grin.

Her concentration shifted when she saw his hands tremble ever so slightly as he taped a piece of gauze into place over the weeping wound. She had never seen Dante's hands tremble before.

The sight shook something loose. Her gaze flew to his face and she gasped. "I remember now. I know what the voice said!"

He went still, staring at her for a few seconds while his right hand rested on top of her left thigh. "You're making me guess?"

She'd swear that if Dante didn't lift that hand right now, it would leave a scar. Interestingly enough, the heat came from within her, not out of him.

"Sorry. He said, 'Pele's Tears — or you.' "

He reacted to the words by exhaling a string of Hawaiian curses. He ran out of air long before he ran out of curses.

"What? Tell me." Her brain was suddenly working too well. "And why did you come looking for me so soon? You found another note, didn't you?"

He sighed so hard he ruffled her hair. "I found it here on the kitchen island when I came in to make coffee. It said, 'Pele's Tears — or her.' " He pulled the familiar paper out of his back pocket.

She repeated some of his curses in a hoarse, breathless whisper as she read it.

"Nice. Watch your mouth."

"You're not my keeper, Kahoa. Besides, you just said most of them." She could tell him about her underwear, but now was not a good time to tell him what she had to tell him. She really, really shouldn't.

He took the bowl and the other things to the sink. She used the opportunity to put on her T-shirt.

Disappointment was plain on his face when he turned around and found her fully clothed. "After I found the note, I went to the shop first. The girls told me you'd taken the *lei* so I knew where you'd gone. Nice sign, by the way. You'd better come up with something Maile and Kalana can use to field customers' questions."

"Thanks. Already working on it. A special bouquet with a romance card telling the story of Pele and Lohiʻau. Or something. Are you ready to listen to me now? Ready to hear the truth?" she asked in a ragged whisper. "Please, Dante. I can't carry this knowledge alone. Not after what just happened."

"Okay, okay. Tell me what you're bursting to tell me."

"Rosemary found them," she blurted. "She says so in her journal. I didn't know how or when to tell you, but I certainly didn't imagine telling you like this."

He went still, staring silently at her for a half minute. "Found . . . *them?*" he croaked.

"*Them.* The same Pele's Tears your Kahoa ancestor somehow came into possession of, perhaps illegally." She couldn't stop talking now that he was finally listening to her. "The same Pele's Tears he named with great imagination and *naʻau* —. That's 'guts,' right? By loosely using the events in a Pele and Lohiʻau chant. The same Pele's Tears he hid away after most of his family died and he became convinced the gems were bad luck. Nothing got by that Kahoa."

She stopped to breathe and waited for the unbeliever standing dumbstruck before her to say something more. Anything. When he didn't she continued.

"She didn't say where or when or how, just that she hoped to atone for the bad luck they'd brought on the Kahoa family by giving them back to the light. 'They live again in the light,' she said, and it's up to us whether we want to find them and sell them to help Lehua or to do anything else we want with them."

His voice sounded like it came from a far, far away place within him. "And someone else knows all this and wants them?"

"After today, it sure looks and feels that way to me. Whoever is threatening us is willing to set us up to hurt ourselves in order to make his point that he wants Pele's Tears. I can't believe this is happening." She looked down just to check. Yep, his hand was still there.

He was concentrating on her now. "Today was more than threatening."

"I know, but I wasn't pushed, just like the temple dog statue wasn't dropped on your head but placed where you'd fall over it in the dark. We did these things to ourselves."

"He laid hands on you. He could have pushed if he wanted to. And he had to have been disguised in some way. On an ordinary day, you'd have turned around and slapped him stupid or screamed him deaf."

She felt her eyes widen. "You're right. I hadn't thought of that. But how did he know I'd be there?"

"No idea."

"Whoever is doing this knows our history. He knew that one note to you would probably be enough to make you angry enough to come to Maine to drag me back home. If that didn't work, the flurry of notes to me just might push me enough that I'd want to come home long enough to give you the stink eye and slap you upside your Hawaiian head."

"I hate it when you're right."

"You should be used to it by now."

He made eye contact again but the shutters were in place. "Tutu talked to a lot of people in her family research."

"You think?"

The paper and pendant she'd taken from the journal were hidden upstairs in her room, but she felt the weight of them as if one was still on a chain around her neck and the other in her pocket.

He continued. "Tutu worked so hard to find them then apparently stash them, and we lost Dom and everything, and now someone wants us to find them and just hand them over?"

"It's your choice, but who says we have to hand them over? We can probably figure this out if we're given the time. Meanwhile, we're each other's soft spot, each other's incentive to cooperate, aren't we?" She hiccupped softly, her childhood reaction to stress. "He can hurt you by hurting me. And vice versa." Hiccup.

"This is crazy." He swallowed. Hard.

"Like I said, he knows us and he's playing us. You had to think I sent your note. You had to bring me back here, or I had to come back here on my own, to read the journal so we'd know she'd found them because we didn't know, and you wouldn't look at the journal on your own to find out."

"You've got that right."

"This person had to know we weren't aware they'd been found. I wonder if he knew about the clues Rosemary left in the back of the journal. The cottage was searched. He probably was looking for them, or the journal, or both, to try to find them himself. It's someone close, Dante, to know all this and to be able to put a note in Lehua's big house kitchen."

His hand had been moving gently against the skin on her thigh but stopped abruptly. "Clues? What clues?"

Her hiccups stopped. At least now she

knew his hand wasn't stuck.

"There are two. I hid them in my room. I'll show them to you in a minute. This creep knows how you feel about Pele's Tears, Dante, and he knows that I was interested in them, so that means Rosemary must have confided all that to him. Close, like I said."

"Helluva plan."

"And it's working well so far. We both know now that being incentive is no fun. I had a feeling this wasn't over and that's why I changed the sign. I hoped that sign would keep him happy, keep him from touching or threatening or writing notes, until we can find them and take them to the bank, or call the cops, or use them to lead him into a trap."

"Did you hit your head on the way down?" His angry-tiki face descended over his features. "You're in danger. Go back to Maine or somewhere else, Lani. Remove yourself as incentive. I'll look for the stones."

"What? No way! I'm home, Dante, and I'm not leaving again. Besides, you need me. Residency, remember?"

"And maybe you still just want to find them."

"I'm not immune to the thrill of finding

hidden treasure. So sue me." She crossed her arms over her chest. "Those two clues in my room, taken together, are our only hope of finding where Pele's Tears are hidden because I'm clueless otherwise. When you're ready to see them and help me figure out what they mean, let me know, just like you had to tell me you were ready to hear that Rosemary had found them."

They glared at each other in silence, a Hawaiian standoff.

He sighed again, with less force this time, before he looked down at his hand. "Sorry. Let me take this in first. Digest it. Harvest some anthuriums. Maybe get drunk. Meanwhile, be careful and forget about moving into the cottage."

Her gaze had wandered to her thigh again. Now it shot to his face. "How did you know?"

"Keep your *ʻōkole* next to mine until we find Pele's Tears or whoever's behind this, while we try to keep up with everything else going on around the farm. Maybe we can find out if there really is a Santa Claus and an Easter Bunny while we're at it." His voice was hoarse, probably from exasperation, but his eyes were strangely warm, she noticed.

She couldn't ignore his hand any longer. "*Mahalo* for getting me off that outcrop and for patching me up. Now, unless you're going to kiss it to make it better, I need to get down and do some work. And aren't you supposed to be helping Shaka install a conveyor belt?" Her voice was none too steady, she noticed.

He looked down again, moving his fingers in a caress that made her heart trip before he let his hand drop to his side. "We were both pretty good at kissing away each other's hurts when we were little. But we're not little anymore. Do you remember I kissed you once, before Dom and everything?"

Breathless, she tried to make light of the situation. "I do. In fact, I remember exactly how it went. My arms around your neck. Your arms around my waist. My nose suddenly in the way. Your lips against my lips."

"Smart ass. I'm being serious here. We've always, somehow, been a part of each other, and best friends because of it, but never brother and sister. You and me. Two sides of a triangle. With Dom."

It was difficult to express proper outrage in a breathy whisper, but she did her best. "So you said. And you got a tattoo when you preached at me and wouldn't let me get one!"

In answer, he planted his palms on the

granite, one on each side of her, and stepped closer until she felt his jeans against her bare knees. He gently nudged them apart so he could step between them, moving up against the edge of the island.

Breathless yet wary, she leaned back a little. Her personal space was no stranger to Dante's footprints. When they were younger, they would invade each other's at the drop of an insult. But now he was suddenly looking at her the way he used to look at a shave ice or a teriyaki steak before he dove into it.

"I've thought about that kiss for a long time, Lani. I've wanted to ask you if it made your toes curl under and your breath stop, like mine did. And if you knew that I wanted to crawl inside your skin with you during that moment."

She shivered as she remembered the kiss, exactly as he described it. He noticed her shiver and glanced down at her arms.

"And I've wanted to ask if you get chicken skin just remembering it. Like I do." He held his forearm, covered in bumps, against hers.

Her mouth was hanging open by that time, so she closed it with a snap. "Yes to all of the above, and we can't go there, Dante," she whispered.

"Why not? Don't you wonder what would have happened between us if our world hadn't fallen apart?"

"We both know what would have happened then, and taking this trip into that part of our past now will only complicate things for us and Lehua."

"Complicate things? You mean more complicated than diversifying our livelihood and maybe losing Lehua to developers? More complicated than discovering that someone wants something from us that I didn't believe existed until a few minutes ago? More complicated than keeping this creep from hurting you if we can't find what he wants? Complicated like that, you mean?"

As he named each hazard in their lives, his face drew nearer until his lips were a flower petal's thickness away from hers.

Her eyes drifted close all by themselves. "Yeah. Complicated like that. So shut up and kiss me already, Kahoa."

She heard him laugh softly. Then his lips brushed hers, soft, fleeting, sweet, and not at all what she expected — and her nose wasn't in the way this time. Whether it was what she expected from him or not, if he didn't stop, she'd soon melt down into a puddle right where she sat.

Then he got serious. He deepened the kiss to hard, lingering, and hot. This was what she expected from Dante, what she remembered from that first kiss, and her melting would be the same, only faster.

His mouth slid over hers, pressing and tugging, until she opened to him. Meanwhile, her heart tried to beat its way out of her chest. Surely he could hear its thumping because she could hear nothing else. Or maybe someone really was setting off fireworks outside.

And then the second most devastating kiss of her life ended, abruptly and ignominiously, because they were flanked on two sides, and in numbers, in what ancient Hawaiian warriors probably would have called a pincer move, plus a head-on attack.

Mei had appeared on Lani's right and made a little squeaking sound in her throat as she put on the brakes.

Dante abruptly pulled away, almost removing Lani's one and only filling as he did so.

And, on Lani's left, following a peremptory knock, someone stood in silhouette in the kitchen doorway and a horrified male voice choked out, "Oh, I'm so sorry. I didn't mean to interrupt."

Then the second wave arrived.

Helen said, again on the right, from behind Mei, "Who's hurt and how bad?"

Then, on the left again, a slight figure, following in the man's wake, crashed into the stranger when he tried to reverse. A different, louder squeak sounded when he trod on the woman's foot.

"Is someone hurt?" the woman, peeking around the man, asked in a wispy little voice once she and the stranger had sorted themselves out.

Dante recovered quickly, she'd give him that. "It's just a scrape, everyone. And an important partnership meeting," he added hoarsely.

Then, over Dante's left shoulder, she saw there had been an unnoticed but head-on surprise attack. Aidan stood in the doorway to the *lānai.*

He caught her eye, and his grin told her he'd seen enough. "Good on ya, Lani. I told you so, didn't I?"

CHAPTER 11

Dante's hoarse voice and his subsequent actions told her that he hadn't been totally unaffected by what they'd been doing. He stepped away, letting go of her to run both his hands distractedly through his thick hair while she struggled to breathe. She was aware of a sensation like lava flowing beneath her skin and fully expected to liquefy the granite upon which she still perched.

A small portion of her feelings stemmed from mortification at being caught in a compromising position with Dante — by no less than five people at one time. The larger portion of it, however, stemmed from the effects of being *in* that compromising position with Dante. Thank God she'd had the foresight to put on her T-shirt.

She slid off the granite island, gave Aidan a weak wave to come inside, glanced up at Dante, then found something absolutely riveting to look at on the tile floor until she could gather her wits.

She was aware of Mei doing a tight one-hundred-and-eighty-degree turn and going back the hall toward the office, followed by Helen who went up the stairs again. Aidan's gaze followed Mei's swaying hips, and he wandered in that direction, after dropping a backpack on the floor near the door and giving Lani a thumbs-up. Then movement drew her eyes as the woman, who must be Agnes, crept past them on her way to the office, with a shy look first at Dante then at Lani's bandaged arm.

Dante had told her a little about Agnes, Lehua's part-time accountant, who always reported for work on time and who was always flustered. What he didn't tell her was that everything about the woman was gray, in coloring and, by her expression, in outlook. Today, she wore her salt-and-pepper hair subdued in a tight bun, while her thin body was shrouded in a pants suit in an oatmeal color. For someone who lived in paradise, she certainly didn't embrace tropical colors and fashions. It would take a newly transplanted, uptight mainlander to still look like that, especially while sharing an office with an exotic bloom like Mei. For some reason, Lani decided on the spot to be extra nice to Agnes. It was the pale blue eyes that did it, sad and possibly hopeless.

The stranger, the last one standing, again backed toward the door, crowded in that direction by Dante's glare. Lani felt a mixture of sympathy and gratitude toward him and the others, whoever he was — a stray apprentice farmer, perhaps — because their interruption had derailed an emotional train that would have carried her and Dante to disaster.

She quietly studied the mystery man since she was incapable of speech, noting he was a head shorter than Dante, well-muscled, and a study in browns and greens, from his tanned skin, light brown hair, and slightly darker milk chocolate eyes behind glasses rimmed with brown metal frames, to his jungle camouflage shorts, T-shirt, and hiking boots. He reminded her of a sexy Indiana Jones with modern eyewear.

"What do you want, Pepper?" Dante bit out.

Pepper?

The man pushed his glasses higher on his nose. "You said I should check in every week or so."

"I meant a phone call from town when you come down for supplies and R and R." Dante's voice was laced with frustration and disgust.

He must have noticed at that moment that she stood beside him like a pillar of salt. She felt his glance.

"Lani, this is Dr. Kern Pepper, ornithologist, who's studying honeycreepers in the rain forest up on our *pali.* Tutu invited him. Pepper, this is Lani Beecham, my business partner, owner of half of Lehua."

The newcomer smiled his skepticism and his willingness to play dumb. "Ah. Pleased to meet you, Miss Beecham."

Not a stray apprentice farmer then. "Um, Dr., er, Pepper. Call me Lani," she managed on her second try.

"And I'm just Kern. Or Pepper. It cuts down on the jokes." He advanced on her, right hand extended.

She was aware of Dante giving that hand and the man who owned it the stink eye. Lani shook Pepper's warm hand then released it.

Dante attempted to stare her down. "Now that we have that out of the way."

She tilted her head and shot him a meaningful look. "Exactly what I was thinking. Now we can move on with clear heads."

He dragged his disbelieving and dismayed gaze away from hers to narrow it in scrutiny of their visitor. "So how's it going up there all by yourself, Pepper?"

If Dante had no manners, she certainly did. This man was Rosemary's guest, and they now represented her. "Would you like some coffee, er, Pepper? I'd like to hear about your work." She definitely felt in need of a cup. Several cups, in fact. Maybe laced with something stronger.

"Really?" Here, apparently, was another surprised male, though for quite a different reason. "If it's not too much trouble. I haven't had a good cup of coffee in weeks."

"I'll leave you to it. *I* have work to do," Dante growled. He turned to Lani, pointed a finger at her, and lowered his voice so only she could hear. "We'll talk about this later. And don't go wandering around alone. Don't trust anybody." He shot another look at the good doctor and strode out.

She glanced away from the coffeemaker, but her hands continued their work, taking up with it where Dante had left off earlier, apparently when he had found the note. "What you saw just now, Pepper," she began slowly.

"Is none of my business." He held up both hands as if fending off embarrassing confidences.

"Oh, you're right, it isn't." She continued, however, needing to explain to herself what had just happened more than needing to explain it to him. "What you saw just now was two people overcome by an episode from their past, reliving a moment of teenage attraction that never came to fruition."

He shrugged. "Okay. No matter which way I jump, I can't avoid hearing this, can I?"

She grinned at him. "No, you can't. As someone recently told me, best to give in gracefully. It's just that Dante can really kiss," she added softly, a wistful note in her voice. "I'd forgotten how good he is."

"Okaaay," he repeated slowly.

She looked at him in exasperation, knowing he didn't believe her. No matter what she told him, Dr. Kern Pepper had decided that he knew what had been going on when he really didn't.

"Sit down and start telling me about your work, Pepper," she ordered.

"Yes, ma'am."

While the coffeemaker made noises like Kilauea preparing to erupt and The Colonel strutted and crowed outside the back door in the middle of the day, just in case she was trying to take a nap, Pepper talked.

"Are you familiar with honeycreepers?" he asked, a gleam of almost religious intensity glinting in his eyes.

"I've seen them and heard them in the

forest up on the *pali.* The four of us used to hike a lot up there. And they're in the garden sometimes."

"Well, they're endemic to Hawaii, evolving differently on each island, wonders of evolution. Take the *'i'iwi,* for example. It feeds only on the nectar of the *koli'i* flower, its bill and tongue adapted, specialized, for that flower alone. They —. Sorry, I tend to go on."

"I asked. How did you know Rosemary?"

He added milk and sugar to the cup of rich Kauai coffee she poured for him, then he sipped it. "Mmm, this is good. Thanks! We met in a tiny, private research library in Honolulu."

She smiled. "I can guess what you were researching, but what was she looking for?"

"Lost or misplaced handwritten records about or written by her ancestors who lived in this valley for hundreds of years — or anything published about them by others. She indicated it had something to do with her work, this need to learn more about those who had come before. She said she was designing a window that was very different from her usual style."

"When was this? I think I know the window you're talking about. It's in her cottage, now my studio."

"It was over a year ago, maybe. May I see the window sometime?"

Suddenly it struck her that here was a perfect candidate for being the note writer. He came here through knowing Rosemary and her research, and by her invitation. He had access to the house, or at least felt no need to wait after knocking before walking into it. He was free to move around wherever and whenever he wanted on Lehua land under the guise of studying honeycreepers.

Of course that description also fit everyone else with a purpose around the place, the apprentice farmers, Mei, Agnes, Helen, Shaka, and anyone who came to cut flowers for them, because the house was open all the time. Pepper's voice didn't sound like the one she'd heard earlier, but men could make their voices sound very different simply by lowering them. Or maybe there was more than one person doing this.

"Um, sure. The next time you check in," she said carefully. "I should be settled in by then."

She and Dante should spread the word on the Hawaiian grapevine that they were taking the threats seriously. Look what happened to her today after she had changed the sign at Beans and Blossoms. They somehow needed to get the word out more efficiently.

So she leaned forward, snared his gaze, and said loudly and, she hoped, meaningfully, "Right now, Dante and I have to find something that's been misplaced." Then her mind weighed in with a list of her other responsibilities. "In between Dante's work and my own unpacking, working on my stained glass projects, helping with Beans and Blossoms, and being drafted to help cut a major shipment of anthuriums, that is." Then that morning's adventure showed up. "Unless one of us is injured or killed, which we want to avoid. So please tell everyone you meet that we get it. That we're looking. For something."

"Uh-huh," he said, standing up and inching toward the hall, his coffee cup in his hand.

No guilty reaction there, just the need to get away from the crazy woman. "But you can tell me more about your honeycreepers while you finish your coffee," she added in a normal tone.

"Another time. Maybe we'll talk the next time I check in. And I'll just say hello to Mei now. And, um, I think I went to school in Australia with that blond guy. Aidan something. I'll just, er, . . ." he said, edging

188

toward the hall doorway.

So that's how things are, she thought to herself. *Good luck with that since Mei doesn't date older men.* Pepper might still be hormone-driven, but he certainly wasn't a kid. Neither was Aidan. But maybe two older guys vying for her attention was just what Mei needed.

After Pepper left, at a rather improbable but effective side-stepping trot, she went upstairs, got rid of most of the grime from the lava outcrop, and changed clothes. When she came down again, she went to the office.

She wanted to ask Mei a question, but the girl wasn't in the office. Agnes was alone, a spreadsheet open on the office computer's screen. In front of her on the desk was a row of pastel pills, lined up neatly. As Lani stepped inside, Agnes chose one and dropped it with a ping into the wastebasket.

"I don't believe we've met, Agnes. Ships in the night and all that. I'm Lani Beecham, Dante's partner."

Agnes covered the pills with a piece of paper and looked up with a fleeting smile, taking Lani's outstretched hand. The woman's opening volley left Lani temporarily speechless.

"You're both beautiful. Of course you

189

would be kissing each other. I understand that."

"Good. Thank you. But we won't be making a habit of it. Can I get you anything, a cup of coffee or water, to take your vitamins?"

Agnes looked down at the concealing paper. "Yes, my vitamins. No, thank you. I appreciate the offer."

"Well, if there's anything I can do for you, just let me know. We appreciate the work you do for us."

Agnes bobbed her head. "Why, thank you. Mr. Kahoa has never said."

Mr. Kahoa? Dante would love that. "If you weren't doing a good job, Dante wouldn't keep you on. Ask anyone who works for us. If you ever have a problem, come to me. Okay?"

"I will. Yes."

"Now I have a question. I can't ask Dante this because he wouldn't have noticed. Have any dress shops opened up in Kalele? Some old high school friends have invited me out for a fancy girls' night out, and I need something to wear."

Agnes told her of a new shop in Kalele that sold Hawaiian designs, prints, and patterns to tourists and locals alike, at reasonable prices. Lani thanked her and told her that if Agnes ever wanted to go shopping in Lihue, Lani was up for it.

After that, she took her still-ruffled self and her coffee to the cottage. She worked at setting up her laptop in the roll-top desk and checking out and ordering merchandise for the shop online.

Aidan knocked on the doorframe a while later, carrying Aumoe in his arms, belly up, like a baby. The big cat was in paroxysms of delight at Aidan's attentions to his chin and throat and stomach.

"Well, you were a surprise," she told him.

"I could tell. We all were a surprise, I'm guessing." When she felt herself blush, he added, "I heard the *kahuna* moaning in Maine about the anthurium cutting. Did I miss it?"

"No. It's happening soon. But our foreman and the *kahuna* say who works, so have a care."

"I cleared it with him in Maine. And I already met Shaka. Nice guy. Reminds me of my dad."

"You're quick, on all counts."

He looked abashed for a moment. "A bit homesick, truth be told. I've been on the North Shore of the Big Island for a few days. Good waves. Regular reunion hereabouts, it turns out. I have a surfing mate who's one of your apprentice farmers. I'm stopping awhile with him out at the platforms. And I went to school once with Kern Pepper. He can use me for a few days on your *pali,* helping with the mist nets to catch his honeycreepers. Then I'll head home."

She studied him as he spoke. Handsome guy. Healthy. Personable. Good body. And Aidan's outgoing and friendly personality was so very different from Dante's. She couldn't help but briefly wonder how she would have reacted to his kiss back in Maine. Heck, she wondered how she'd react right here, after Dante. Unfortunately, there was only one way to find out. And she couldn't. Really. He caught her assessing look, and she felt her face grow warm but didn't break eye contact.

"You shouldn't look at a bloke like that, Lani. It makes him imagine all kinds of things." He smiled, but his eyes were alight with more than good humor. And questions.

"Sorry. I was just wondering what it would be like to kiss you, Aidan. We never got around to it in Maine."

"And what about the *kahuna* in the kitchen not so long ago?"

"Well, this would be the surfer in the cottage *now.* And I'd be using you to compare my reactions to the *kahuna* in the kitchen not so long ago, emphasis on using. Never mind. I'm being silly."

"And what if I'm curious about my own reactions?"

She was struck dumb, wondering what she was doing, wondering what was wrong with her. "I apologize. I had an accident earlier today, and I'm not thinking straight."

He gently put down the cat on the sofa. "Oh, I'm game if you're serious. As an experiment, as anything you want to call it. I never pass up an opportunity to kiss a beautiful woman. Besides, I've thought about kissing you often enough," he answered, his voice soft.

She nodded, and he came to her, enfolding her in his muscular arms and snugging her close to his body. And she was disappointed when his lips were merely warm and gentle on hers, his body merely warm and hard against hers.

"No good?" he asked when he raised his head.

He certainly didn't have the fireworks, earthshaking, meltdown effect on her that Dante had. But she remained standing close to him with her arms around his neck and her forehead resting against his as she shook her head.

"It's not you. It's me. Friends?"

"I'm willing to keep trying until I get it right, you know." He added a devilish grin to his offer.

She gave a little laugh deep in her throat then kissed him. Even willing herself to respond to him didn't make it happen.

"Sorry. Friends." She let go of him with her right arm and brought her open hand between them at chest level.

He did the same, and they shook hands. "I enjoyed the audition. It's a deal. Cheers, Lani."

"I can only imagine what that deal is about. Taking up where you left off in Maine?" Dante's voice from the doorway was cold and sharp. "I thought Aidan might want a ride to the tent platforms. But maybe he'll be sleeping here instead."

She would have stepped away from Aidan, but he still held her firmly with one arm and didn't let go. She admired his cool defiance while her heart pounded and her face burned. Dante raked them with an icy-hot glance and turned away.

Aidan looked at her again and smiled. "Are you sure you wouldn't like to experiment some more?"

She shook her head, and he released her.

"Well, if it doesn't work out with him, I'm available to help you get over him. I'll show you Australia. Then we can surf our way around the world."

She nodded, tears welling up in her eyes. "Thank you, Aidan." She kissed him on the cheek.

"Cheers, luv." Then he turned and bolted for the door. "Hold up, mate!"

She rushed to the door after him, throwing her words at Dante's stiff, retreating back and clenched fists. "Don't hurt him, Dante!"

CHAPTER 12

Don't hurt him? Really? He was aware of the Australian behind him, trying to catch up. He didn't dare turn around because he couldn't do that without driving his fist into the guy's face.

"Thanks for the ride, mate."

They reached the truck before Aidan spoke again. "Look, I know what you want to do to me right now, and I appreciate your not doing it. But it's not necessary. I'm no danger to you."

Dante looked at him across the hood, feeling his fists clenching and unclenching at his sides. "I'm not blind. Or stupid."

"Neither am I. I was an experiment just now. She asked me to kiss her so she could compare what she felt earlier, with you. Didn't you notice? She wasn't just embarrassed when all of us walked in on you two in the kitchen. Crikey, she could barely stand. You had rocked her world, mate.

Now, back there, she didn't react to me at all. She was just embarrassed and worried when you walked in."

Dante studied the face across from him through narrowed eyes. Lani had gone awfully quiet for a minute after that fiasco in the kitchen. Unfortunately, it didn't last. And he had seen her face after he kissed her, felt her reactions to him during it, and saw her willingness beforehand. He knew when a woman wanted him. And he knew he wanted this one, knew that they'd been born to love and hold each other.

Lani. The love of his life? As in the whole love-of-his-life thing he'd mentally disparaged most of his years on this earth? He'd even caught himself thinking about green-eyed little girls, twins maybe, but carbon copies of Lani, who would have a natural talent for *hula,* who would be unteachable when it comes to driving a stick shift, who would drive him crazy, again, when boys started hanging around them. Just like their mother.

So it looked like he had plans with Lani, and knocking this guy senseless wouldn't help his cause. He wondered what Dom would think of all this. He was probably laughing his *ʻōkole* off in heaven right now. *If you're listening, little brah and God, please help me get this right with Lani.*

"I'm not saying I believe you. But I am saying don't touch her again," he said in a deadly quiet voice that would have driven Lani elsewhere, at a run.

Aidan raised both hands, palms out. "No worries. I won't be invited to experiment again. You're in, mate!"

Lani dropped onto the sofa. Was there anything else she could screw up today? Rosemary's CD player sat on a table beside her, so she reached out and pushed Play. Soft big band World War II music wafted into the room. She and Dante and Dom had grown up with this music, occasionally dancing to it with Rosemary, with each other, and sometimes all four of them in a cluster. Rosemary said it reminded her of her "beloved," as she called him, who had passed away before they could marry.

She flopped sideways on the sofa then stretched out to rest and think. Aumoe looked down at her from the back. Sleep wasn't a possibility because of her racing thoughts. After all, she'd nearly been killed today and slightly injured in the process, then thoroughly kissed, then not so thoroughly kissed and caught at it by Dante. *Oh, God! Just kill me now.* All in rapid succession. Naturally, Dante's thorough kiss rose to the top of the pile of things to be considered.

Was she totally out of her mind, or had it just been temporary insanity to allow that kiss in the kitchen to happen at all? Then for him to catch her with Aidan not two hours later? What was Dante thinking right now? What might he be doing to Aidan right now? And what would he say to her when she next saw him? *I can probably make it to another island before that happens if I start swimming right now.* Still, he had his own reputation to consider. He was a lot more experienced than she was; he began experimenting with girls long before their first kiss and Dom's death.

Before Dom's accident, Dante had been liberally sampling the delights the island girls offered, and that's when their own attraction had flared. Dante A.D., After Dom, was the Dante who protected his heart, Rosemary had told her. He became notorious for taking only what he wanted — and making sure the women knew it going in. Rosemary had added in the spirit of fair play that he also made sure they were never disappointed, unsatisfied, or sorry they had given in. Their only complaints, as far as she had known, were that the affairs didn't last.

Lani paused to wonder if his interest would have been temporary and fleeting with her, if she had stayed at Lehua and their relationship had progressed.

Also, the reason for this change in him was first proposed to her by Rosemary. Dante kept his relationships light, floating above commitment because everyone he loved, or who had loved him, had died: his parents, his brother, and now Rosemary herself. Or, Rosemary had added, she suspected Dante might already be in love and had been for a long time, but wouldn't say more on that tantalizing subject.

She knew she shouldn't dwell on what Dante had made her feel that day — or allow herself to fall under his spell of dimples, charm, and Hawaiian-sky eyes. The last time she had succumbed to them, with Pele's Tears in the mix, Dom had died. She couldn't, wouldn't, risk getting up close and personal with Dante until the gems were out of their lives, just in case the trio was cursed, as Captain Talbot-Kahoa had thought. After that, all bets were off.

What made her feelings so difficult to restrain was that she knew Dante better than anyone else, knew him to be so much more than the sum of his charms. But in order to get this partnership off the ground and reinvent Lehua, and until Dante and Lehua were safe, a cool head was called for by both of them where their magnetism for each other was concerned. If he tried to get friendly again, it would be up to her to figure out some way to temporarily dowse their attraction to each other.

As for Pele's Tears, she'd have to study Rosemary's journal from the beginning to the part just before Dom's death in order to revisit her own youthful reasoning for focusing on caves on the *pali* face. Totally ignoring the tragic consequences of that reasoning would be impossible for her, despite her session with Dante in her loft in Maine.

After that, she'd have to read beyond that point, hoping for something more telling, something she could connect to the clues hidden in her room, something that had sent Rosemary to wherever she'd found Pele's Tears. Because she was sure that wherever that was, the gems had been safe there for a very long time, and she believed that's where Rosemary would have left them, where she would have "given them back."

She rolled onto her left side and reached out to the wicker storage chest in front of the sofa. Rosemary had added a long, rectangular Hawaiian-quilted pillow on top so the chest could be used as a footrest or a seat. With the pillow removed, it served quadruple duty as a coffee table when Rosemary conferred with clients. She'd put Rosemary's journal, sketchbooks, and project notebooks inside it yesterday. A nearly invisible clasp facing the sofa kept the lid tightly closed and thus well disguised.

She took out the journal and flopped back against the cushions. Rosemary's voice in her head as she read the journal's words reminded her again of how lucky she had been to have Rosemary and her boys in her life. She'd been reading for an hour or more when a no-nonsense knock on the doorframe announced Dante's arrival.

"I wanted to make sure you're all right, after the overlook and everything else you got up to today," he said, stepping into the room.

She sat up, avoiding his gaze. "Does Aidan still live? And does he still have all his body parts?"

"Thanks to you begging for his life. And he told me about your little experiment."

"In that case, I'll have to kill him myself. I feel like an adolescent fool, if that makes you feel any better."

"Somehow it doesn't. So how's the arm?"

"It doesn't even hurt. I would swear sometimes that you have magic fingers."

"I've been told that before," he said, a hint of a grin in his voice.

"Grow up, Kahoa."

"Look who's talking. The Experimenter."

She pressed on — and pressed her palms against her flaming cheeks. "Healing hands, then."

"Seriously, I've also been told that."

He paused, but she remained silent, wondering how long he'd beat her over the head with The Experimenter handle and whether she was going to cry.

"Let's do ourselves a favor, Lani. No more experimenting until we sort out ourselves and this mess we have on our hands. Unless, of course, you feel the need to experiment some more to get it out of your system. Do you want me to send Pepper over here so you can test-drive him?"

She threw the quilted pillow at his head. He caught it before it hit him, threw it on top of the wicker chest, and nodded toward the journal. "Know where to look yet?"

She swallowed, thankful he wasn't insisting on analyzing their kiss, or teasing her about it, or being really, really angry about her experiment with Aidan. She doggedly followed the Pele's Tears conversational opening he'd offered.

"If Rosemary found them, we can find them too. I've started reading at the beginning of the journal to see what made me think of the *pali* face the first time."

"And how do we let this jerk know we're working on it? Put up a billboard on the *pali?*"

"I don't know. I proved earlier with Pepper that telling everyone we know that we're looking for something, without telling them what it is or why we're looking for it, will make us sound like idiots. The new sign at the shop should have given our guy a clue. Maybe he didn't see it on his way to the overlook to terrorize me. When we find them, what will you do?"

"They belong to *us.* We'll sell them and use the money to help Lehua. I know we're not just handing them over to some nutcase." His voice was cautious, half question, half declaration.

Surprise made her look at him. "Really? I was afraid you'd want to do exactly that. They'd be out of our lives."

"They'll also be out of our lives if we shove them into a safe-deposit box, have the stones appraised, and then send them to Sotheby's or Christie's for auction with a nice reserve on them. A large sum padding our bank account will offer Lehua a lot of protection. We've already paid for them in blood."

"Speaking of blood, will we be safe? If we don't know the identity of this person and we don't hand over the gems, what stops that person from seeking revenge? We'll handle this however you want to handle it, Dante, but we have to find them first." She patted the sofa beside her.

He sat down, staring at the open journal and his grandmother's written words. Then he reached out and took her left hand, lacing his fingers with hers. They quietly listened to the big band music, the music of a generation at war, a generation whose young people lived in uncertain times but loved totally and in the moment.

"Do you remember the four of us dancing to this stuff when we were kids? If our friends had ever found out . . ." Dante whispered, moving restlessly beside her.

"How could I forget?" Her mouth went dry. He wasn't actually considering asking her to dance with him?

"You and Pepper got on well?"

"Swimmingly until I nearly tied my mind and my tongue into knots by telling him to tell everyone he met or knew that you and I were looking for something. Now he just thinks I'm nuts."

"Ah. And you haven't eliminated him from your Sour Note suspects?"

"Is that what we're calling this creep?"

"His notes are certainly striking a sour note with me."

"I can think of lots of other names to call him, most of which I learned from you. And how can we eliminate Pepper? We can't eliminate anyone because it could be anyone. One of the workers even. Anyone. Someone just walked in and put that note on the kitchen island for you to find. And I hope Sour Note saw the new sign at the shop on his way out of the valley. Because if he saw it before, then he terrified me, almost killed me, just to make a point."

"If he even left the valley."

Silence fell as they considered the points they'd just made. She was suddenly very tired and very conscious of how she still felt. That outcrop and this day had definitely left their marks on her and on her mind.

"Tutu would only confide in someone she trusted, or maybe someone involved in her research," he finally said.

"She says in the journal that she kept a low profile in her research to avoid attracting attention." Her eyelids were so heavy she could barely keep her eyes open.

"That worked well, didn't it? The conveyor belt is in, by the way, and works like it's greased. Well, parts of it are greased. Shaka is amazing."

Dante was dirty now. She hadn't paid any attention to the state of his clothes. "Everybody around this place is pretty amazing, in case you haven't noticed."

"Oh, I've noticed," he said softly, his breath on her cheek. "And how could Tutu do research without asking direct questions, just like us and the whole 'We're looking for something' thing? Pepper's not the only one who will think we're crazy if we do that. And questions make people curious."

Dante still held her hand, neither of them mentioning what had happened in the kitchen, although it was right there between them and she could scarcely think of anything else.

She forced her thoughts back to their predicament. "We'll probably have to go back to the *pali*."

"Not until after those anthurium fields are cut, we don't."

"Unless I find something new beyond where I stopped reading the journal all those years ago, I don't know where else to look. I think we can eliminate the cliff face because I don't think Rosemary would have or could have gone up that way after Dom and everything. Then there are the clues, of course. The clues you haven't asked me about."

Like a spring uncoiling, he suddenly jumped to his feet, pulling her up with him. "Dance with me."

She found herself on her feet, wide awake, and feeling her cheeks flush. Did she dare voluntarily step into those arms again?

"Not a good idea. My, um, arm?"

He shot her a look, reading either her mind or her face. "Right. Your arm didn't stop you from kissing two different men today. Of course, those are just the two I know about."

She snorted a weak laugh, too weary to respond in any other way.

"A dance is no big deal, Lani. And we've danced to this music before. We're just taller now. I'll behave, I promise. I just want to dance with you the way we all used to do, to Tutu's favorite music. There's scarcely an ulterior motive in sight," he ended with a grin.

She nodded, feeling the pull of Rosemary's heaven, back to a time of short, passionate love affairs, where the memories often had to last a lifetime. The notes of "Moonlight

Serenade" surrounded them.

"Come out on the *lānai*," he said and pulled her toward the doors. "It feels crowded in here."

She gulped. Maybe she wasn't the only one who imagined another couple dancing here. "Crowded?"

"Like another couple is dancing around us." He ended with a shrug.

She nodded once. "It's Rosemary and her beloved."

"I thought that's who it might be," he whispered. "And when this dance is over, you should take a hot bath and lie down for a nap," he ordered gently. "This day has already been two days long for you."

"Sounds like a plan."

Dante lifted her left hand to the back of his neck, clasped her right hand against his chest, and pulled her close. His heart pounded beneath their hands, and she wondered if he felt hers as clearly.

And he lied. This dance was definitely different, and it wasn't just because they were taller.

She snuggled her head between his jaw and his shoulder, giving herself up to the music and breathing in the scent of him for the second time that day: damp cotton, his familiar aftershave, and fresh air, all overlaid with a hint of axle grease this time.

There went her resolution about not getting close to him. But how could she honor it when holding her was surely what this man had been born to do, just as she had been born to hold him? Praying that she could keep him safe, and with a smile of contentment curving her mouth, she relaxed into him, the beauty of the moment, the music, and the company.

Then exhaustion, mental, emotional, and physical, overwhelmed her. Was reaction to the whole package of today finally setting in? Was it possible to sleep standing up? She was all for finding out.

CHAPTER 13

The next morning, The Colonel called Lani to flower duty. The anthurium fields were well and truly ready for harvest and shipment. Bleary-eyed at the crack of dawn, she bracketed sunglasses over her eyes and hitched a ride in one of the trucks going up to the first field. In the front seat, and nearly too tired to enjoy it, she was the filling in a man sandwich, packed between two big, handsome college students home on break, guys looking for a last injection of cash before classes started. The truck bed was full of them too. Other vehicles, including bicycles, followed them. The apprentice farmers were elsewhere, not involved in the flower side of the business.

Dante's truck, at the head of the line, had its crew cab and truck bed full of laughing, giggling, beautiful girls and women. When their little convoy got to the fields, the crews piled out, met up with other crews, received their equipment and assignments from Dante or Shaka, and set to work. She noticed that Dante teamed Aidan with a bevy of island beauties, including Mei, and sent them as far away from her as possible.

Shaka had made a leather tool belt for her that she'd used since Dante had taught her how to harvest Lehua's blooms many years ago. He'd put enough holes in it so it grew with her. The leather was still soft and flexible. Someone, she discovered, had been giving it tender loving care through the years of her absence.

She uncoiled it, kitted out its two loops, each with a shallow cup made of plastic pipe, filled her cups with disinfectant, screwed on the squeaky membrane lids, and pushed well-oiled shears through each lid into the cups. She fumbled while trying to strap the belt around her hips.

Dante came over to help her. "Let me," he said and deftly tightened it into place around her hips, pulling her up close to him with his tugging. "It's been a while since you've done anthuriums. Do you remember what to look for?"

He was close enough that all he had to do was reach out, remove her sunglasses, and hook them over the neck of her T-shirt, all the while looking into her eyes.

Hawaii was fraught with superstitions, legends, and myths, and she, having Hawaiian blood and a healthy dose of Hawaiian upbringing, was not immune to them. She just couldn't shake the superstitious belief that she was bad luck for the Kahoa brothers. Dante's body heat reminded her of how close they had been several times the day before. She'd been on edge ever since their dance, constantly reminding herself that the last time their attraction flared, Dom had died.

She studied the second button of his denim shirt and recited what he'd drilled into her when she was tall enough to follow him down the rows. "I'm looking for blooms with bright yellow tips on their noses, no longer than this," she held up her little finger between them and used her thumb to isolate its tip.

She'd been taught that an anthurium's nose was the long, pointy spike in its center, the spadix, which turned white from the bottom up in six to eight weeks. Cutting anthuriums at the right time made them keepers, lasting two weeks or longer in a vase. And this made them favorites of florists and customers alike.

Spying a perfect bloom nearby, she stepped away and pulled out a pair of her shears. With gloved hands, she parted the glossy foliage and placed the cut an inch from the base so the tropical beauty was long-stemmed.

"Okay?" she asked, twirling the flower in front of his nose.

"Like riding a bicycle, you never forget." He pointed over her shoulder. "I've partnered you up with someone else who's rusty. Play nice," he said and turned to leave, his parting shot drifting out behind him. "But then you already have an in with the Takei boys and their great smiles."

She would kill him. Slowly. Because she had turned to find that her partner was Keneke Takei, one brother up from Noa. That would make him the motorcycle nut who didn't talk much but who had always been nice to her. So she decided to remind him he could be nice.

Her resolve wavered as she faced the scowling, tough-looking, tattooed man across a row of heart-shaped, scarlet anthuriums, a surreal picture in itself. She searched for her second flower of the day — and a way to turn this around on Dante. She should have known he wouldn't let that kiss with Aidan pass so easily.

After a hesitant hello, she said, "How are you, Keneke? It's good to see you again."

He grunted in response.

After a few more blooms, she added, "I think Dante put us together because he thinks we don't know each other very well. He doesn't know you were nice to me when Noa and I hung out together. Or that you gave me a ride on your Harley once. So why don't we try to enjoy working together today, just to get up his nose? Are you willing to talk to me a little, maybe flirt with me a little, smile a little?"

Oh, he was willing, with a smile and a sideways glance at Dante that spoke volumes. Ah, those Takei boys and their unnerving, glorious smiles!

"Thanks for being a good sport about this. I haven't been to the library yet to see Noa. How is he? I thought he was going into the law." She ended with a big grin.

Keneke's smile transformed his face a second time, and they were off. "Mama told my brah he be preacher or lawyer 'cause the rest of us need one or da other most of da time, but he liked da books."

She laughed and continued laughing, naturally and at regular intervals, as they talked back and forth across the rows. She was getting a look at the softer side of an older Takei brother — and it was surprising. When they exhausted one subject, she just asked another question.

Sunlight was filtering through mesh covers and gave the area a glow, protecting them from the climbing sun. But Lani knew the shade cloth wasn't there for them but for the flowers. It kept the sun from burning the rich, velvety blooms, saturated with color, that they were cutting.

They were working rows in a terraced, two-acre field 2,000 feet above sea level on one of Lehua's valley slopes, a miniclimate that received 200 inches of rain per year. The first Kahoa flower growers had amended this soil for anthuriums years ago by adding volcanic cinders and Canadian peat. To this day, Dante and Shaka watched the mix closely. When it became impossible to amend the soil in new fields, they put anthuriums in pots in those fields, with volcanic cinders as their growing medium.

"This is like working in two acres of rainbow," she told Keneke, during a burst of enthusiasm.

That was too girly for him, so he just nodded and looked uncomfortable. She smiled an apology. She had to keep in mind that he was a long way from his leathers and his bike up here.

White, pink, peach, orange, deep ruby, bright red, and variegated anthuriums grew from knee-high in height to five feet in these fields. She'd been surprised when Dante told her that Lehua Flower Farm now cultivated 100 different varieties that they shipped to mainland florists. A small percentage of this crop would be diverted to Beans and Blossoms, to their local customers and hotels, and to their small but healthy online mail-order business. Plantings were staggered in some fields so blooms could be cut every day for orders coming in for tropical flower arrangements.

"Are you still into motorcycles?" she asked, to put Keneke on familiar ground. "Why don't you tell me about them?"

He was and he did. "If I geeve you another ride on my bike — I'll go slow — dat will really worry da *kahuna*." She watched Keneke give Dante the stink eye, and they each got one in return.

Other than coordinating with the Takei brothers on the intervention in the flower prep shed and their working for Lehua during harvests, Dante and the Takei brothers went their separate ways.

She pushed the shears she had just used through the membrane in the lid of one plastic-pipe cup on her belt and reached for the other pair in the second one, switching back and forth with each cut. The disinfectant discouraged the spread of blight. Dante and Shaka insisted on this precaution.

"Da *kahuna* use to warn guys off you." Keneke ended the sentence as though he wasn't quite finished with the subject.

She sighed. "I know. He more or less admitted it to me once." She threw Dante the stink eye on her own. "Other than killing him, I didn't know how to stop him."

Keneke leaned across the row toward her, so she stopped and leaned toward him. "You maybe tell me to keep *hāmau,* quiet, but I think maybe da *kahuna* was in love with you himself before you went off-island. He din know how to go about it 'cause you live under same roof."

Keneke was on a conversational roll so she didn't want to throw any sounds into his path, especially the surprised squeak that almost escaped her. She'd never heard him speak so many words at one time.

"I seen how it was with him in da prep shed when we was scarin' Noa straight. I'm thinkin' things no change, da way he's geevin' us the stink eye. An' I'm also thinkin' you still don't mind."

She made thoughtful noises for him. He shot her a look from under his lashes that was so like Noa that she blinked — right before everything around her shifted.

First, there was the mental picture of Dante not knowing how to go about anything. Then she recalled his dimples, his eyes, their first kiss, their second kiss, their dance. After what they'd been up to together lately, she thought maybe they were both ready to bring it on. She wouldn't mind if her best friend morphed into something more after their Pele's Tears mess was sorted out.

She shook herself out of her open-mouthed trance in front of a bloom she was unsure about harvesting. She flicked the edge of the heart-shaped lobe, a leaf really, not a petal, just a little too hard. It sprang back quickly, feeling firm and waxy, so she harvested it without another thought.

"I'll have to think on that, Keneke," she whispered. "But I'll tell you what. I think you're a wise man."

Since the anthuriums they were cutting had no scent, the humid air smelled simply of moist green plants. Black volcanic cinder in the soil crunched under her hiking boots. Dante had drummed into her years ago that anthuriums, like orchids, are epiphytes, air plants, and don't need soil to grow. So a big chunk of this side of the valley, with its elevation and its amended soil, provided the plants with good drainage and stability.

Lehua harvested flowers year-round since its climate made temperatures constant. The farm also propagated its anthuriums, which produced well for three to five years, by transplanting the sprouts that grew around the base of the plants.

As lovely as these blooms were, she was looking forward to the new, scented, potted anthuriums coming up in the next field.

At the end of each row, they took their flowers to a cart slowly pulled by a tractor. Dante, who was driving for their section this morning, scowled at them every time they approached, resembling more than ever a tiki god. She ignored him at first. Keneke gave as good as he got and urged her to do the same. Instead, she started to wink at Dante and give him a thumbs-up, every row. She hoped he didn't grind his teeth down to nubs.

But he had problems of his own keeping up with the steady stream of workers that approached the cart with their harvests. The older women had warm smiles for him. The younger women's smiles were beyond warm. She and Dom had enjoyed watching Dante squirm and trot out the fancy footwork when eager girls or their mothers hove into view, as they frequently did when Dante was around. They had decided between them that Dante liked to play with the opposite sex only when he initiated the games. Apparently, nothing had changed.

With a knowing grin in his direction, which was met with a thundering frown, she sorted her flowers by color and stem length into buckets of water set into holes on the flat cart's floor. She then rinsed her gloves with disinfectant and went back to work.

Showers rolled in during the morning and they worked through them.

After lunch, Dante separated them, not before hearing Keneke's rather loud invitation to take her for *another* ride on his bike, and her response, "I'd love it! Just like last time."

"I'm putting you with Mei for the rest of the day," he responded, throwing Keneke a look, and left them.

She gleefully realized he was too busy to do much of anything about any of this. She joined Mei in their assigned area where cup and saucer anthuriums grew. The flowers had an extra curved petal, which looked like a cup sitting on top of the larger one. Next would be bright pink anthuriums that smelled like bubble gum, another variety would be minty, another cinnamon-scented. As she carried armfuls to Shaka's cart, she breathed in their lovely scents, a big smile on her face.

Facing the young woman across a row, she asked, "Did Aidan introduce himself yesterday? And did Pepper find you?"

Mei nodded and smiled warmly.

Lani waited a few beats then said, "I think they both like you. And they're both really cute."

"I think so too. We all went to a party at the platforms last night. But we're just friends." The girl's rosy cheeks said otherwise. "Some people won't believe that, though."

"Shaka can be stubborn as a mule sometimes. Like Dante. Does Shaka think Pepper is too old for you? And you know Aidan's going home soon?"

"It's not just my grandfather, it's me. I've never dated older men, like I said, but I suddenly want to date both of them. But I wish Dante would mind his own problems."

"I think Dante tries to protect any young woman he cares about from players like himself."

"Maybe that's it. You should watch out for Melika, who owns the gallery in town. She has a weird thing for him."

Lani felt her cheeks grow warm, remembering that Mei had seen her and Dante in the kitchen yesterday. "That's nothing new. Women tend to like Dante, a lot, but he likes to do the chasing. It irritates him when they reverse the roles."

"Well, this one has been after him ever since she set eyes on him. He steers clear of her. I think she scares him. He says she's *pupule*."

Crazy? That stopped her in her tracks because she didn't think the woman had been born who could scare Dante Kahoa. She decided to steer the conversation elsewhere. She wondered what else Mei might have seen.

"Mei, who was in the house yesterday before, um, Dante and I got there? Especially in the kitchen."

The girl grinned then shook her head. "I was in the kitchen before I went to the office."

"Did you notice a folded white piece of paper on the table?"

"It had Dante's name on it, so I didn't open it."

"Who, besides Pepper, came to the house yesterday?"

"Melika stopped in earlier, pretending to want to meet you, but Dante wasn't around and you weren't there so she left. Then there was Aidan, Agnes, Helen, and me." Their

223

conversation ended when Mei, who cut blooms much more quickly than Lani, got too far ahead in her row.

Dante had casually mentioned Melika and her new gallery in town, and that Lani should check it out for placing her work there. Tomorrow, she promised herself, she'd have a look at this woman who scared Dante Kahoa and who had been in Lehua's kitchen yesterday.

She'd forgotten how much she enjoyed this work, hard though it was. The next plant Lani chose for her attentions showed brown blight spots on a few of its leaves. Frowning, she snipped off the offending leaves and put them aside to be raked and burned.

Soon after that, Dante took her off flower harvesting. Around the edge of the field grew rows of hot pink and green *ti* plants. The upright stalks reminded her of cornstalks. She snapped off the perfect leaves near the top for use in their bouquet mixtures, much easier work. She suddenly felt something that Dante must have seen in her. Her falling off the overlook was still taking its toll. And, unaccustomed as she now was to the bending, pulling, and humidity of harvesting, she was wiped out. She was grateful he hadn't sent her to the sloping acre of orange, white, and purple bird-of-paradise plants with sharp leaves.

After that, he sent her to the grading shed. By that time, she was really thankful he had seen her problem, forgave her for the fun she'd had at his expense with Keneke, and was pacing her, looking out for her, again.

So, sitting down and laughing with the chattering women on both sides of her, she graded anthuriums, measuring each bloom against a marked board. She spread the waxy hearts gently to judge the widest part. Nine-inch jumbos were the largest she handled. The two-and-a-half-inch buttons were graded at another table.

Dante finally told her to stop when she wanted to and wait for him in his truck. She knew he would guarantee her a ride back to the house just to make sure she didn't climb up behind Keneke Takei on his bike. While she waited for him, she wandered through the cleaning area, where each flower was checked for insects and weed seeds before being packed. In the mail-order shed, she pitched in to fill the long cardboard boxes lined with foam sheeting and wet newsprint shreds.

Ti leaves went into the box first, topped with more damp shreds. Bird-of-paradise and anthuriums went in next, each bloom in a paper bag. A foam sleeve was folded over each anthurium before it went into the box. The labeled, finished boxes went onto the new, slow-moving conveyor belt, Shaka's brainchild, which carried them to shipping. There, the orders were loaded into waiting refrigerated trucks for their journey to the airport in Lihue.

She looked in on the *lei*-making shed. The craft involved ten-inch needles, heavy thread, plumeria, orchids, and other exotic flowers. It was an art, one she'd never been good at, so she left the *leis* to the experts and made her weary way to Dante's truck, longing for a shower, a snack, and her bed.

She was almost asleep when he climbed inside. "Where's your crew?" she asked, glancing behind her at the truck bed.

"Some of them are working a second shift or a few hours over. I'm taking a break. Shaka and I will be in and out all night."

"I forgot how intense harvest days are. Sorry I folded so quickly."

"You did well for your first day back and after everything that's happened to you the past few days. Besides, you're an owner now. You shouldn't have to work this hard. Tomorrow's cut will be smaller. And you're excused from it. Both of us are. But I'll do half the night shift in the sheds tomorrow night."

"You work hard all the time, no matter what's going on."

He shrugged. "Lehua's reputation is all about quality. One of us has to be visible just about all the time."

"Well, I think we should rotate the packing and shipping night shifts, once I'm up to speed with it all again."

He glanced at her. "*Mahalo.* You and Keneke Takei have fun?"

"Yes, we did. He was nice to me when Noa and I were friends, and he gave me a ride on his bike once." She couldn't help grinning at the look on his face.

"How did I not hear about that?"

"Oh, I don't know. Saturation point, maybe? Maybe everyone on the island decided it was time you didn't know everything. Like I said, he was nice to me."

"Keneke Takei is good with motorcycles, but nice? Keep your *'ōkole* off that bike of his. He's still too old for you. And he still has a reputation."

"Not your problem anymore, Kahoa," she reminded him before pinning him with a look. "It's okay for you, as an adult, to ride a Harley and get a tattoo, but still not okay for me?"

"Okay, I'll say please. Please keep your *'ōkole* off that bike of his. If you want the thrill of wind in your face and bugs in your teeth, you can ride with me. So how did you get on with Tutu's journal yesterday?"

He was playing his mental leapfrog game again, and she let him. "There are long gaps in the dates, after Dom, when she didn't make any entries. I took a closer look at the two clues you still have to ask me about."

She hesitated, giving him a chance to ask. He didn't speak, making a point of not asking about the clues. They rode in silence after that.

Just before Aidan had come to the cottage yesterday, she found what she thought had set her off last time. Rosemary had been eager to look for caves on the *pali* based on something her father had put on paper when Rosemary was just a girl. That had sent Lani to the parchment the ugly pendant had been wrapped in. When she dragged herself to her room after dinner, she took it out and examined it with a magnifying glass. It was part of a page where he had written about finding a cave on the *pali* as a boy, a cave with glowing eyes, he'd said. He had ended by saying he was afraid to go back.

"House or cottage?" he asked as they approached the buildings.

"Home." She managed to exhale the word and pack it with feeling when she finally saw the house.

Dante parked in back. "At last."

On harvest days, the house was usually unlocked and empty from dawn until dark. But she just couldn't leave it unlocked that morning, not after what had happened to her yesterday. Today hadn't been one of Agnes's days to come in, Helen had helped with the harvest, and Aumoe had a cat door. So she had felt it was okay to humor herself and lock up. Dante didn't comment, even though he had to dig in his jeans pockets for his key.

Still, she glanced warily around the kitchen as they passed through, locking the back door again behind them. She had hoped, uselessly as it had turned out, that changing the sign at the shop would make her feel less jumpy. Instead, after the overlook, she was now really nervous, maneuvering under a cloud of doom, sure something was about to happen.

Dante was apparently too exhausted to notice her mood. They climbed the stairs together, with her behind him, admiring his tight Hawaiian butt. He reached back a hand to help pull her up the stairs after she gasped, caused by an unidentified, unused muscle suddenly making its displeasure felt. He disappeared into his room, muttering a good-night, while she continued up the attic steps to her room at the top of the big house, with no warm, callused hand to help her up the last flight.

CHAPTER 14

The next day, she coordinated with Dante then chose and packed a few samples of her work, including the *pikake* lamp she'd made for Rosemary, which she would never sell, to show Melika, the mysterious gallery owner. She planned to stop at the shop first and show the girls some catalog pages she had printed out of new products she had ordered to be delivered via Overnight Express Mail. She wanted their input; Dante had told her to order whatever she wanted — just so it sold.

She hitched a ride with Shaka again, and Dante promised to pick her up in an hour or so. He had errands in Kalele. After what Mei had told her yesterday about his reaction to Melika, she was eager to see if he even came inside the gallery with her.

The first customers arrived at the shop when she did, and she took a moment to add one more word to the tracking sign.

The girls were wearing their new cobbler's aprons with Beans and Blossoms' *pikake* logo embroidered on the front. She'd had them overnighted from Honolulu. Another clerk, a guy, was coming on soon because they were expecting their first tourist van later. The girls approved Lani's choices and were eager to sell the new product lines. Helen, at Lani's request, had hurriedly purchased outright some local crafts for resale, so the shelves weren't nearly as empty as they had been. The big switch for the shelving units was tentatively scheduled for next weekend. The stereo system was on order.

She was describing to the girls the special bouquet called Pele's Tears they would offer soon, making it up as she went along and asking for their suggestions, when Dante strolled in. The girls almost quivered.

"*Aloha,* ladies." He flashed his dimples, but the blue laser beams he used for eyes were aimed at her.

His smile fried long before his eyes could grab it. He'd seen the sign — and he wasn't happy. She wondered if it was a combination of the sign and her interaction with Keneke yesterday, or if he was simply grumpy from his coming and going at the sheds all night. Maile and Kalana didn't notice, but if their eyes had hands, their fingerprints would be all over him.

Lani sent a bright smile his way, grabbed the envelope with the invoice she could fill in if Melika took any of the stained glass items in the box she'd packed, pointed to the box, sweetly saying, "Please," to Dante, and went out with a wave to the clerks.

"Another nice sign," he said through his teeth when they got outside.

"I added 'Really!' hoping it will make Sour Note get the idea that we'll look."

She saw him wince when she slammed his truck door. Dante never abused his truck, even when he was upset, other than smacking the steering wheel the other day with his fist.

He reopened her door and put the box on her lap. "Softer ride," he muttered.

"So are you going to ask me what I found in my trunk?" she asked after they set off.

"No. I. Am. Not."

This was not going well. It was time to divert his anger and frustration, whatever the cause, away from Pele's Tears because she did not want to go up on the *pali* alone.

"I've been told that this Melika makes you nervous. Is it because she's beautiful?"

He didn't answer, but the following look he sent her was loaded with *Oh, please.*

Silent miles passed.

"Or you could just tell me why you think she's crazy."

They were approaching Kalele before he answered. "Or I could just take my hands off the wheel and strangle you," he ground out.

"Guess I'll have to steer, huh?" She followed through by reaching toward the steering wheel.

He laughed, long and loud, his bad mood gone with the first sound of it. "Sorry. I just hate to go near Nohea right now, for reasons I won't go into. That's the name of the gallery, by the way. Its owner is unique. Stunning, but not as beautiful as you are."

She gasped. "Me? You think I'm beautiful?"

"Here we go. I've told you forever that you're a Hawaiian hottie, Lani. Dom thought so too. I don't know why you have such a hard time seeing it. The way you move . . . If people couldn't see feet at the end of those beautiful long, long legs of yours, they'd swear you had wheels. And those cat eyes of yours, with that mane of hair . . . Don't you have mirrors?"

He didn't even give her time to digest the compliments before he plowed on. "When you meet Melika today, take a good look at her. Especially her eyes. And wait until you see her office. And you will see it because your stuff is as good as Tutu's. Melika's from the Big Island, and she takes herself very seriously, all wrapped up in Hawaiiana and Pele legends. Just wait." He swung the truck into a parking space.

He went on to tell her that Melika's new gallery was part of the chamber of commerce's attempt to make Kalele a shopping destination.

"I'll contact them. Beans and Blossoms can be part of the shopping destination thing. And have you thought of giving tours of the fields and sheds?"

Dante didn't answer as he opened her door and took the box she had carefully packed earlier.

Lani had seen quite a few galleries on all the islands, but always in Rosemary's company. *Nohea* meant lovely, and the wide, small-paned bow window in front, as far as she could see inside, showed lovely things indeed. One of the corner panes was covered with a notice, and the word "chant" caught her eye.

"Dante! Alepeka is doing the Pele and Lohi'au chant in a few days. I didn't realize she was still doing chants. Do you still record them?"

Lani memorized the date and time as she spoke. This was the chant behind James Talbot-Kahoa's naming of Pele's Tears — and she was going to be there, with or without Dante.

Alepeka had been the best chanter in their part of the island when they were kids. Lani had spent a lot of time traipsing via foot, bicycle, or a bummed ride before Dante could drive, from beaches to hills to fields while he pursued his hobby of recording chants. He had her broken in as his assistant early on, and she became hooked on chants because of his interest.

"Believe me, I know all about it," he said in a tight voice. "If you really want to go, I might record it."

"Yes, please. I'd love to hear it."

She stepped back to admire the building. Melika had turned what Lani remembered as an abandoned storefront into a replica of a New England saltbox house. Judging by the number of vehicles parked nose-in along the main street in front, this gallery was as successful as Melika's other galleries that Dante had mentioned, on the other islands. She was sure that carrying Rosemary's work had helped make it so.

"I'll meet you here at the truck. I'll probably be napping inside," he said and set off down the street toward the hardware store.

She watched him go, then went inside. All around her, paintings and drawings in different mediums, sculptures in various stones, figurines done in glass with Hawaii's volcanic ash added to their formulas, carved *koa* wood bowls and boxes, scrimshaw — old and new — and other fine handicrafts were arranged in tasteful groupings and in lighted displays. Every piece was Hawaiian in theme or, as in the case of the glass items and the *koa* bowls and boxes, some natural part of Hawaii had been used in their creation, according to the small, tasteful signs accompanying them. A cluster of tourists, wearing silk aloha shirts or *mu'umu'us,* and with Italian leather sandals on their pedicured feet, whispered among themselves, apparently liking what they saw.

Lani sensed a purposeful ripple in the air and looked up to see a woman flow toward her across the space, gliding around tourists and displays alike, as though *she* had wheels instead of feet. In a slow-motion moment worthy of a TV commercial for the Hawaiian tourist industry, the woman's long, full, dark flowing hair appeared to move in a wind that wasn't blowing — at least not one that lifted Lani's hair like that.

She wore a red *holokū,* the long, fitted

dress of Hawaii, minus the train, and the material had a tone-on-tone plumeria pattern in it. Being tall and slim, she looked really good — she could have carried off the train.

Lani remembered what Dante had told her and struggled to ignore her first impressions in order to "take a good look." She smiled at the idea until . . .

Melika's beauty and grace skewed slightly when Lani got to the woman's eyes. They were the color of mud that had been made with blood instead of rain. Then she noticed something else that wiped the shreds of her smile right off her face. When the light caught her eyes just right, they appeared to glow with an inner fire.

"*Aloha,* and welcome to Nohea. I'm Melika. You must be Noelani. I've been hoping you'd come to show me some of your things," she said in a voice that sounded like Dante when he had a cold, all whiskey, leather, and smoke. "Let's go up to my office."

Lani nodded, speechless, and simply followed her. She was sure that men would follow Melika's amazing voice anywhere and wondered what Dante's reaction to it had been the first time he heard it, before he decided that she made him nervous or that she was crazy.

Melika paused before starting up the stairs, catching the eye of every employee. One of them was Agnes, who moved away from the front window. Her pale blue eyes widened briefly when she saw Lani. Lani waved and Agnes's head dipped in a self-conscious nod. So Agnes did accounting for Nohea too.

The stairs took them to a mezzanine, which had skylights and a glass-fronted office that filled one corner of it. Most of the gallery was visible from here, but it was the wall beside Melika's desk that made Lani's breath hitch.

An unbroken slab of what looked like lava rock was lit from floor level, with light fanning up over it to the top. She had the feeling someone watched her from its shadows, a face hidden in the textures of the rough surface. She studied it for a few moments, like it was one of those hidden pictures in a kids' magazine, gasping when she finally saw a woman's face, a woman whose long hair swirled around her head as if it floated on the surface of the stone.

Melika went behind the desk and gracefully folded down onto a leather executive chair, inviting her to sit down. Without looking away from the wall, Lani stepped sideways then dropped into the first chair she felt touch the backs of her knees, still clutching the box in her arms.

"Do you like it?" Melika asked, a smile in her voice. "It's a cast of a rock face, no pun intended, which I accidentally found while hiking. I shone my flashlight upward and there she was. I had to have it. It was meant. A miracle."

Images of Pele had always inspired fearful respect in Lani's heart, despite her fascination with Pele's Tears. "It's . . . amazing," she managed, her throat so dry she croaked the words while chicken skin prickled her body.

"I believe Pele formed this image of herself naturally, in her own medium on the Big Island, for me to find. Watch this," Melika invited and pushed a button on her desk.

Those two legendary words made Lani yearn for an O.S. handle on her chair to hang on to, like the one in Dante's truck, especially when the lighting on the floor switched to red, creating a misty effect that made the stone come alive as magma. The eyes of the image captured within it glowed with an otherworldly light.

New chills crawled over her body. "But Pele is temperamental and angers easily," she whispered. "Why would you —"

"Because she's like me, or so I've been told," Melika replied, laughing. "Now I'd like to see whatever you have there." She turned off the glowing nightmare on the wall.

Thankful for that, and with unsteady hands, Lani unpacked the small *pikake* lamp. "This item is special to me and isn't for sale. I brought it as an example of what I can create in a practical piece."

Melika stood, sucking in her breath. "I can almost smell jasmine from here." She came around the desk and took the lamp from Lani's hands, continuing on to the glass wall overlooking the gallery. She held up the lamp to the light pouring in from the windows below and the skylights above.

Lani moved to stand beside her, carrying an oval panel. Agnes was coming up the stairs, she noticed. She then heard a door close nearby.

"And this is stained glass enhanced with painting. The beauty of the *'ōhi'a lehua's* pom-pom blossom doesn't translate well to the medium."

Her voice faltered when she realized what she'd just said — and what was behind her on the wall when she said it. The lava-red *lehua* blossom of the *'ōhi'a* tree was called the flower of Pele and was sacred to the Hawaiian volcano goddess, and as such is the official flower of the Big Island, home of Pele.

"I understand." Melika set the lamp on her desk and reverently took the panel, holding it higher in the light. "*Nohea,* indeed. You have every ounce of Rosemary's talent overlaid with your own impressive style. You're truly an artistic craftsman, Noelani Beecham, and I want you for my galleries."

While Lani stared, numb with shock, Melika rattled off an outline of her commission fee scale. She paused before asking Lani's own pricing philosophy.

After exclaiming over a second panel that had been layered in the box, this one featuring plumerias, Melika called in Agnes, who went away again with Lani's hastily scribbled invoice, and with instructions from Melika to pull the invoice and cut a second check, for an amount that made Lani blink, to purchase outright the items in Rosemary's last delivery to Nohea.

Melika continued talking while Lani continued to throw sideways glances at the wall, wanting to get out of there. When Dante tapped on the open office door, she wanted to jump up and hug him. She also wanted to tell him that Melika made her nervous too and that the woman was likely leaning at a sharp angle toward *pupule,* crazy, when it came to Pele.

"Dante. Come in," Melika purred.

He wouldn't. Instead he draped himself in the doorway, about half as much as he had done in Lani's doorway in Maine. "Melika," he said, taking off his hat and holding it by its brim. He watched the woman closely, every relaxed line of his body shouting tension to Lani.

Lani had the oddest feeling that, besides the effects of Dante's hat, denim shirt and jeans, and his boots, if these two were armed, they'd draw on each other like this was a showdown at high noon.

"Tell me you've changed your mind, Dante." Melika made the statement sound like an order wrapped in cajoling. "You will be the perfect Lohi'au for the chant."

Ah, now Lani understood the standoff thing — and the nervous thing. Dante was very touchy, bordering on cagey, when it came to his Hawaiian side. Rosemary and Lani had agree that he found his Hawaiian niches in working the land, in the language, which he spoke fluently, in his acquired *paniolo* look, and in his lifelong hobby of recording chants as spoken history.

Dante also spoke a mean Hawaiian pidgin when he was with his friends. Then it was all "da kine" and "howzit" and "mo bettah" and "no can" and "geev'um," all of which Lani understood. But when those were mixed in with more pidgin, she was in trouble. She always found herself a sentence or two behind, translating in her head.

And Dante would never, ever, be caught dead in a *malo,* the loincloth Hawaiian men wear when they perform *hula* and interpret chants. He enjoyed watching *hula* and would dance in shorts at a *lū'au,* but that was it.

Lani, however, celebrated her Hawaiian side with dance. She had taken *hula* lessons every summer in Hawaii, and had joined a *hula hālau,* a *hula* troupe, in California in between visits. It had crossed her mind to join one since she returned to Lehua, although she felt terribly out of practice.

"I haven't changed my mind." His quiet words could have echoed off the glass if they wanted to.

Lani's gaze jerked back to Melika when she heard her name. "Noelani, how about you? You'd be perfect to interpret Hi'iaka's part."

She froze. Hi'iaka was Pele's sister — the Other Woman, and one of the patronesses of *hula* dancers — who stole Pele's man in the chant. Wide-eyed, she looked at Dante again, he looked back, and they held a conversation without saying a word. "No, thanks. I haven't danced in years. I'd need weeks of practice to catch up. Besides, I'll be helping Dante record the chant."

Melika's eyes flashed red. Maybe it was the dress or a trick of the light? "You'll need permission to do that, and I don't think you'll get it." Her threat wasn't even thinly veiled.

Icy calm still laced Dante's voice. After all, Melika had been one of Rosemary's patrons — and was now one of Lani's. "I already have it. I have a written agreement with Alepeka. I record all her local chants for historical record."

Lani cringed, expecting Melika to send fire out of her fingertips, like a flamethrower, and fry both of them crispy. Instead, the woman nodded and leaned back in her chair, never taking her eyes off Dante.

"I see. Why do you fight your blood, Dante? You disbelieve Hawaii's myths and legends yet record chants for posterity. Your own family's lost treasure takes its name from Pele. If Madame Pele wanted them found, someone would have found them by now, don't you think?"

She knew about Pele's Tears! Lani heard a gasp then a voice. Her own.

"But in Rosemary's journal she says —" She stopped when she saw movement beside and behind Dante. He stood upright so Agnes could enter.

They stuck to business after that then got out of there.

"Okay, it's official," she said as soon as they stood on the sidewalk. "She makes me nervous. Thank you for rescuing me."

"And?"

"And she's very possibly obsessed with Pele. Her and her wall of horror." She shuddered. "And, as you said, unique and stunning. No wonder she has you on the run." She gulped at his sharp look. "I mean, I hear she has you on the run. Or not."

"I'm not on the run. Someone's been gossiping."

"But I just listened. You're one of the biggest catches on the island, Dante. You can expect gossip. You should be used to it by now. Your love life is the Kalele version of a soap opera."

"Really? So when are they going to start gossiping about you? You're the other half of Lehua now. Doesn't that make you a catch? How about your love life?"

She stared at him, horrified. "Oh, crap!"

"Yeah. Let's see how you like it. Maybe I'll start a rumor about you and Pepper and Aidan."

"Don't you dare! Pepper and Aidan are spoken for until a decision has been made."

"Oh, right. Mei. Although she won't admit it. Then how about your old friend, our local male librarian, Noa Takei or his brother Keneke?"

She said something extremely rude in Hawaiian, but his snort of laughter made her suspect that, again, she hadn't gotten it quite right.

He glanced at the check for Rosemary's items Lani had handed to him. "I'm taking this to the drive-through. I don't want to go inside today to put you on the bank accounts. But we have to do that soon. Remind me."

She glared at him. She wanted full disclosure from him about any moves put on him, or anything else Melika might have done or said to him, besides asking him to dance at the chant.

"Aren't you even interested that Melika mentioned Pele's Tears to us? That she knows about them?"

"No, I am not. Do you have any errands while we're here?"

She paused, skewering him with a look.

"Yeah, I do. You can take me to see my old friend, our local male librarian, Noa Takei," she said, enjoying how his face went slack for a moment before his features arranged themselves into his tiki frown.

CHAPTER 15

Earlier, she had felt the sudden urge to find out more about the stones that made up Pele's Tears, so she had called ahead to the library from the shop. All she had to do was pay for the photocopies at the reference desk.

Dante dropped her off at the foot of the three broad, shallow steps that led up to the graceful Victorian house that served as Kalele's library. She passed through the snug vestibule, gently opened the double inner doors with their original stained glass windows, done by Rosemary's father, and paused in the carpeted hallway with wide stairs running up the left side of it.

Through a doorway on her left was the main collection room, where the reference desk, the circulation desk, and the main collection areas were located. To her right was the Talk Story Room, or meeting room, which also held overflow books, young adult books, and was dotted with reading chairs. Behind it was an enclosed room, the smallest, known as the Keiki Room, which housed the children's collection. Judging by the number and volume of small voices coming from that direction, she guessed something big was going on.

A fireplace of charcoal gray smooth stone faced the doorway of the long, rectangular meeting room, and a portrait of Kolenelia "Cornelia" McMullin hung above the mantel. Lani always visited Miss McMullin's portrait when she came to the library, to thank her for leaving her house and fortune to Kalele for a library. A brass plate at the bottom of the white and gold wood frame gave her name in black letters. A handsome woman, her painted blue gaze allegedly followed library patrons as they walked around the room. Lani had spent many hours here with that portrait, reading.

"*Aloha,* Lani."

The man's voice behind her made her jump and turn around. It took a moment to realize it was Noa Takei watching her. She immediately felt the beginnings of her unfailing reaction to Noa from their high school days. A smile. It was hard to believe that the reluctant bad boy, who had made her feel so good when she needed to feel good, was now a librarian.

"Welcome home," he added. And there on his broad face was his answering grin.

"*Aloha,* Noa." She hugged him, and he still felt good in her arms, like in their make-out days. Noa was her height, but sturdy, and he looked like he worked out now. They'd never gone all the way simply because she hadn't been ready and he, reluctantly, respected that. When she thought back to those times and how close they came to it, she was amazed they hadn't.

"I'm sorry about Rosemary." His voice was appropriately grave. "And I just wanted to say *aloha.* We have a *keiki* program going on and I need to keep my eye on things. Could we have dinner some time and catch up?" He flashed his bare ring finger at her.

She flashed hers back then caught up his hand in her own. "I'd like that, Noa. Very much." And she meant it.

Noa didn't have the compelling good looks Dante sported, but he was attractive and a gentle soul as well. He reminded her a bit of Dom. She'd always suspected Noa had been going through the motions of being a bad boy simply because all his brothers before him had been. He'd proved her right when he'd shed the image so readily. She had witnessed his hulking older brothers scaring their little brother straight that long ago night, while Dante tore a strip off her. As a concession to their frazzled mother, they had put the feet of her youngest son on the path he now traveled. Afterward, Lani never doubted the effect that night had on her. She didn't have so much as a speeding ticket against her name.

"Can I help you with anything?"

"No, I came to pick up some photocopies and to visit Miss McMullin's portrait." That would sound stupid to most men, but she had shared with Noa years ago this little habit of hers, and they had talked about it. That should have given her teenaged self another clue that he wasn't really the bad boy he wanted everyone to think he was.

Her mind led her astray again. At the thought of kissing Noa, she realized she wasn't breathless and didn't have chicken skin from remembering a kiss from their past or by imagining a potential kiss now. In fact, she couldn't think of one man she'd dated who made her feel that way — except Dante, in the kitchen of the big house, asking her if she'd felt what he'd felt all those years ago. And then he had gone on to prove he could still make her feel those things now. However, here was a local male who was willing to ignore Dante, even if she couldn't.

"Um, I do have a quick question, Noa. Can you tell me who Rosemary might have asked to help with her, uh, family research? Besides you, of course."

He still held her hand and gave it a squeeze. "Everybody. She interviewed the old ones. She went to the other islands for information when she had exhausted Kalele's small collection of Hawaiiana. She'd talk to anyone."

Lani chewed her lower lip while she quickly thought. This was an impossible task. They would never find out if Rosemary shared the full Pele's Tears story with anyone outside the family, unless someone admitted that she had. She and Dante simply would have to find Pele's Tears then see what crawled out of the woodwork.

When she started paying attention again, she noticed that Noa's gaze was locked on her mouth. Then a movement made her glance over Noa's shoulder; a familiar figure was silhouetted in the open doorway. She wondered how long Dante had been standing there watching them. Her temperature ratcheted up several degrees under his calculating look, which was quickly followed, again, by his tiki frown.

He crossed the room to stand beside her,

eyeing their clasped hands. Noa let go and retreated a step. In a heartbeat and without effort, Dante towered over Noa, smiled his widest, most charming smile, thrust out his hand, and asked after Noa's parents. She swore the man could make himself taller when he wanted to.

When Dante pulled back his hand, he casually draped that arm around her waist. She followed the direction of Noa's gaze, looking down at Dante's hand resting on her right hip, in disbelief.

"I have to get back. The natives are restless," Noa said softly, with a smile, and turned away.

Lani elbowed Dante and flung his hand off her hip, delighting in his huff of expelled air. "Give me a call, Noa. I'd love to have dinner with you," she called after her old teenage flame.

She turned on Dante as soon as Noa disappeared around the edge of the doorway. "What was the wandering hand about, Kahoa?"

Now he looked like a tiki in pain, first rubbing one hand along his ribs before he shrugged. Then discomfort and puzzlement played a duet on his features when he moved his palm along his stubbled jaw, creating a rasping sound.

"I'm not sure. Side trip, maybe? Or maybe I thought we should present a united front and not let people think you're running around the island unprotected. You know."

"Do I? And what about you running around the island unprotected? The target's painted on your back too, you know."

A look of utter disdain crossed his features. "I can take care of myself. *I* didn't fall off the overlook."

"No, *you* managed to fall over a moved garden statue and open your head. Running out into the night to check on a sound doesn't count?"

Apparently it didn't. Her fingers and toes tingled because she, once again, wanted to slap him stupid and maybe kick him for good measure. But she had to concede those actions for the umpteenth time, mainly out of self-preservation and the fact that she wore sandals.

But she took her normal stance in these encounters. She stepped up to him, feeling her bare toes touch his boots' scuffed leather. "Stop interfering in my nonexistent love life unless you're willing to *become* my love life."

She blinked. Had she really just said what she thought she'd just said?

She was sure of it when his grin built

really, really slowly. She blinked again at the point where his duet of dimples, in stun mode, dove into his cheeks. Every woman who worked in the valley talked about Dante's dimples, and she had been exposed to both barrels from a very young age. Those point-blank dimples made her step back, almost leaping away from him.

Standing as tall as she possibly could, cheeks on fire, she managed, "Forget I said that. I must have had a moment."

Then she turned and marched across the hall to the main room, feeling his gaze drilling into her back and points south as she left the room. She paid for her photocopies and stomped out to the truck.

After her lone, quick, and much-contested but successful visit to the little dress shop Agnes had told her about, neither of them said a word on the way home. Dante turned the radio to a country-and-western station and blasted it the whole way.

When they got to the house, he announced his plans to go out that night. So did she, not telling him it was with high school friends who wanted to dress up for a nice dinner then maybe go to a revue or a movie and for a shave ice after.

The dress she had found fit her like it had been tailored for her. It was a knee-length, fitted tank style in sky blue rayon with a widely spaced pattern of white-and-pink orchids. What gave it attitude was its cascading ruffle hem caught up by a silk white-and-pink orchid somewhere around her left mid-thigh. Each step showed a lot of leg, and the low scoop neck showed the soft upper curves of her breasts. She accessorized it with wicked, strappy stiletto heels and a fresh white orchid in her hair, which she wore up with corkscrew curls cascading onto her cheeks and neck.

She was looking forward to this night out. She wanted to get away from Dante's intenseness for a little while.

He didn't really want to go out that night, but he needed to get away from Lani's intenseness for a little while. Left to his own devices, he was very close to grabbing her and kissing her until she couldn't remember her own name.

He lost his breath when they ran into each other, each dressed to go out, in the upstairs hall. *Perfect example.* He didn't know where to look. Breast or thigh? He made himself dizzy trying to look at both, or maybe it was just the diverted blood flow. Thank God it was dim in the hall.

When he could speak, he said, "Blue.

Does that mean . . . ?" *I didn't mean to say that!*

"Yes, it does. Matching."

At least he sounded normal. "Do you need a ride?"

"No, thanks. I've finally worked up the courage to drive Rosemary's van without her in it."

"I was serious today about your not going around by yourself. I'll follow you in and make sure someone follows you home. Where . . . ?"

She had a flower in her hair, on the right side, meaning she was available. *Damn!*

"I'm meeting friends at the Plumeria. There's a *hula* revue after dinner. Maybe we'll get a shave ice after. How about you?"

"Meeting some brahs. I don't know where we'll end up."

He watched her go down the stairs ahead of him, curls floating or bouncing with every step. And long, long legs. And wearing heels you could poke out your eye on, given the right circumstance.

He gripped the banister, white-knuckled, to keep from grabbing her and kissing her into submission right there on the stairs. Howling at the moon was a definite possibility for him by the time they got to the bottom.

He met the brahs all right but cut out early, pleading three A.M. work in the sheds, to swing by the Plumeria on his way home. He wanted to make sure that the boyfriend of one of Lani's friends, whom he'd talked to earlier and who was keeping tabs on the women from a distance, was present, sober, and remembered he and the girlfriend had promised to follow Lani home. He caught the guy's eye and they spoke briefly.

He got there in time for the audience participation part of the revue, just in time to see Lani being pulled away from her table of old high school girlfriends and up onto the stage. The two guys in *malo* cloths who were doing the pulling had been in her *hula hālau* while she was growing up. He watched them, hating them every microsecond their hands were on her, as they tied a *ti* leaf grass skirt around her luscious hips. All the while, she protested that she was out of practice.

Better get out now while you have the chance, Kahoa.

Her hips, her hands, all of her proved her wrong when the music started. And he was a goner from the first drumbeat. Toward the end, you could have heard a pin drop, along with jaws, including his, when the pace picked up and everything cut out except the drums. She ended with *hula hue,* rotating her hips as fast as the drummer could beat time.

He decided in that moment that at some point in their future he'd challenge her to *hula kolili,* the *hula* with love penalties, a kind of strip poker and spin the bottle all rolled into one for the old Hawaiian chiefs. When he had her exactly where he wanted her, he'd remind her of this night.

There are at least four adult women, and those are the ones I'm aware of, in this place who are checking me out right now, one college, one cougar, and two that are just right. And I won't even count the two jailbaits. And what am I going to do about it? I'm heading home for a cold shower. Because I'm well and truly hooked and nobody but Lani will do, ever again. How scary is that? Or, as Lani says, how lame is that, Kahoa? Adolescent hormone payback at my age is no fun.

Dante was already in when she went to bed, probably because he was due at the sheds early that morning. Shaka and his crews had done the second, smaller cutting that day.

God, Dante had looked good tonight, black chinos, black silk shirt open at the neck, short black boots. Good enough to tackle in the hallway and kiss until he agreed to let her have her way with him.

After her shower, she slept awhile and woke up hungry in the wee hours. All was quiet behind Dante's door when she headed to the kitchen for a snack. She turned on one small light and ate cheese on crackers and drank a glass of passion fruit juice.

She noticed that Aumoe wasn't in his basket, and he hadn't greeted her when she had come in earlier. He was probably just asleep in the cottage—oh, crap, had she closed up and locked the cottage after she and Dante had danced? She wanted to be sure on both counts. But she shouldn't go over there alone at night. Maybe if she shook a bag of treats and called Aumoe's name from the *lānai?* But, at the side door onto the *lānai,* she noticed a tiny clothes-basket stacked with clean towels that Helen had left for the cottage's galley kitchen and half bath.

It would take just a minute to run over to the cottage. And she would turn on the lights and be aware of her surroundings. She put the treats in the basket on top of the towels and picked it up, resting it on her left hip. *Clothesbasket as weapon. What a concept. I can throw it at someone's head, at least.*

She turned the corner of the *lānai,* stopping when she realized she had forgotten to

261

switch on the lush garden's lights, just as Dante hadn't done the night he did this same, not very smart, thing. She dithered, undecided whether to go back and turn on the lights or to just shake the treats bag from where she stood and leave the basket for tomorrow. It was in that pause that she saw a moving light in the cottage, sending elongated shadows ricocheting everywhere inside. Unless Dante had taught Aumoe how to use a flashlight, somebody was in there. She froze at first, not even breathing. Then she was scared. No way was she going over there alone. What had she been thinking?

Anger struck when she was halfway up the stairs to wake Dante. How dare someone manipulate them like this? How dare someone violate their privacy and, since they had no idea who it might be, perhaps even their hospitality? How dare this person drag her and Dante into the midst of his own selfish obsession when Lehua needed them and their full attention so desperately? And the creep had better not have touched Aumoe.

She maintained a good head of steam as she paused outside Dante's door. She tapped on it and called his name none too softly. When no response came, she opened the door slightly, intending to say his name again, louder. Instead, she glanced around the now-larger room in amazement before mindlessly stepping over the threshold. Rosemary had told her on her last visit that Dante had renovated and redecorated his room. But this? He had taken over a much smaller bedroom next door to create more space, a walk-in closet, and an *en suite* bathroom. She itched to get a look at that.

Auras of moonlight glowed through the new, open plantation shutters that covered the windows. Dante's old, familiar mismatched furniture was gone. The pieces had been replaced with a lovely mahogany plantation-style suite that made it a stylish man cave, sans electronics. She nodded approval of his choices to herself. The man had decorating chops as well as dimples. And this room reflected the man he had become. She was impressed solely with the room until she looked toward what appeared to be an acre of bed and, more importantly, its sleeping occupant. *Now that's impressive.*

Dante still slept on his stomach, but on the far left side of the king-size mattress, which put him exactly where his old extra-long twin bed used to sit. That old bed had seen many games, discussions, plans, councils of war, minor skirmishes, and warfare among the three of them and their friends.

In that space now, a well-muscled expanse of tan satin shoulders and back showed above a tangle of almost-glowing white sheets. *I hope he isn't naked under there.*

Getting a grip on her hormones, she moved closer, calling his name softly and lightly touching him on his left shoulder. Too late she remembered the game the brothers had inflicted on each other every morning of their lives, and on any friends who had happened to sleep over. Whoever woke first stalked the other and attacked.

As blindingly fast as a startled gecko, Dante twisted within the sheets, grabbing her by the shoulders and rolling her onto the bed beside him, his upper body pinning her down and his left forearm across her throat. Through the flurry of settling sheets she glimpsed a pair of colorful sleep boxers while the forgotten clothesbasket, which she'd still had balanced on her left hip, arced gracefully through the air and landed upside down on the opposite side of the bed.

Dante glared down at her before he sighed and moved his forearm, releasing the pressure on her throat. "Lani? What are you doing? I thought you were Dom."

Unexpected tears sprang to her eyes at

the name and the memory that skittered away. "Sorry. I forgot about wake-up war."

He relaxed onto his side, resting his head on his left hand, with his left elbow thrust into a pillow. He was still close against her right side. He rubbed his eyes with his free hand after examining her sleep shorts and sleep tee.

"You looked good tonight, Beecham."

"You too, Kahoa. But I —"

"Did I hurt you?" He gestured toward the basket. "What's all that stuff? This better be good."

She ignored all his questions. "Oh, this is good." Then she told him what was going on at the cottage.

"Much as I'd like to talk about your dancing tonight, and explore various aspects of this interesting situation, I can't. All I can say about that is damn it," he told her in a normal tone of voice.

He rolled onto his back and off the edge of the bed then scrambled around on the floor for his clothes. Meanwhile, she jackknifed her body to the opposite side of the bed where she crawled off with her back turned toward him.

"That too. I forgot to say that."

"So much for your revised shop sign. Again. Maybe Sour Note decided to have a little look-see around the cottage, or maybe he's just leaving another note."

She told him what Sour Note could do with the sign and his notes, and Dante laughed.

"Let's go." Bare feet showed beneath today's jeans, and tonight's black shirt was unbuttoned and flapping with every step.

She scraped the towels off the edge of the bed into the clothesbasket and dropped the whole mess in the hall. *Stupid things.*

Anger struck again as they carefully made their way along the path through the old, established plants of Rosemary's garden, without benefit of the outside lights or a flashlight.

"This must be *déjà vu* all over again for you," she said in a whisper.

She slapped at a broad leaf with one hand, almost wishing their tormentor would step out in front of her right then. She was just in the mood to force-feed him some of these plants.

"Upstairs or down?" Dante whispered.

"Down." She didn't see light in the cottage now. But the front door stood ajar. "I left the place open. After we danced. I was too tired to lock up."

Dante's breath tickled her ear as they reached the door. "Tutu left it open all the time anyway. Stay here."

"No way. We go in or we stay here, but we do it together."

As soon as they stepped inside, together, she sensed it. A presence lingered in the air, as if someone had just walked out, leaving an invisible trail behind. Dante didn't turn on the lights as he checked behind the sofa and in the kitchen.

Aumoe meowed at them from the sofa cushions where he'd been sleeping in a tight black ball. She stroked his soft fur, thankful he was okay.

And that was her last coherent thought. She had an immediate and total brain disconnect caused by what Dante did in the next moment. He hesitated at the foot of the stairs then let loose a Hawaiian war cry, freezing her blood, as he leaped up the stairs two at a time. Surprised, shocked, and terrified, she covered her head and simply dropped, cowering, to the floor where she stood. This, of course, happened once her feet actually touched the floor again after her initial leap into the air. Capable at that point of making little whimpering noises only, she crawled over to the light switch and flipped it.

Dante came down into the light. "Everything checks out in the studio and storage room. Why are you on the floor?"

Since she couldn't speak, she had to ignore his question. She'd explain why she was on the floor when she had him alone, in the dark, in the big house where she could tie him up and subject him to sudden, unexpected, and varied female war cries as long as she liked, or at least until he had an inkling of why she was on the floor now.

Someone had searched the place. From where she sat, trying to breathe, she could see that the long wicker chest in front of the sofa wasn't completely closed. She had removed Rosemary's journal from it the other day and hidden it in her room, along with the sketchbooks and project notebooks. She also saw a paper sticking out of a drawer in the desk. She'd have noticed the stark white of the paper against the dark wood if it had been there when she sat on the sofa reading the journal the other day. A feeling of violation crawled over her.

Dante held out a hand to her, and she found her feet, although her voice was still missing. Aumoe now stood on all four of his on the sofa, eyes dilated, with his fur puffed out like a black bush. She sympathized. She was sure her hair looked much the same.

Dante apparently wasn't finished with their nerves.

He suddenly yelled, "Hey! Stop!" This was followed by some colorful Hawaiian language as he tore outside through one of the open sliding doors.

What she heard next made her heart bungee jump to her feet then recoil up into her throat. It sounded like someone smacking a watermelon with a baseball bat.

Somebody was down.

CHAPTER 16

Urgency pushed her through the same doorway Dante had just used, darting first one way to flick on the cottage's outside lights, then the other way to grab a Hawaiian war club off its display beside the door. If someone had hurt Dante, she was ready to make war and use his ancestors' club to do it.

Sure enough, Dante lay on his left side on the *lānai.* She glanced around, hefting the club, as someone crashed through the vegetation behind the cottage. The person Dante had been chasing was getting away and she let him. She knelt beside Dante, tears wetting her cheeks. There wasn't any blood she could see, but she was afraid to move him. She ran into the galley kitchen, soaked paper towels with cold water, and laid them carefully across his forehead and around the back of his neck. He groaned, rolled onto his back, and eventually insisted on sitting up.

"Should I call an ambulance? Should I call the police?" Though hoarse, she sounded surprisingly calm, she thought, despite the state of her mind and nerves. One sound, one tiny movement, would set her off screaming.

"No, I'll be fine. No cops. We know what this is about. Just let me sit here a minute."

"Did you see who it was?"

He started to shake his head then thought better of it. "All I saw was a black shape in front of me, running away. Then bang, from the right side."

She was glad she was kneeling because the implications of that statement made her weak in the knees. "That means there are two of them. Just what we need. Can you stand up and walk to the house if I help you? I want to take a look at you in good light."

He got to his feet with no help from her, although she insisted on keeping an arm around him as they went inside the cottage. She led him to the now-vacant sofa.

"Sit down while I close up. And keep talking to me. What was all the yelling about in here a while ago?"

"Shock and awe. I wanted to scare anyone

hiding upstairs into moving or making a noise."

"Well, it worked on me and Aumoe instead. Warn us next time. Are you still okay for a minute?"

"Yeah. And Lani? I'm asking. When things settle down, I want to hear all about those clues you found in your trunk. Now it's really personal."

"Well, it's about time!"

She hesitated for only a moment before running up the stairs. The trunk was sitting in its place in the storage room. She'd locked it, yet the lid now lifted at her touch. When she looked closely, she saw scratches visible around the shiny keyhole. Many days would have passed before she would've noticed that the trunk was unlocked.

Everything inside was neat. It wasn't until she let down the lid liner that her breath stopped. The space was empty. Rosemary's primary sources, heaps of books, papers, and maps, were gone. She gasped at the loss and at the feeling of violation slithering through her again.

Dante still sat on the sofa where she'd left him. She told him about the trunk then took the keys to the cottage out of a pigeonhole in the desk. While she was at it, she slid out the offending, very white piece of paper and put it into the pocket of her sleep shorts. At that point, she was more concerned about Dante than interested in looking at it.

Aumoe was probably halfway to Lihue by now, so when they left, for the first time in her memory, the studio cottage at Lehua was securely locked.

Dante was too tall to sit on the kitchen island. Besides, it was occupied. Aumoe sat there, his tail slashing, glaring at them as if to say, "Have you people lost your minds? Don't forget that I have the SPCA on speed dial!" They gave him a wide berth.

She jerked a chair away from the table and folded Dante down onto it. He had a lump the size of a small egg near his hairline on the right side of his forehead. She tipped his head forward to rest against her sleep tee while she parted his hair with her fingers and ran them over every inch of his scalp.

"The skin is barely broken on the lump. I don't see or feel any other injuries."

In answer, he said, "Umm," then, "That feels good. Don't stop."

He had been strangely quiet up to that point and she suddenly realized why, registering four things as she looked down: one, his face now rested between her breasts; two, he'd had to move his head slightly to position his face there; three, his arms were wrapped around her hips; and four, he was enjoying this way too much.

She lightly tapped on the bump on his forehead and stepped back. Four problems solved, accompanied by appropriate and satisfying exclamations of pain.

"Ouch! Thank God you didn't go into nursing."

His pupils reacted evenly when she made him look up at the light. She found a bag of frozen peas, wrapped it in a tea towel, and gently placed it on the bump.

Then she drew up another chair and faced him, knee to knee. Before she could speak, and without him missing a beat, he pulled her chair closer to his and did the knee thing, rearranging his long legs until one of her knees was sandwiched between his. She glanced down, then pointed the conversation in practical directions.

"I found two things in a pocket at the back of Rosemary's journal. Both are hidden upstairs with the journal and some other things I took out of the trunk."

"Good thinking. You saw that the chest in the cottage was open?"

She nodded. "Interesting that this happened right after I mentioned Rosemary's journal in front of Melika. And she mentioned Pele's Tears in front of us. She has a husky voice. Maybe she and Rosemary were friendly enough that Rosemary confided in her. I wonder who her accomplice might be."

"We don't even have proof that Melika is Sour Note, let alone who her sidekick is. And I wasn't aware that Tutu and Melika were close. Melika might have simply guessed that if Tutu was keeping a journal, it might be in the cottage and easier to get at than something here in the house."

"Whatever. On a piece of parchment was something Rosemary's father, your great-grandfather, had written, signed, and dated when she was just a girl. He found a cave when he hiked the *pali* as a boy. No climbing mentioned, only hiking. 'A cave with glowing eyes,' he said."

"Glowing eyes." He paused. "Olivine, maybe? It's light-green and transparent. It sometimes stands out in old lava flows."

"An olivine deposit in an old lava-tube cave on Lehua land will help the budget if it's gem-quality peridot, olivine's other name. Rosemary kept quiet about the cave. That has to mean something. And a cave with a hidden or overgrown entrance on private land would be a good place to hide something of value for years, and a good place to put the gems 'away from loved ones' for a long time and to 'give them back' once both were discovered."

"If she found the cave and the gems after Dom, she might not have told us about it because she was afraid we would go haring off to the *pali* again. Is there a way to pinpoint this olivine cave before we go up there? For my sanity."

"Maybe. The second thing I found was a gold pendant inside the folded parchment. Rosemary mentioned to me a few years ago that she was playing around with gold and making some jewelry. If she made the pendant to pinpoint the cave's location for us, we have to figure out how it can do that.

"I wondered why this thing was so ugly, but she'd have had to make it a certain way so it could tell us what she wants us to know. There are three olivine stones set in it, so you're probably right about the 'eyes' being olivine."

She was suddenly aware of him, his body, being close to hers. Something, a force, gently tugged her toward him, and her insides hummed with a jittery awareness that sharpened her nerves to points as sharp as *'a'ā* lava, and turned her stomach into a quivering jellyfish.

"Whoever these two are, they're not going to give up or let up."

"And now they have Rosemary's primary sources," she grumbled.

"We'll be able to go up to the *pali* in the next day or so. Meantime, try to figure out what the pendant means."

"I'll do my best."

Dante looked at the clock, shoved his chair away from hers, and stood. "I have to change clothes and go."

She put herself between him and the back door. "Go where? I'm not finished yet."

"Hold that thought. I have to relieve Shaka at the sheds."

She couldn't argue with that. Lehua came first. "But you saw me dance tonight? How did that happen?"

He closed his eyes and took a deep breath. "A sudden need for self-torture, mostly. You haven't lost it, Lani. The hips remember." He took the stairs two at a time.

She shoved a couple of painkillers at him, along with a glass of water, when he came down. While he took them, she reached into her pocket and pulled out the paper she'd taken from the cottage.

"Keep your hat on tonight," she told him. "If Shaka and the girls see that lump, they'll think I'm slapping you around."

"Promises, promises," he muttered.

She had ended her words with a grin. It

slid off her face as she read the words on the paper.

He started to say something but broke off when she handed the note to him. He read it, his lips compressing into a thin line. "Lock all the doors, lock your bedroom door, and go to bed! The alternative is to come along with me."

The note had said, big surprise, "Pele's Tears. Now!"

Exhausted, angry, and defiant, she did what Dante suggested, adding a chair under her doorknob for good measure, and went to bed.

Early the next morning or, rather, later that same morning, she sat at the kitchen table, mentally gnawing on kisses, other up-close-and-personal encounters with Dante, how good it had felt to dance again, and last night's late-night events. Her mental gnawing kept her from physically gnawing on her own leg. She could *feel* Pele's Tears in a cave on the *pali.* How could Dante not be excited, not be galloping up the *pali* this minute? Also showing up regularly, if she let it, was the thought Keneke had put into her head the other day, and resulting developments along that line. Then there was Rosemary's cryptic statement that Dante had been in love for a long time.

She found a black, peppery seed she'd missed when she scraped out her papaya. Turning toward the open kitchen door, she spat it toward the opening. It was meant as a general comment on her lack of self-control, but was also sent off with the vague hope that it might take out The Colonel, whose dawn greetings appeared to be on a constant loop that morning. The small, round projectile pinged off the doorframe beside Dante's shoulder as he stepped into the kitchen.

"Nice one. You haven't lost your touch."

Seed-spitting contests had been a big draw with the three of them in the old days. She had been the reigning champion when Dom died and the contests stopped.

"Trust me, I've lost my touch. I was aiming for the open doorway at a level somewhere around your knees."

She took a good look at him. What with his interrupted sleep, his sore head, and his having to monitor the packing sheds and make runs to the airport off and on all night, even his voice sounded exhausted.

"There's fresh coffee. Can I get you anything?"

"I must look really bad."

"You do, actually. How's your head?"

"Still attached. I'm going to bed. Blood or

279

smoke, Lani. Anything else, you handle it. Don't forget that we have the chant to-night."

She spent the morning in the fields and sheds, clearing debris and helping wherever she was sent, doing whatever she was told. The Kahoas had a work ethic that she had adopted, as a satellite of the Kahoas: They never asked Lehua's workers to do anything they weren't willing to do themselves.

By early afternoon, she was free. She took the parchment, the pendant, the photo-copies from the library, and the cottage key and followed Aumoe, whose tail stood as upright as a beacon, along the narrow garden path to the cottage.

It was hot and stuffy inside. She threw open two of the sliding doors, waiting until a breeze, with the scent of flowers riding it, moved freely through before she settled onto the sofa. She hit Play on Rosemary's CD player. Aumoe studied her, apparently undecided about joining her since the sofa had turned on him last night. When he ignored her patted invitations on the cush-ion beside her, she read over the photo-copies from the library then opened Rose-mary's Pele's Tears journal.

She started at the front again, and this time noticed Rosemary's small, faint, and faded one-word notation in the margin, "caves." There it was, Lani's long-ago trigger. She, a teenager at the time, had seen the possibilities of caves in the cliff face because the three of them had been on top of the *pali* many times and had never seen signs of any caves. Rosemary had spent time on the *pali* through the years, and Lani and the boys had usually gone with her, camping, hiking, and keeping tabs on the tame ornithologists Rosemary turned loose up there every so often to study their honeycreepers.

If Lani had chosen to look for caves *on top* of the *pali,* she and Dante and Dom would have been well on their way to finding Pele's Tears, and Dom wouldn't have fallen. *Forgive me, Dom, and I'll continue trying to forgive myself.*

Lani plucked a rough map of the trails on the *pali* from between the pages of the journal. Rosemary had drawn it as a reference for them, marking the safe trails they had hiked and the areas where the birds had been studied. Lani put it aside to take with them when they went up the *pali.*

She worried at the problem of the cave's location, while alternately studying the pendant and the watchful cat.

Lehua's hefty black cat gave her a last,

disgruntled look, stood up, stretched, and took off like a rock shot out of an erupting volcano, much like Dante had gone up the stairs last night, in fact, only without the sound effects. She watched in startled amazement as he banked off surfaces, including the bottom of the sofa beneath her drawn-up legs, and finally the back of the sofa beside her cowering body.

Aumoe rose ever higher, like Keneke Takei and his motorcycle would rise if both were turned loose in a large, empty silo, until the cat was able to launch himself high enough to reach the thick molding that defined the parlor's one nearly solid wall, and from there to the lip of the round stained glass window above the door. Amazed, she knew Dante would never believe it when she told him how their cat attained the great heights necessary to rest on that particular window ledge.

The cat's presence on it drew her attention there. She crossed to the stairs and sat on the bottom step. Aumoe, as if having achieved his purpose of making her notice the window, pushed off in a graceful leap that brought him safely to the back of the sofa. His dismount from the window wasn't nearly as impressive as his method of getting up there.

She studied the pattern of the glass representing the cliffs. And the view of Lehua looked different from this new vantage point. If she imagined the cliff edge at her feet, looking at the view from where she was now . . .

She moved up one step higher then another and another until she was almost level with the window across the room. Her memory dragged up an image from its deepest, darkest depths and clanged it into place. It couldn't be, yet she dreaded that it was.

"No, no, no. Oh, please, no," she chanted to herself.

She flew down the stairs, trotted across the room, snatched up the pendant, and ran back to her perch on the stairs. The window was beautiful; the pendant was not. Yet they represented the same thing.

The window appeared smaller across the distance from the stairs. She held up the pendant so that the window floated beside and behind it in the distance, and she could look from one to the other easily. The pendant trembled when her eyes confirmed what she suspected.

The puffed, quilted pattern of the gold represented the fields. The bottom edge of the ugly pendant roughly matched the cliff edge in the window. The round, smooth olivine stones set above it matched the grouping of glass cabochons in the window, depicting the sun, moon, and a star. And she knew which trail on the *pali* to take.

Because both the window and the pendant represented the view from the top of the cliff where Dom had died. This was the view of her beloved Lehua that she had stared at, unseeing at the time but apparently imprinting it on her memory, after she and Dante had hauled themselves over the top of the cliff to look down on Dom's broken body, lying face up, his eyes wide open with fear, and possibly accusation, on the rocks below.

She wanted to curl into a ball on the stair, protect her soft parts, cover her ears, try to breathe, maybe even suck her thumb. She saw Dom fall yet again, in her mind, as always in slow motion, just fall away from his place between her and Dante; heard his scream; recognized the pose he could never have adopted in life.

Apparently, she and Dante would have to go back to where Dom had died, God help them. The pendant and window were telling them this was the area where Pele's Tears lived. This jagged golden edge was as close to giving the location of the olivine cave as they could hope for. "The glorious trio shines and lives again in the light. And I gave them back to the light. . . . Remember, look for them through the light," Rosemary had written. Rosemary hadn't seen that vista in the way she and Dante had seen it and would remember it until their dying days.

Lani gulped and took a firm hold on her emotions. If Dante recognized where they were going, he'd have to come to that realization on his own because she couldn't tell him. And even if they stayed well back, away from the edge and weren't rock climbing up the face, what if Dante died this time?

CHAPTER 17

If something happened to Dante because of her, how could she live in a world without him in it? If she was the cause of his leaving it, how could she live with herself?

She didn't know how long she sat on the stairs, but that's where Dante found her.

He took one look at her and said, "Now what?"

"Come up here." She patted the step beside her, tamping down the new, damning knowledge she possessed. "Take off your hat," she added when he sat down. She paused to look at his thick, dark waves before continuing. "This is the pendant."

"You weren't kidding. That's ugly. It looks like something took a bite out of the bottom."

She held it up and sighted past it. "Look at the window and the pendant sort of side by side." She beckoned him closer until his cheek touched hers. He put his arm around her so he could get closer. "Do you see it?"

He made a little sound of disbelief. "They're the same. Sort of. How . . . ?"

"Aumoe helped. I know how he gets up there. I'll explain it later."

He gestured toward the window. "I think that star is Hōkūle'a, 'Star of Joy.' "

"Arcturus. Good call. It's centered directly above everything else in the window, and it's the Big Island's zenith star."

He didn't scoot away but tightened his arm around her. "I remember learning in school that prehistoric Polynesian navigators used it to find these islands. They sailed east then north to the latitude where Hōkūle'a appeared directly overhead in the summer sky. Then they hung a left and sailed west to the Big Island. Should its being in the window mean something to us, like where this cave is located?"

"We can add that to our we-don't-have-a-clue list."

"Are you sure the gems aren't in the window? It would make life so much easier." He glared at the stained glass as if it was the window's fault it didn't hold a treasure. "That's what you were doing on that ladder that day when you nearly killed me, wasn't it? Checking, not studying."

"Guilty. I hadn't told you yet about Rosemary finding Pele's Tears. You can see up close that the cabochons are just glass. Besides, the colors don't match the story. I think we have to find this cliff edge pattern on the *pali*."

He held up the pendant, squinting first at it then at the window. "These stones better be worth enough to help Lehua if we go to the trouble of looking for them."

"Egg-size gems with their provenance laid out in Rosemary's journal? They'll help, all right."

"Maybe you'd better give me the short version of the Pele's Tears story again, before the chant tonight, especially the part about the stones. As incentive. I'm running low."

"I'm primed, Kahoa. That stuff I picked up at the library was research on gemstones. James Talbot-Kahoa, clipper ship owner, captain, and your ancestor, loved Hawaiian legends, mythology, and chants. Somewhere, somehow, he acquired a set of three gems and called them Pele's Tears, based on the ancient Hawaiian love story chant of Pele and Lohi'au. He sailed the Orient and South Seas, so he could have gotten them anywhere.

"Since Rosemary didn't correct or confirm in her journal what the gems really are, we'll assume the stones are what we were told they are."

She knew he was looking at her, studying her, so she kept her gaze on the window.

"The first stone is a diamond, probably clear, or what's called a white diamond, Pele's Tears of Pure Love. We should hope for a D or E colorless. Pele left her goddess's body on the Island of Hawaii, became mortal, and followed the sound of lovely music, a *hula* festival, to Kauai. She fell in love with a young chief there, Lohi'au, probably a real Hawaiian hunk, with broad shoulders and legs like tree trunks. He'd have to have been muscular to ride Kauai's surf on a log, the way the *ali'i* did in the old days."

Dante's voice brought her back from visions of silky, tan wide shoulders amid a sea of white sheets. "You'll be drooling in a minute."

She risked a sideways look at him, cleared her throat, and continued. "Next is Pele's Tears of Sadness, a sapphire, probably blue. We should hope for a Cashmere. Pele had to leave Lohi'au on Kauai and return to her spiritual body on the Big Island. She sent her sister, Hi'iaka, to bring the hunk to her on Hawaii.

"Then comes Pele's Tears of Rage. A ruby.

We should hope for a Burmese. The hunk and the sister fell in love, but they had control of themselves until they were in Pele's sight. Pele was enraged when she saw them making love. She killed the hunk a couple of times but the sister, who was a goddess in her own right, always brought him back to life. The couple lived happily ever after, but Pele is still in a rage, hence the active volcanoes on the Big Island."

She looked at him then. He grinned at her colorful retelling, the same little-boy smile that made her heart trip. "We'll Meet Again" started to play on the CD player.

"I love this one." She closed her eyes for a moment and felt a tiny smile play on her face as she let the notes wash over her.

She opened them to find Dante watching her with a look of hunger and longing on his face. He quickly glanced away. and so did she, to wonder at this solid friendship that was once again laced with an almost painful awareness of each other.

"I need more incentive. How big do you think Pele's Tears are?"

She shifted uneasily. "I don't know. The Hope Diamond is roughly forty-five-and-a-half carats. It was a hundred twelve and change originally, before it was cut and faceted into a cushion cut."

"And Pele's Tears are the size of eggs, and just polished not faceted?"

She nodded. "So their value really depends on what kind of egg, doesn't it? Goose, chicken?"

"Pigeon? So you think the diamond is clear and the other two are blue and red? That's what you meant when you said the colors of the cabochons in the window didn't match the story."

"Ah. I could be wrong about that. According to the pages I had photocopied at the library, sapphires and rubies are both corundum, but rubies are the only red corundum. And sapphires can range from sunrise to sunset colors, and from tropical blue to a deep dark blue. The rarest is a pink-orange called lotus blossom."

She paused when he lifted a strand of her hair, testing its silkiness between his long fingers. She watched out of the corner of her eye. Somehow she didn't think he was going to ask what conditioner she used.

"So our diamond is probably clear. But our sapphire just might be pink instead of blue. And, if we have a red stone, we hope it's a ruby?" His smile was in his voice. He was making her nervous — and enjoying doing it.

She pulled her hair out of his grasp. "That

pretty much sums it up."

His blue eyes were dilated when his gaze met hers. "I need some air. This is a lot to take in."

Somehow, she didn't think he was talking about Pele's Tears anymore.

He stood up and went down the stairs. "We'll hike the *pali* sometime tomorrow, but I don't want to stay overnight unless we absolutely have to. We'll leave for the chant in about an hour."

She gave him a minute then followed, closing and locking the sliding doors. When she turned, he blocked the cottage doorway, his hands resting on each side of it, his fingers keeping time to "Moonlight Serenade."

Oh, no.

He bowed from the waist. "May I please have this dance, ma'am? The weather's clearing. That means we're flying a mission tomorrow. I might never feel a woman's touch again. I might never —"

"Shut up," she interrupted, "and lose the boots this time."

"Yes, ma'am!"

He grinned, hopping on one foot as he slid a boot off the other, then reversing the process. He tossed them onto the mat outside the door, punched some buttons to restart and replay "Moonlight Serenade," and advanced on her.

He placed one hand on each of her hips this time and pulled her flush against his body. Then he draped her arms around his neck, meanwhile bringing his hands behind her waist.

"You're taking liberties, flyboy," she said, her voice husky.

"Only little ones. They don't count."

"Well, then. As long as they don't count." She tucked her head against his jaw and let the music take her away.

There was no doubt in her mind that this is what they had been born to do — hold each other. Though every moment she held him, and let him hold her, possibly made him vulnerable. *What if something happens to him, like Dom, because of Pele's Tears and me? Because, God help me, I've loved him since I was four.* The realization and the voice in her head made her stumble.

"Easy," he whispered, his breath warm on the side of her face.

They were quiet after that until the song ended.

An hour later, she was riding shotgun in Dante's truck as he turned it inland. She was relaxed, letting the warm breezes from the open windows play over her face and arms, until he spoke.

"So we have to find that pattern of *pali* edge?" he asked. "It could have changed by now."

"But not that view from the *pali*." Their view of it would never change as long as they lived. "Once we find one or the other or both, then we start looking for the cave. And bring some rope so we can tether ourselves if we have to get close to the edge."

"Really? Tutu was probably in her late seventies or early eighties when she found them in the olivine cave. Do you think she —"

"Who knows? Your grandmother hiked that *pali* all her life. She was as strong as a *koa* wood log up until the day she died. This cave could be anywhere up there. And here's a thought. Have you heard of any ornithologists who suddenly came into money and abandoned their life's work?"

He glanced at her briefly, his face slack with surprise and shock. "I didn't think of that. They've had access to the *pali* for years. Perfect. One of Tutu's Bird Men might have beat us to Pele's Tears." He sighed heavily, really getting into his scenario. "What if Pepper is the one who wants them, the one who scared you off the overlook? What if the Pepper Bird Man is really up there looking for Pele's Tears? Or Aidan? He turned up right after the overlook incident. He could have sent your notes in Maine."

"Then we'd better get up there ourselves and find them first!"

Twenty minutes later Dante turned onto a dirt road. After a few miles on packed earth, he parked on the grassy edge along with a few other cars, pickup trucks, and a bicycle or two.

Opening one of the crew-cab doors behind their seats, he handed her a blanket, put a tripod under his arm, and picked up a full HD camcorder in its case. His free hand, callused and warm, reached back for hers to help her down the path. Her fingers nestled within his like they belonged there, sending familiar heat up her arm.

"You bought new equipment. Nothing for me to do."

He grinned. "Have to keep up with the times, you know. Besides, you're moral support — and really good to look at."

They walked single file down a path through thick tropical growth that ended in a natural clearing lit by torches beneath a rocky outcropping, returning many *alohas* because a lot of people they knew were there. They searched for a place away from the others, so no unwanted sounds would reach them while Dante was recording.

They climbed halfway up a small hill to a flat area, unrolled the blanket, and sat down on it Indian-fashion. They were above and behind the chattering crowd. She watched while Dante checked the camcorder and its battery then got to his knees to set up and secure the tripod. He put it a little farther away from them than in the old days. Probably due to newer, more sensitive microphone technology, she decided.

She found she enjoyed his excitement more than her own. "You're still really into this, aren't you?"

"You've been away too long or you'd be excited too. Just wait until it hits you again, like at the revue."

A respectful hush fell when Alepeka, a stately Hawaiian woman in a voluminous *mu'umu'u,* knelt on a woven mat beneath the outcropping. The torches threw wild shadows onto the concave rock walls behind her. Her head was crowned with a *haku lei,* a head *lei,* and a long, open-ended, elegant braided strand of *maile* leaves rested around her neck. She placed a large *ipu,* a hollow gourd, in front of her and sat quietly for a moment with her eyes closed.

Slowly, rhythmically, she began slapping

the gourd with one hand then lifting and thumping it on the mat with the other. Her voice, a husky singsong, was projected into the clearing by the natural acoustics of the rock above and around her. Two female dancers appeared to interpret the chant. Lani didn't know either one, but they were good.

She gasped as the ancient chant and primal rhythm filled her body and her mind to overflowing, amazed all over again that her second language, one that used only twelve letters, could be so beautiful. Her hands moved against her knees, keeping the beat, while her body swayed to the rhythm. But, after the other night at the revue, her hands wanted to do so much more. When they finally lifted into the air and performed several graceful motions, interpreting, along with the dancers, something Alepeka had just said, she shoved them under her knees.

Dante brought his mouth close to her right ear, exposed because she had tied back her hair with a pretty hibiscus-patterned scarf. "Go ahead. Nobody will see you back here."

Instead, she let the power of the words flood through her, leaving her frustrated at times because she couldn't keep up. Her Hawaiian wasn't good enough to under-

297

stand all the words of the chant. She reacted to one particular line, about two-thirds of the way through. It left her flushed and breathless.

She leaned toward Dante, putting her lips close to his left ear so the camcorder's sensitive microphone wouldn't pick up her words. "Where are we in the story? What did she just say about a flower?"

He grinned and moved his lips close to her ear. His warm breath tickled, making her tuck her chin to her chest, which only brought her closer to him.

"Geeze, Beecham. You weren't kidding about misplacing your love life. It's Pele's Tears of Rage time. The ruby we might find tomorrow on the *pali*. Hi'iaka, Pele's sister, has just embraced Lohi'au on the rim of Kilauea, in full view of Pele. Hi'iaka tells him he is the *lei*-making needle and she is the flower. Get it? I can see I'm going to have to take your sex education in hand. Meet me in the flower prep shed at midnight."

She made a choking sound and elbowed him in the ribs. "Sorry I asked," she muttered, keeping her gaze straight ahead. *Why, oh, why, was the most erotic line of the chant the one I asked him to translate for me?*

She felt his soundless laugh when he

leaned close again, and she expected more words. Instead, she froze when the tip of his tongue caressed her earlobe so lightly that she wasn't sure she had felt it . . . until he pulled back far enough so she could look into his eyes when she slowly turned her head toward him, the unspoken question on her lips.

Her breath hitched when she saw warm light, like reflected sunlight, in the blue lagoons of their depths. And then she was sure he'd done exactly what she thought he'd done because the warm tropical air pressed coolly against her wet lobe.

"Does it freak you out that I want to do things like that to you, Lani, along with a lot of other things I can think of?" he whispered. "Because it sure freaked me out at seventeen. And now, just like then, when I kiss you, you kiss me back. And I can sense something like lava flowing just beneath the surface of your skin." He drew one finger down her forearm. "I still can't stand the thought of another guy kissing you and maybe feeling that."

When she got her breath back, she said, "No other guy has ever brought forth lava, Dante. Trust me. Only you."

No more thought process was necessary on her part — and no more words, at first.

That he wanted to kiss her and that she desperately wanted him to, despite what was going on in their lives just then, was so right, like the next step in something they were destined for. If she had any feminine wiles for a time like this, she didn't know where she kept them, and they weren't needed anyway. And so her lips curved in a smile that held only her, the Lani he'd always known, the Lani he knew at this moment, and the Lani he might help her become in the future. From that first day on the beach when Dante was five and she was four, they had been forever bound in some way to each other. Questioning it, doubting it, was at an end.

As usual, speech was the first faculty to recover. "And this won't . . ." She gulped, unable to put her question into words. It's a good thing Dante could read her mind.

He drew closer with every word. "Change our friendship? Never. How could being a part of each other and being best friends change, except to grow in new ways?"

When he briefly hesitated, it was the most natural thing in the world for her to outline the two sculpted points of his beautiful upper lip with the tip of her tongue. Then, in a hungry move, his lips covered hers like warm surf flowing over a sunlit shore. She wondered if she were sleeping and only dreaming that she could respond to him this enthusiastically in public. A sound deep in his throat brought her back from the sleep fantasy she had sunken into.

He finally sat back and stared at her. "Shock and awe of a different kind." He ran both his hands through his thick hair while she struggled for a full breath.

Dazed and shaken, she looked around to see if anyone was watching them, only to see Melika, her lovely face twisted with a mixture of anxiety and anger, looking right at them. Melika sat on the side of the clearing that curved around toward the "stage." The heat of that gaze rested briefly on Dante then beyond him before she looked away. Lani glanced at him to see if he was aware of it, if he had felt its power. Apparently not. He got to his knees, peering at the camcorder's screen, oblivious to the volley of emotions that had just been shot across their bow.

She continued to scan the clearing. Love was definitely in the air. Mei perched on the ground in front of Pepper, whose arms were wrapped around her from behind, his back against a rock. Aidan snuggled with a beauty not far way. They were just two of many couples engrossed in the love chant

— and touching or holding each other while they listened. One of Dante's old friends caught her eye and gave her a thumbs-up. She felt her face flame.

Still aware of the camcorder's microphone, she whispered, "Pepper and Aidan aren't on the *pali*. If we avoid them up there tomorrow, we'll avoid their questions."

He looked at Pepper and Mei. "Maybe Mei can keep him busy for a couple of days. She has a break from school."

The lovely chant came to an end. Dante turned off the equipment, packed it up, and left it in her care before going down to speak to Alepeka.

A small rock rolled to a stop beside where she sat on the blanket, waiting for him. She glanced behind her, up the hill that crested a few yards above and beyond their little flat area. The moon was floating in the dark blue, star-shot velvet bowl of the sky. She caught a flash of movement by its light, and a pebble rolled down the incline. It could just be kids up there, but she didn't think so. She jumped to her feet and climbed to the top of the hill as fast as she could.

No one was there. Not even a gecko was in sight. The only thing out of place was a lone, jumbo, blood-red hibiscus bloom lying on a flat rock in the moonlight.

Lani thought it was just about the shade of the Pele's Tears of Rage ruby she imagined.

CHAPTER 18

She and Dante finished making their plans for the next day on the ride home.

"I can get away around noon or so tomorrow," he told her. " 'Pack lightly but well,' " he quoted Rosemary. "We sure had fun up there, the four of us, in the old days."

"Yeah, we did," she said, and gulped at the memories.

If Rosemary were here now, Lani would ask her what to do about a friendship that was catching fire. Again. And what to do about someone who wanted the Kahoa family treasure enough to hurt her and Dante to get it. She told Dante about the rock, the pebble, and the hibiscus.

"And you think it was Sour Note?"

"I don't know, but it wasn't Melika up there. She was giving us the stink eye from below." She felt her cheeks grow warm again at the thought of his friend's thumbs-up.

Then she swiped another nagging thought

out of the air. "Dante, what if James Talbot-Kahoa had it right? What if Pele's Tears is bad luck for the Kahoas? I'm dragging you right into it again."

"Don't hold back, Lani. Tell me how nervous you really are." He slowed the truck and studied her for a long moment, frowning, and she knew he was exercising his mind-reading abilities again. "If I suspected for one minute that you really believe some superstitious crap about being bad luck for the Kahoa brothers, I'd —. I'm too tired to finish that sentence. I can't even think of a decent threat. I could probably come up with an indecent one if you give me a minute."

If he was too tired to verbally spar, then she was too tired to take advantage of him — but she couldn't stop thinking.

Could she talk herself into going up on the *pali* without him, just in case she was right? She reasoned that she had just a drop of Kahoa blood compared to Dante, and only half as much as her mother had carried. Maybe the curse, if there was one, would be weak in her. Her stomach did a graceful dive to her feet at the thought of doing this alone. And how could she distract him until she got up there and had a look around?

She doubted she'd get a minute of restful sleep that night, and she proved herself right with a night of horrible dreams about Dante, lying at the foot of the *pali,* much like Dom.

The next morning it took several slices of toast, a whole papaya, and some Kona coffee before she came up with a plan. Even then she didn't know if she had the guts to put it in motion.

She glanced at the clock. It was midmorning by then. Dante would soon be in to get ready for their hike up the *pali.* Pretending to be sick was the best she could come up with, but she couldn't tell him face to face. He'd know in a heartbeat she was lying to him.

Half an hour later, she read over the note she'd hurriedly written in the big house kitchen, biting her lower lip in uncertainty over using this way to communicate after their recent experiences with notes. Her use of colorful, flowered notepaper and no envelope made this one look as different as it possibly could from the others.

Dante, I don't feel well. It's just a sick headache-type thing, and I'll be fine in the morning. Can we leave then? Under pain of death, don't check on me! I took some

meds, so just let me sleep this off.
Lani.

P.S. Helen already knows.

She had tried out the same story on Helen when she stopped in before going food shopping in Kalele. Luckily, Lani had eaten like a pig and cleared away the evidence before Helen got there.

She shoved the unfolded sheet under a small *koa* wood bowl in the middle of the granite island, slung her hastily prepared pack over one shoulder and her rolled, lightweight sleeping bag over the other, and sidled cautiously out the kitchen door. This was the most dangerous time, when she might simply run into Dante. She didn't dwell on that thought, in case it conjured up the very person she was trying to avoid.

She'd managed well enough to stay out of Mei's way when she arrived for work and went into the office. Helen and Mei had been easy. Uncomfortable, but easy. But Dante was a different animal altogether. She almost broke out in hives thinking about that note. She doubted her lie would make it through the afternoon, and she was thankful she wouldn't be anywhere near Dante when he realized what she'd done.

Her plan had flaws you could drive Shaka's truck through. For example, Helen would find she wasn't in bed when she brought soup to her room later that day. Lani was sure Helen would, despite her request to be left to suffer alone. And, at some point, Shaka would tell Dante about his missing truck. She'd had to write Shaka a note too, which she would leave where his truck usually sat so he didn't call the police or somebody.

At either of those points, Dante would start looking. He'd find Shaka's truck at the trailhead, and she'd be toast. But with luck, she'd be at the cliff by then — and he wouldn't. That was her goal and the reason for this deception.

Or maybe Dante would just know even before her plan crumbled. She could face Dante's anger, eventually and fully, but she couldn't face his death. She was more sure of that now than of anything else in her life.

Dante's intervention in Maine had been good enough to get her home to Lehua again. But a voice from deep in her Hawaiian blood stubbornly insisted that because she had again found clues to the whereabouts of Pele's Tears, she might be an instrument of the Pele's Tears-Kahoa family curse for a second time. And, if she were slightly tainted herself, maybe she could deflect the risk from Dante.

She made her cautious way, from plumeria tree to plumeria tree, to the long open shed where Lehua's vehicles lived when not in the best of health. Shaka's truck was almost a resident patient these days. She stuck her note on the tractor beside Shaka's old wreck.

A manual transmission. How she hated them! The sounds she generated when driving one was like someone grinding coffee beans. The truck's engine, serviced yesterday by their regular mechanic, roared nosily to life, making her stomp down the clutch and gas pedal and grind the gears to get herself out of the area as quickly as possible. She swore she felt Dante's eyes and anger boring between her shoulder blades as she sped toward the high fields. The feeling was so real she flexed her shoulders and shifted uneasily on the seat.

She rattled and rolled upward, waving to the group of workers clearing debris from the harvested fields. *Witnesses!* Beyond the high flower fields, the narrowing road wound slowly through a tangle of trees, and she was grateful for the cooling trade winds today that blew through the truck's open windows. She glanced at her pack beside her on the seat. She was hungry already, a nervous hunger.

The road worsened, rutted by runoff, and finally disappeared into the beginning of a trail. She left the truck where she had braked to a stop, stalling the engine. From there she'd travel on foot.

Five steps in and she was engulfed in a bamboo thicket. The tall stalks met overhead in a Gothic arch that blocked the sky. Then came wild cane and *'ōhi'a*. She recalled a long-ago day when the four of them had set out for the *pali*. Dante had carried a *pahi ka,* a cane knife that resembled a long machete, for the first time. She could see him still, three strides ahead of her and Dom and Rosemary, with his free hand held behind his back, carefully slashing at the vegetation, while Dom put forth a steady flow of words about the plants around them, not caring if any of them listened to him, answered him, or ignored him. Just to be among the plants he loved, with the people he loved, had been enough for him.

Now the trees gave way to ferns and vigorous vines, whose tendrils reached out for her and her pack, and the trail became steeper. She physically and mentally fought the urge to hurry, to run because she felt Dante's anger behind her, pushing her now, crowding her, closing in on her like flames.

It was only her vivid imagination. She hoped. He probably didn't even know she was gone. Yet.

I'll soon be hot on your heels, Lani. And, big surprise, I'm really huhū, *although angry doesn't do justice to what I feel right now!*

He knew on his way back from Lihue that she was up to something. He could feel it. He suspected she was heading for the *pali* without him, caught up in some middle-of-the-night meltdown about the gems being cursed and her being the instrument to unleash it on him, like she believed in her weak moments that she had unleashed the curse on Dom, or some such crap.

He had picked up her note as he passed through the kitchen and read it on the way to her room, hoping she'd be in her bed with a sore head. When she wasn't, he'd blazed through the house, questioning Mei and Helen, scaring the bejabbers out of Mei in the process. Then Shaka had shown up with, what else? A note from Lani. Shaka's old truck would never survive Lani's assault on its clutch, and its transmission would probably seize from her famous gear-shifting deficit. Well, if he didn't strangle her first, she was going to learn to drive a manual

311

transmission vehicle as penance, and drive it well.

The workers in the high fields confirmed she had passed that way, *wikiwiki,* a couple of hours earlier. Well, she'd have to be a lot quicker than that to stay ahead of him. He just hoped he could control his temper when he found her.

Funny how she had usually been able to defuse him when he saw red as they were growing up, when Dom and Tutu couldn't. Well, not this time. The thought that she would come up here alone when some maniac was after them . . .

I'm hot on your heels, Lani. And I'll bet you can feel me. I'll bet you can feel the heat from wherever you are right now!

And why am I wondering what color of underwear you're wearing today to hike the pali?

Both Lani and Dom had carried a healthy mixture of respect and fear of Dante when he was in the throes of anger, righteous or not. Enough of each still lingered so that she had to force her feet to set a slower pace. Maybe when she explained, or better yet, if she could show him a nice, safe cave — because she wouldn't go in without him — well back from the dangerous edge, maybe he wouldn't be quite so angry with her.

As the afternoon lengthened, the noises surrounding her became more tranquil. Unseen birds trilled from within a quivering cover of foliage. Leaves drifted silently to earth while something scurried in the brush, sounding very untranquil. She prayed that wild boars hadn't moved in since she had last been up here.

She knew that Dante and Shaka kept a close watch for domestic animals gone wild, a close watch on anything that threatened Lehua and its livelihood. She spent an enjoyable time imagining how she might pin a threatening behavior on the lone, and lonely, Colonel then point the Terrible Two in his direction. By the end of this self-indulgence, she was debating with herself whether or not wild pigs scurried. She doubted it.

The winds deserted her as she entered a layer of thick, rampant growth. She wished again that she had thought to bring Dante's *pahi ka* with her. *Right.* He had never, ever, allowed her near the thing. She'd probably have amputated something by now if she had borrowed it. She shuddered for a moment, mentally adding a "borrowing" charge to that of lying to Dante, which she could

313

only achieve on paper, piled on to what she was doing now.

She saw signs of passage on the overgrown main trail. Kern Pepper, probably, and maybe Aidan. What excuse would she use if he and Aidan had come up this morning and she met them? Not that she needed one. This was Lehua land, after all. She could always use the honeycreepers as a subject, of course. She'd deal with them if she stumbled upon them, but she hoped she wouldn't. She hated lying in general and to Dante in particular.

She rested when she came to a guava whose oval, light-yellow fruits littered the ground. Planted and abandoned when Dante's ancestors cultivated this high ground at some point in the past, volunteer plants of all kinds still pushed through the earth. She pulled off the fruit's skin with her teeth to expose the sweet, dark pink flesh. While she ate several, she spied a pineapple plant and some sugar cane, both wild and stunted now, and maybe a patch of wild taro.

Her plan had been to save the food in her pack for later and, possibly, the morning, if it turned out she had to spend the night up there. The truth? She felt guilty and inadequate, and it was no fun at all without

Dante. To save worry at Lehua, she should just chuck her plan, hope for a quick look around at the top, and make her way down by lantern light. But at that moment she was alone, as in all by herself, with an angry Dante waiting for her at any ending to this mad idea and grueling hike.

Eventually, she came to a small, familiar stream that still murmured to itself, fed by the rains on the *pali* higher up where the ornithologists usually hung out. She followed it, letting its voice calm her as it spoke of simpler, happier times. Its low banks broadened as she climbed, the clear water becoming noisier and appearing colder. She stuck in her hand to test it. Finally she came to the waterfall she'd been hearing for the last half hour, and the large pool at its base. Both looked smaller than she remembered, and it had taken her longer to get to them than in the past.

Still, the cool water invited her in, and she decided to take time to calm down and think. She'd take a swim and maybe still be able to get to the top and have a good look around before the tropical sunset came down like a curtain around her — or she could just turn around after her swim.

She stripped down to her lacy black bikini panties and hung her black lace bra on a nearby bush. She froze when she heard someone coming up the trail. Maybe Pepper and Aidan had set out after she did, or maybe they had rejoined this trail from another trail from another direction. As the sound of muttering joined the footsteps, she realized with dread that a more accurate description of what she was hearing was someone stomping up the trail and slashing greenery out of the way, with a vengeance. She fervently hoped that Pepper and Aidan stomped when they hiked — or that wild boars muttered in Hawaiian — but the sinking feeling in her stomach told her to stop kidding herself, to admit that she recognized this particular determined stomp. Dante was coming on fast.

Hoping to the bitter end that she was mistaken and that it really was Pepper and Aidan, she slung her jeans over her shoulders, with the crotch at the back of her neck and the legs hanging down over her bare breasts. She also had just enough time to put the width of the pool between them before one angry native Hawaiian strode into the clearing. Hot Hawaiian curses trailed out behind Dante like wisps of smoke.

"Oh, no," she whispered, followed by, "Crap!"

Dante ground to a halt on his side of the pool, throwing down his *pahi ka* so that it stuck upright in the dirt, quivering. And she knew just how it felt. He shrugged off his pack and sleeping roll while his angry gaze scorched her from the top of her head to her bare feet. He went very still when he came to her lacy black panties then his eyes cut to the matching bra hanging by one strap on a bush. He studied it before he studied her again, more slowly this time.

"What do you think you're doing?" Each word was enunciated carefully and crisply and quietly, all bad signs.

She felt a flash of envy that he wasn't even out of breath, although his sweaty denim shirt stuck to his chest, molding itself to the bumps and curves of underlying muscle. Envy morphed into alert awareness when he casually moved toward her around the pool's edge. She moved the other way and there was nothing casual about it.

Time for damage control. How could she best explain her treachery? If she told him the truth right away, it would only make things worse. So she decided to stall for time by answering his question in the literal sense.

She held the damp legs of her jeans tightly against her chest. "I was going for a swim," she managed on the second try.

Head down, like a bull, he came around another section of shoreline. Again, she trotted an equal distance in the other direction and didn't stop until he did.

"Let me tell you why I think we're dancing around this pool right now, other than you keeping me from getting my hands on you," he said, breathing heavily now. A very, very bad sign.

"Sometime in the night, after we finalized our plans to come up here, you had one of those moments when you're really in touch with your Hawaiian side. In that moment, you talked yourself into some superstitious nonsense about a Pele's Tears-Kahoa family curse and decided to save me by coming up here alone. How am I doing?"

She knew her face told him he'd got it in one. "Busted. How did you figure out what I'd done? Before I die, I'd like to know, just out of curiosity, which part of my plan was the weakest link."

He looked heavenward and took a deep, deep breath before he spoke. She was thankful to see that at least he was trying to control himself.

"I had a feeling. Then I found your note on the table. Then I checked your room. Then I terrorized Mei and Helen with questions. Then Shaka showed me his note, that you had borrowed his truck. Then I packed. Then the workers burning the last of the waste from the anthurium cutting told me they'd seen you coming this way. Then I found Shaka's truck at the trailhead. And you left a trail a blind man could follow, including guava skins."

"Like a house of cards or a line of dominoes," she said aloud before she could stop herself.

"And, in case you haven't noticed, it's still falling. You're a *wahine* who's run out of shoreline. Damn it, Lani!" He lost the battle and headed her way.

And he was right. Other than a few feet of ground, she had nowhere left to go. When she looked around her, she realized she was as close as she wanted to get to the place where the waterfall crashed into the deep pool. So she pranced in place for a moment. Then she mentally surrendered, begged for mercy, and finally prepared to dive into the pool so she could tell him everything from its safety. She left the dive a little too late.

"No, you don't! Not yet." Anger rolled off him in waves, enveloping her in its heat.

His warm, callused hands shot out to grip her upper arms. She cringed when he opened his mouth to heap more anger upon her head. But for some reason he didn't. Instead, he looked from one hand to the other, and she watched a change come over his face as vivid awareness replaced anger.

His thumbs moved against her skin while his gaze snagged hers and held. "You have the softest skin I've ever touched."

She tracked the moment on his face when he registered just how much of that skin was exposed at the moment. Hot knowing flared before he looked down at his hands again. She felt herself go limp with relief. The anger had gone out of him. She'd rather deal with an amorous Dante than an angry Dante.

His thumbs stopped their gentle stroking. "You scared the devil out of me," he finally said, his voice hoarse. "Lehua is posted, but we don't have security, electronic or otherwise. Anyone or anything could be up here, Lani. You don't ever come up here alone. You've known that since you were a kid."

She closed her eyes for a moment and held her breath against her guilt. They were friends, allies, and a lot more. A sincere, abject apology was all she had to offer.

"I'm sorry, Dante. Really, really sorry I lied to you and worried you. Everything I did today was dumb and dangerous, and you're right about all of it. I plead temporary insanity on my Hawaiian side. I make myself crazy sometimes."

"I know that feeling well."

She looked up at him, let go of her jeans legs, crossed her arms, and pressed one of her hands over each of his on her shoulders.

Her voice caught on the edges of her next words. "I was afraid. For you. I couldn't bear to lose you too, Dante."

He was silent for a moment. "I can understand that because I feel the same about losing you." Then his expression changed and flames of anger burned away the other heat in his eyes. His fingers tightened their grip. "But, Lani, you make me crazy *huhū* sometimes. Some nutcase makes you fall off the overlook and lays me out on the cottage *lānai* and you come up here alone? I could just —"

She knew what was coming and made a preemptive strike. His voice cut off when she uncrossed her arms, grabbed two fistfuls of his shirtfront, and pulled him toward her, off balance.

"You need cooling off more than I do before we can talk this through."

Then they were falling sideways into the icy pool. The cold water closed over her head, silencing her gleeful whoop and his outraged howl.

CHAPTER 19

"You could have at least let me take off my boots!" Dante said over his shoulder as he stood barefoot beside the pool, wringing out his shirt.

She glanced up at his profile, a clean-shaven square jaw and one planed cheek, before he turned back to what he was doing. Then she studied the width of his bare shoulders, muscles rippling beneath his smooth skin. He was powerfully built. Like Lohi'au, maybe?

Her thoughts took a detour when she remembered the tattoo he'd mentioned. More than wanting to know what it looked like, she wanted to know where it was. She glanced at his soggy jeans riding low on his hips. It had to be under there somewhere, probably on his tight Hawaiian butt. She wondered if he'd tell her where it was, maybe even show her, if she asked nicely. But now was not the time.

"And lose the element of surprise?" she finally answered. "If I hadn't been barefoot already, would you have given me time to take off my hiking boots? You planned to throw me in anyway, so I decided to throw myself in and take you with me."

She had put a towel into her pack. While his back was turned, she had used it to pat dry her face, arms, and legs. After she used it on her hair, she threw it in his direction.

"Catch."

He plucked it out of the air. He dried his hair and chest then had the nerve to ask her to dry the very back she'd just been admiring. No signs of even a tiny tattoo there.

She had also brought a change of clothes, a pair of his sleep boxers, and his digital camera. She didn't tell him about any of them, but she wouldn't let him suffer through the night in wet clothes.

"Did you bring the grill? We could fire it up and dry out your stuff a little."

She gave no explanation when she offered him the boxers before slipping behind some greenery to put on dry panties, the bra she had retrieved from the bush, jeans, and a tank top.

"Yeah, it's in my pack."

She watched through the leaves as he strolled over to where he'd dropped his pack, her towel hanging over one bare shoulder, and ducked behind a bush to change.

When she'd finished dressing, she took the pressure lantern out of her pack and lit it. Darkness was very nearly upon them. She sorted through everything else she had thrown in there.

"I have cheese or PBJ sandwiches, fruit, nutrition bars, and water. We can save the fruit for breakfast and the bars for later tomorrow."

He set up the tiny propane grill as she laid out her sleeping bag six feet in front of it. He had gone quiet. He unrolled his sleeping roll a few feet away from her sleeping bag, laid down his boots with their openings facing the grill, and draped his socks over them. His shirt, underwear, and jeans went onto a bush near the grill. She had done the same with her wet jeans and underwear.

Sitting on their sleeping gear, they finished their sandwiches and split a candy bar she'd forgotten about. Except for a grunt when she handed him his food, he didn't make another sound, tense and preoccupied.

She broke with scarcely a whimper. She couldn't take his tense silence another second. "Look, you have every right to still be mad at me, so if you have more to say, go ahead. I can take it now that I have food in me and you've calmed down."

He smiled. "No lecture, but there's something I want to talk to you about."

He got up and started pacing back and forth in the corridor between the grill and their sleeping areas. This was infinitely worse than his tortured silence, although a part of her managed to enjoy the sight of all those muscles and tan skin on display. Still, if he didn't stop that animal pacing soon, she'd have to get up and chart a course in the opposite direction to his because his unease was catching and watching him struggle was painful to her. She felt her eyes go round when he suddenly hung a left and hunkered down in front of her, in the space between their sleeping gear so he could look into her eyes. Now she was nervous *and* scared.

"Look, Lani, I don't know how to say any of this, so I'm just going to jump in." He pulled in a deep breath. "First, you don't have to stay at Lehua all the time if you really don't want to. It's not fair to you. Just because Lehua is my world doesn't mean it has to be yours unless you want it to be. I want you to be happy. We can keep up your residency requirement somehow."

She didn't like the sound of this. Not at all. And why was he looking a question at her?

"Thanks, Kahoa, but no thanks. It's my world too. How did you put it? I'm 'an orchid in a sunflower patch anywhere but Lehua.' My world is Lehua, and I hope it always will be." She almost told him she'd discovered that her world was where he was, but she stopped as a new thought hijacked her into misery. "Oh. Are you telling me you want me to go away, and not just because of Sour Note?" Her voice skittered to a halt.

"No!" He let one finger trail down her cheek and continued in a quieter voice. "Just the opposite. I want you to stay for all the right reasons. We need to be honest with each other about this attraction thing going on between us. Maybe you're wondering when I might . . . try to move things along. Why I haven't . . ."

"I haven't, actually," she said, surprised at herself. "And you usually move pretty quickly. Or so I've been told," she added.

"You have good sources. It's because I want to get it right with you. I want this to be right between us. Just hear me out before you start laughing. Okay?"

"I don't think I'll laugh. You're being too

serious for that. I'm almost ready to run."

"That's what I've been afraid of. I wanted to give you the chance to run before I say this to you."

"I won't. I promise."

"Okay. You've grown into a beautiful woman. I know there have been other men in your life, and you know there have been other women in mine."

She wondered what the count was up to by now in his love life. She knew hers to be tiny.

He continued with a half smile. "And I know what you're thinking. But, despite my track record, I want you to give me a chance. I want you to stay here at Lehua and give me a chance to, um . . ."

She got it — and relief made her dizzy. "You want to court me? Romance me. Date me. Sweep me off my feet. Let the whole island know we're a couple." She paused. "You want to remind me that I've loved you since I was four," she ended quietly on a gulp.

He stared at her before a grudging smile tugged up the corners of his lips. "Yeah, all that and dibs. Most of all, I want to tell you that I finally get it. I get that I've loved you since I was five. You okay with that?"

"I am. But I want the same things from

you. I want you to stay at Lehua and give me a chance to court you back, romance you back, date you back, sweep you off your feet back, let the whole island know we're a couple —"

"And remind me that I love you back?" he inserted.

"Yeah, all that and dibs."

"I promise."

"So do I. And meanwhile?"

"Ah. Here comes the most laughable, unbelievable part. I'm giving you control. *You* say when our relationship moves to the next level. But I want you to understand, believe, and know without doubt that I want you more than I've ever wanted any woman, but that I'd like to take it slow with you, give us time, let *us* evolve. Because I never have, or wanted to, before. I've never had a serious relationship.

"Meanwhile, we'll work together, dance together, and talk together, go surfing, to movies, and to chants, get a shave ice, get used to each other again, as best friends who are now a couple, before we jump into being engaged."

"*Engaged?* You mean I'll eventually be a Kahoa? At last?"

He laughed. "Tutu wanted this to happen between us. She could see it when I couldn't. I thought she was crazy until I saw you again at the funeral, then in Maine and finally back here. No one could have been more shocked than I was when I realized I was in love with you and had been for most of my life. I never thought I was a one-woman man." His dimpled smile stretched from ear to ear. "Turns out I was a one-woman man from the first time you came to Lehua."

She was so happy she wasn't sure she was still touching the ground. "Deep down, I've always known I was a one-man woman. I've never dated much, never had a serious relationship either. I think I realized why when I saw you standing in my doorway in Maine. We'll have to tell Shaka and Helen first." Another thought squeezed in. "Oh, I hope you told them where we are so they won't worry."

"We're good. I did some damage control. We should get some sleep now. And you'd better hope my boots are dry by morning."

"Or?"

"Or I'll throw you in again, Beecham."

"Technically, you didn't throw me in the first time, Kahoa."

She had a lot to think about. They settled down for the night, she in her single sleeping bag and Dante on his bedroll. But she

329

had forgotten how profound the darkness was up there when clouds hid the moon. And how overhanging branches and vines trimmed the edges of the pool's clearing, leaving ragged edges around the bit of sky that showed lighter when the clouds moved away from the moon's face.

"Dante?"

"Hmm?"

"As part of this getting-to-know-you stage, may I drag over my sleeping bag and cuddle? It's awfully dark over here."

He made a little sound. "You call the shots, but I was going to suggest the same thing myself."

And so they nested, like spoons. Close.

"Is that . . . ?"

"The flashlight. Shut up."

"Uh-huh."

Sometime in the night, something rustled or scurried through the plants on the other side of the pool; she was too sleepy to debate the point with herself. She wasn't scared and went right back to sleep. Nothing could hurt her in that moment or intrude on her happiness.

Dante's boots were dry, the small propane tank was empty, and his clothes were still very damp the next morning. By the looks of the sky, they would be wet all over again before the day was finished with them. They each ate fruit and a nutrition bar before they pulled on their footwear. She went into the bushes for a pit stop. When she came out, she shoved the camera into one of her pockets.

"Let's leave everything except the food and water and necessities. We can pick up what's left on the way down," he suggested.

He divided up the load between their packs. She snickered when she watched him put the flashlight into his, but she didn't see the rope she had requested. They headed up the trail, holding hands when they could.

They were at the cliff edge in less than an hour, gazing out over Lehua below. She thought the view was still breathtaking, a colorful patchwork quilt of various fields in bloom, despite the memory of what happened below here on the face. Green pleats of narrow, steep valleys, covered in *uluhe* ferns, rippled away on both sides, like folding closet doors.

Dante went still beside her, more frozen than unmoving. "It was here, wasn't it? This is where it happened. On the cliff below us," he whispered.

She nodded, tears suddenly streaming down her face. "I wasn't sure. Now I am."

"Can we name our first son Dominic?" he asked in a strangled voice.

She smiled through her tears. "Dom for short."

Dante tore his gaze from the view and looked up at the overcast sky. "Let's do this thing before it rains. Okay, it depends on the season where the sun and moon will be, so we can eliminate them on the pendant as markers."

"And we would need an aerial shot to match the pattern of the cliff edge to the pendant edge."

She reached into her jeans pocket where her fingers found the saw-toothed and rounded edges of gold and the smooth, rounded lime-green olivine stones of the pendant. She pulled it out for reference. It was simply too dangerous to get close to the edge.

Dante frowned. "Let's just look around. And we'll do it as far back from the edge as we can. I don't see how we can possibly find that shape in the cliff edge. It must mean something else."

They went to the right for a short distance first. When they came up against the side of a green, vertical valley, they took a break.

Dante disappeared for a pit stop, and she walked away from the view to explore the formations created by an ancient lava flow. The weak sun had climbed, and a flash on top of a formation on the left caught her eye while she was still some distance away from it. When she got to it, she walked around it, looking for an easy way up. The back side of it sloped, the top wasn't too rounded, and the whole thing wasn't high enough to be too scary. She was able to climb the back like a stepladder set up at a lean.

The *uluhe* ferns, covered with dew, were slippery. She crawled to the area she thought the flash had come from then carefully stood. It was safer to stay in one spot and just turn, using her feet or hands to push the fronds aside to find whatever had glinted. Shadows chased across the *pali* as the sun broke free of clouds for a moment. She saw the flash again. She separated the ferns over the spot with both hands then shot upright in surprise. Glass was set into a fissure in the solid rock, angled to reflect the sunlight, now overgrown with roots and dark with dirt but still capable of catching the sun. She recalled Rosemary's words from the Pele's Tears journal. "Remember, you'll find them through light. I was very careful about that."

She was afraid to believe . . .

"What did you find?" Dante's magnificent voice said.

It was a good thing they were nowhere near the edge of the *pali.* She spun around at the sound. Big mistake. Her feet slipped out from under her on the dewy ferns and she sat down on her butt.

"Ouch! Glass. I found glass set into the stone."

"Come down so I can get up there. Just slide down toward me, and I'll catch you."

She wriggled toward him, planning a slow, dignified descent. Instead, she shot down the side of the formation, feet first, as if she were on a water slide, right at him. In a video byte, she saw Dante reach out for her. In an audio byte, she heard screaming. Somehow, Dante managed to grab her around her hips and bring her to a halt, upright, in his arms. Bless him.

"Magic hands," she said, hugging him in relief.

"At your service."

She took a time-out to brush herself off while she described in detail what she had found. He'd brought the packs, so he handed her a bottle of water. She turned to face the *pali* edge while she drank. When she looked beyond the end of her water bottle, she saw a pattern of solid and open,

334

dark and light, a pattern that tolled recognition inside her head like a church bell.

"Dante," she whispered — and choked on her water.

CHAPTER 20

After some coughing on her part and some backslapping on Dante's part, she held up the pendant so he, too, could compare it with the pattern of sky showing between or behind the ragged or rounded or flattened lava formations that marched toward the cliff edge. On the pendant, the pattern wasn't in the gold that remained but in the shapes of the parts that Rosemary had cut away.

In the distance lay Lehua's fields and Kauai's rivers, like in the window above the cottage door. When they turned their heads to the right, the formation she'd just dismounted so spectacularly was beside them. Dante climbed it to see the glass, and she saw him use the flashlight. She heard squeaking as he rubbed the glass with his shirttail.

"The cave must be inside this formation,"

he called down. "Start looking for an opening."

Then it thundered. She looked up and dark clouds were rolling across the sky like smoke. Dante, of course, knew what she was thinking. Again.

"Pele does lava, not storms."

He climbed down, with dignity and efficiency, he pointed out. Only because nobody scared the bejabbers out of him, she pointed out.

"Let's find the opening and get inside before we're soaked again," he said, smiling to himself.

They walked around the formation, which was furry with plants, pushing them aside as they went. The wind picked up suddenly, finally showing them the way in. The entrance wasn't a hole, as she expected, but a slit. Then the heavens opened. She grabbed the lantern from her pack with her free hand. Dante pushed through first, using the flashlight and towing her along behind. The entrance turned out to be two slits, one to the left and the other to the right.

Slightly damp, they half slid and half fell through the opposing slits, driven by booming thunder and lightning that slashed the fabric of the sky behind them. Inside, Dante lay on his back against a large, slanted sheet of rock, catching his breath, and she sprawled beside him. Their shoulders touched in companionable awe as they listened to the sound effects outside.

She finally sat up and blotted her face with the bottom of her black tank top. When she opened her eyes, Dante stood at the foot of the slab, one hand extended to help her. From where she sat, her eyes were level with his sculpted lips.

He pulled her to her feet, close to him, and she suddenly wanted to feel the soft, wet warmth of those beautiful lips moving against hers again. It was the most natural thing in the world to reach out one finger to trace their full outline, this time with a fingertip.

She felt the warmth of his hands through her clothes in the cool cave as he pulled her into his arms, strong and tight and tender at the same time. It all felt so right, she felt so complete, that she was sure, once again, that holding her was what Dante Kimo Kahoa had been born to do. And she hoped it felt the same to him because, at that moment, she was certain she had been born to hold him.

This time, his feather-soft movements against her lips with his own were so gentle that she wanted to weep. The kiss went on and on and on as, damp and chilled by the cave, they stole warmth from each other's bodies. His senses must have been on overload too because an especially violent clap of thunder made them break away from each other.

She stared at him wide-eyed and sucked in a long-overdue full breath. "What you make me feel scares me, Dante," she confided in a whisper before she could stop herself. "I've never felt it before."

He was a bit wide-eyed himself. "Same here, like diving off a high cliff into a sea of electricity. I hope we spend a lot of our getting-to-know-you time scaring the devil out of each other."

"I'm thinking maybe we can move that schedule up a little, don't you?" she said softly.

He grinned. "Fine by me. Now stop distracting me and let's find that glass in the ceiling. Whoa!"

His flashlight's beam picked out thousands of sparkling green points of light, the color of Aumoe's eyes — and her own. For a moment, she was on the point of whimpering, until she realized it wasn't the reflection of living eyes she was seeing. This was what Rosemary's father had seen and written about.

"Olivine!" She lit the lantern and stepped closer.

The cave had once been part of a lava tube, and its black walls were studded with thousands of green globules of olivine trapped in the natural setting of its creation. She trailed her fingers over the rounded, smooth semiprecious gems.

"So how many jewelry makers do we know?" she asked.

"Not nearly enough."

"We can sell Lehua olivine jewelry in the shop."

"Come on, let's start looking."

The storm had passed and it had grown quiet in the cave, so when she heard an unlikely sound, she set down the lantern in the center of the cave floor a little harder than she had planned.

The shuffling and scraping from behind them had made them spin around to face the entrance. A woman stood just inside it. She was relatively dry, her red *mu'umu'u* billowing around her in the determined wind traversing the entrance slits, her long, graying hair wild, her head circled by a *haku lei,* her feet bare and bloody, and her eyes . . . her eyes were as wild as her hair. She held a tall Hawaiian war club, red-brown with age and shaped like an elongated baseball bat, with its smaller end planted in the dirt at her feet.

She extended one hand toward Dante and said in a deep voice Lani recognized from the overlook and her unexpected trip off of it, "Lohi'au! Have you found them?"

Lani stood as still as she could beside Dante, maintaining a death grip on his right arm. She was sure she had passed through a portal into a real Hawaiian myth, and Madame Pele was about to strike her dead, right there in a cave the Hawaiian goddess had formed.

If the woman's words shook him, Dante didn't let it show. His voice came with a studied, casual authority, yet managed to fill the space. "Ma'am, I don't know if you're aware that this is private, posted land and you're trespassing —"

"Have you found them?" She stepped forward into the lantern's circle of light. "Have you found Pele's Tears?"

Her voice sounded totally different this time, and Lani noted that her light blue eyes had calmed. Sudden recognition slapped Lani in the face.

"Agnes?" she said, her voice squeaking as she doubted her own eyes, and certainly her ears, and, very possibly, her sanity.

Dante looked down at her as if she were

crazy. But when he looked again at the woman, his face changed and Lani felt him tense.

Agnes hadn't heard her or had chosen to ignore her. "Because when you find them, I'll be free. I can leave this place and go back to my home on the Big Island."

Just when Lani thought it couldn't get any weirder, a second, and this time a recognizable figure, slipped through the slits. Melika was dressed for the part in an Indiana Jones–style hat and matching khaki pants and shirt, all very wet.

Melika held out both hands to their accountant. "Agnes. Sweetie. What are you doing? You scared me, leaving camp like that in the middle of the night."

Camp? They had to have set up farther down the *pali* trail than her and Dante's little camp. And Agnes passing through their site would explain the rustling sounds she'd heard in the night. Ignoring totally, of course, the creepiness factor. And to stay dry like that, Agnes must have found cover here at the top before the storm. Maybe she had watched them arrive, look around, and find the cave, although their packs right outside the entrance where they had dropped them, and the mashed greenery all around the slit, might have given both

Agnes and Melika a clue.

"Agnes, will you wait outside for me?" Melika looked at them over her shoulder. "I'll be back in a minute to explain. I'm sorry about all this."

But Agnes stepped away from Melika, closer to them. "No. You'll tell them I'm crazy, but I know what you did. You gave me the other pills."

Melika sent them a pained smile, ignoring the words just said. "Agnes is my cousin and has a little apartment in Kalele. I asked Rosemary to give her accounting work at Lehua, as a favor to me. We started out on our hike late yesterday. I assure you I was given Rosemary's permission to hike the *pali*. Long ago. I'm so sorry you've been subjected to this. I thought Agnes was doing better."

"I *am* doing better since I've been throwing away the other pills you give to me."

Lani thought back to that line of pills on Agnes's desk at Lehua, and the ping one of them had made when Agnes threw it into the metal garbage can.

"You'd better explain, Melika. And I mean all of it," Dante said in that rock-solid tone of his. "And permission for you to hike Lehua's *pali* is hereby rescinded. Right, partner?" He glanced down at her.

343

"Me? Oh, right."

Lani beat back her exasperation at his calmness. How could he be so unaffected by all this while she was quivering like his *pahi ka* had done yesterday, sticking out of the dirt like a nightmare? She was about to erupt with questions if somebody didn't start explaining. Immediately, if not sooner.

Melika looked at Agnes and kind of deflated a little, like she knew this was going down Dante's way rather than hers. "I brought Agnes to Kauai with me when I opened the gallery. She's mentally fragile and became obsessed with you, Dante. At the same time, she became caught up in my Pele hobby and Rosemary's Pele's Tears story."

Lani felt Dante move beside her and sensed his discomfort and impatience.

"Agnes had stopped taking her medication," Melika tried to continue.

"Only the pill you added."

"She tricked me, hid her meds, and I didn't notice until very recently that she was fragile again. We haven't found the correct dosage just yet."

"Ask her who took the papers from the trunk, who hit you with my war club the other night when I was running away from the cottage, and who made me help her

344

move the statue out into the path," Agnes chimed in.

Melika gamely continued, still selling. "Agnes knew the cottage was open most of the time. She overheard you mention the journal in my office. She knew that if Rosemary kept a journal about Pele's Tears, it would probably be in the cottage somewhere."

"We couldn't find it the first time either," Agnes added helpfully.

"It won't work, Melika," Dante said. "Both of you were there. I was chasing someone who was running away when I was hit. Try explaining away something else."

Melika ignored him, but the strain of trying to convince Dante was evident on her face. "She wouldn't stay away from the chant the other night. She was lying on the hill above you two. She has acute hearing and said you mentioned Pele's Tears, a ruby, and coming up here."

Lani remembered that just before Dante kissed her at the chant, he mentioned Pele's Tears of Rage, a ruby, and coming up to the *pali* on what would have been the next day, yesterday, to find it. When she nodded confirmation, Melika clung to the gesture.

"Agnes was already jealous of the attraction she sensed between you and Lani long

345

before she saw the two of you kissing in the kitchen at Lehua and at the chant. All I did was try to watch her, take care of her, but I wanted so much to be present when you found Pele's Tears. Rosemary often spoke of them to me."

"And me! Don't listen to her. Ask her who sent the notes. We have a cousin in Maine who sent Lani's."

Melika broke, her voice becoming harsh and demanding, with a little whine thrown in. "In that case, you'd better ask Agnes who pushed Lani off the overlook."

Lani made her voice as gentle as she could under the circumstances. "Was it you at the overlook, Agnes? Can you tell me what happened?"

"Of course. I'm not crazy, despite what she says. I ride my bicycle to work, often on the footpaths, away from the road. I take a blanket and go to the overlook to meditate on the table sometimes before starting work at Lehua. It helps me think."

Melika spoke quickly, carrying on the story. "She heard someone coming and hid. When she saw it was you, Lani, well, you're apparently a trigger for her because of Dante. She used the blanket as a kind of hooded cape. And she speaks in a lower voice when she's . . . not herself."

"I didn't push! You fell. And I checked to see that you were safe on the ledge before I ran away. I didn't know what to do."

Really? If in your mind, at the time, you were Pele and Dante was Lohi'au then I was the other woman, Pele's sister Hi'iaka. Talk about your triggers.

Agnes went on. "I knew Lohi'au, um, Dante would come for you. I just wanted to scare you. You're young and beautiful, and I'm not. I was jealous when I saw you there. I watched Melika make the notes, so I knew what to say. But Melika didn't tell me to do that or to say that."

"So, Melika, let's see if I have this straight. You used my grandmother and abused her trust, wrote the notes and arranged for them to be mailed, even hand delivered one yourself, made Agnes help you move that statue so I'd fall over it in the dark, burglarized the cottage twice, stole items from there, and hit me with a club. It must have felt like a gift when you found out what happened at the overlook. All in the name of watching over Agnes and taking care of her? Nothing at all to do with stealing Pele's Tears? Does that pretty much cover it?" Dante said the words in his calm, watch-out tone that Lani knew was the equivalent of a bull pawing the ground.

347

Melika's chin lifted. "Yes." She hissed the word. "Rosemary told me everything except where she found them and where she hid them. The more she told me, the more sure I became that they should be mine. Then she died. But she had told me all about the dynamics of the relationship you two have.

"I sold Rosemary that captain's trunk for Lani after I searched the cottage the first time, messing it up to look like kids had done it. I knew the journal would be in that trunk. When Lani mentioned the journal in my office, I decided to look in the cottage again.

"I want Pele's Tears. I simply used who and what I had to work with. I was willing to do anything to get them, not that I wouldn't have enjoyed it, but you, Dante, wouldn't play."

Lani felt anger build. Melika was calculating, ruthless, and devious. And Agnes was as much a victim in this as they were. But Agnes, in her most lucid moment yet, spoke to Melika before Lani could.

"I might have overheard Rosemary discussing Pele's Tears with you. Everything might have become mixed up in my head. Dante might have become Lohi'au, and Lani might have become Hi'iaka, and I might have become Pele for a little while because of the pills. I couldn't help that. But you. You would have done anything to make them find Pele's Tears and give them to you."

"Pele is part of me, my life. They should be mine!"

Melika had slid her right hand into her pants pocket. Now it emerged, gripping a small, yet vicious-looking, gun.

Lani felt Dante go very still, yet very loose, beside her. Her knees trembled, and she hoped they would continue to hold her upright if she was meant to die beside him. Just when they had acknowledged this love between them, were she and Dante about to become the last Kahoa victims of the Pele's Tears curse?

"Give them to me," Melika said in a voice that rippled with hysteria just beneath its surface.

Agnes, who had been staring at the gun, came to furious life. "I won't let you hurt him again!"

She brought down the bulbous end of her club on Melika's right wrist. The sound of a bone breaking was sickeningly clear in the confines of the cave. But Melika had seen Agnes move and had gripped the gun more tightly. It went off when Agnes struck the blow.

The percussion and the echo of the shot nearly deafened her, but Lani sensed the bullet hitting the cave wall beyond them. Before the pinging of ricochets around the cave began, and before she even realized what the sounds were, everything went dark. Dante had tackled her, face-first into the dirt on the cave floor, and landed heavily on top of her. Just as quickly, his weight lifted, and she raised her head to watch him lunge on his belly across the grubby floor to where Melika's gun had come to rest.

He carefully scooped it up, got to his feet, and turned to Lani. "Are you all right?"

When she nodded, he looked at the two women huddling separately against the slanted rock where she and Dante had shared a special moment earlier. Agnes had a small cut on her face from a flying stone chip from a ricochet. Dante gave her his red bandanna handkerchief.

"Okay, I've had my fill of you two. We're done here," Dante said in a voice that brooked no argument. "Agnes, you're on suspension until you're feeling better. And she'd better be feeling better real soon, and under the care of a new doctor. Do you understand me, Melika?"

"I understand." Melika agreed sullenly and glanced around the cave, her gaze lingering on the olivine-studded wall.

"I'm not finished. We *will* be taking you to the police to file a report about this incident, requesting that social services monitor Agnes, and consulting our lawyers. Meanwhile, we want everything you stole out of the trunk in the cottage returned to us immediately. Get some help for yourself too, Melika."

Lani high-fived him in her head.

"Not only did you drug and use a vulnerable person in your care for your own ends, you placed our lives in danger and caused us mental anguish, violated our home, disrespected the memory of my brother and how he died, and used my grandmother's trust in you to gather information to steal from her and us."

"I'm sorry. I got carried away."

"Right. I'd say pulling a gun on us and firing a shot in an enclosed space qualifies as being carried away as well as being an idiot. We're all lucky no one is dead in here right now. And Agnes. Everyone knows what happened to my brother and that Lani and I saw it. I'm sure you knew it too, so it was cruel of you to approach Lani and say what you did at the overlook."

Agnes nodded, tears streaming down her face.

Melika went into pitiful mode, clutching her broken wrist as she spoke. "Are they here, Dante? If Pele's Tears has led you to this place, please, please, forgive me and let me see them. That's all I ask. I'm not a bad person, just obsessed with Madame Pele and things of beauty."

Sure you're not a bad person, Lani thought. *Or, as an English friend once told me, pull the other one.*

"You'll never see them if I have anything to say about it. And I think my family, past and present, would agree with that decision."

When a shouted hello filtered into the protected cave, Dante added, "What is this, rush hour? You two, out."

Dante ushered Melika and Agnes outside ahead of him. Lani followed. He answered the shout, and Pepper and Aidan soon hove into view.

"Oh, it's you guys," Pepper said, relief evident in his voice. "We thought we heard a muffled shot, then saw the packs and wondered what was going on and where exactly it was going on."

"Pepper here was set to run off intruders." Aidan's words were for Dante, but the whole time his eyes were taking in the two women, one bleeding and one nursing an arm, and Dante holding a gun by its butt.

Dante bagged the gun in a plastic storage bag from Lani's pack. He handed a first-aid kit to Aidan and told him to wrap Melika's wrist to stabilize it while he filled in Pepper on what had just happened.

When everything was explained for the moment, Dante added, "Pepper, would you and Aidan do Lani and me a great favor and escort these ladies off Lehua property and to the hospital and then to the police station in Lihue? You'll find Shaka's old truck, keys inside, and their vehicle at the trailhead." He handed Pepper the gun. "We have some unfinished business here. We'll pick up some other things for the police at the house. Then we'll be along. We'd really appreciate it."

Aidan had quickly stabilized the break and now offered Melika his arm to lead her away. "The *kahuna* has spoken, luv. But don't hold it against me."

Pepper was left with Agnes, whom he now recognized, and looked disbelief and un-asked questions at them over his shoulder until he was out of their sight.

"Be gentle with her, Pepper," Lani called after him.

When they were alone, they stood silently, their fingers laced, until the peace of the place settled around them again.

It took a little while because Lani realized that if her plan hadn't fallen apart, if Dante couldn't read her mind, if he didn't know her so well, if he hadn't followed her yesterday, and if Aidan and Pepper hadn't shown up, she and those two might have had an up-close-and-personal encounter there on the *pali* today.

CHAPTER 21

"Are you okay?" he asked eventually.

She nodded because she didn't trust her voice. "You were great in there. What just almost happened really puts Pele's Tears in perspective. Thanks for being you. Hold me for just a minute?"

He wrapped her in his strong, warm arms. "We can come back. We don't have to do this now."

"Yes, we do."

They finally went back inside, and Dante pointed the flashlight beam upward. He took her hand as they trailed around the cave, following its beam.

At last they found the piece of dirty glass fitted to a fissure in the cave ceiling on the *pali* side. They climbed onto a small boulder beneath it in order to reach it, the very place where Rosemary must have stood to create what was above their heads. Having already cleaned the glass on the outside, Dante took off his damp shirt and carefully wiped the inside surface. Light poured through. Colorful light. Because studding the plain glass's surface were three clear, smooth ovals, each held within the glass with leading. One was as clear and pure as tears of love, one was as blue as tears of sorrow, and one was as red as tears of rage. They were set in a simple triangle pattern.

"Another triangle," she whispered.

Facing the final truth that Pele's Tears existed, and that they had just found them, was a lot to get their minds around. They stared at the glass a long time, breathing deeply, before either of them spoke again.

"What are we going to do?" she finally asked.

"My Hawaiian side tells me to leave the glass in place until we can come up here with a digital camera to record where and how Tutu 'gave it back.' But my *haole* side tells me to get this sucker out of here, down the *pali,* and into a bank vault before closing time. Very quietly."

"We can do that. My *haole* side told me to put your digital camera in my pack to record this moment. I haven't found my own camera yet." She reached into her pocket and pulled out his camera.

He turned to look at it, then at her, and

she would have sworn he reached inside and squeezed her heart.

"Beautiful and smart. I've always liked that about you."

They took many pictures of the glass in place, from all angles. By holding the camera away from them and shooting upward at just the right angle, they got a shot of their smiling faces with the glass showing above their heads. She even ventured to the top of the formation again to record it from the outside while Dante lit it from below with the lantern and flashlight.

The glass came out in one piece with the gentle use of the lantern's wire handle, which they borrowed and reshaped to suit their needs. She gave up some of her own awe to capture Dante's for posterity when he pushed up on the glass and carefully turned it sideways to pull it down through the opening. Up close, all the gems were egg shaped, egg size, and nice and fat, each the equivalent of a small goose egg.

After more digital photographs, Dante put on his damp, dirty shirt and tucked the glass next to his body until they got outside to their packs.

Since gravity was on their side, they went down the *pali* a lot faster than they had gone up. In their need for speed, they passed, with scarcely a glance, the stuff they'd left behind. They would gather all of it later, returning the *pali* to its pristine existence. Lani hoped their faces gave nothing away as they passed Pepper, Aidan, and the women. A strange car, Melika's, sat beside Shaka's truck at the trailhead, along with Dante's bike.

"Your motorcycle is red. Why am I not surprised?" she asked as she looked at the small padded square that was upholstered and attached to the back fender with what looked like carpet tacks, and upon which he obviously expected her to sit and cling to him like an *'opihi,* a limpet.

"Show a little respect. This is a 1947 Harley-Davidson EL 1000 Knucklehead. One of the last to come off the line. It took Keneke and me months to fix her up."

"Keneke Takei? Really?"

"Like I said, he's a good man with motorcycles."

"And I still say men's fascination with motorcycles is simply the feeling of all that power between their legs." She ignored the choking sound he made. "So it's okay if I ride behind you but not Keneke Takei?"

"Damn straight."

She snugged Dante's precious pack between her body and his back for the ride from the *pali* trailhead to the big house. And she very much enjoyed the clinging.

At the house, they locked the doors behind them and agreed to regroup before setting off for Lihue. That included taking quick showers, changing clothing, gathering the two surviving notes, finding a couple of pills in the office wastebasket, and retrieving the safe deposit box key. Dante kept his pack and its precious cargo with him.

They met in the upstairs hall, ready for the trip. She quickstepped ahead and turned to face Dante. "Now that some of the pressure is off, I have to know! Where's your tattoo. What is it? Show me. Please?"

His jaw went slack. "You mean the only way I'm going to get out of this hall and into my truck with the family treasure is to show you my *'ōkole?*"

"I knew it! The only place that doesn't show in swimming trunks." She did a little victory dance around him.

He gave her the pack to hold when she stopped, unhooked his belt, turned around, and coyly pulled his jeans and white briefs off his left hip.

She gasped and got all teary-eyed. "Oh, Dante. It's perfect."

The name Kahoa, underlined and twined with manly *maile* vines and leaves, was written in lovely black copperplate with the capital K flowing outward with a long serif. The gracefully angled lower stem of the upright of the K was formed by the name Lani, the extended bottom serif of the fancy K was formed by the name Dom, and both rested where the flowing, twining leaves spelled Dante.

That word, that tattoo, said it all. She belonged to the Kahoas. The proof was recorded right there on Dante's tight little Hawaiian butt. She was the third side of a triangle, with Dom as the other, and Dante as the foundation.

"Happy now?"

"Yes, I believe I am. *Mahalo,* Dante."

He hiked up, tucked in, snapped, zipped, and belted, all of which she watched with pleasure. She carefully handed him his pack with its Pele's Tears cargo when he was ready.

"Whoa. You're not getting off that easily," he growled. "Show me yours."

"Ah. About that. I was pulling your chain. I don't have one yet because I'm too much of a coward to do it without you with me. Besides, I wanted to come back to Hawaii for it. You can help me choose what it might be, although I want it to be small. If you play your cards right, you can help me choose the location . . . and scope it out."

"Hmm. I'm thinking definitely ʻōkole, low enough that it just peeks out of a bikini bottom. Maybe an angel orchid or a hibiscus."

"Not sure about the orchid. Rosemary and I talked about an orchid tattoo. She said that in one of her gardening books it says that orchids symbolize beauty, charm, and refinement. Somehow, it doesn't fit me."

"I disagree, but Tutu also talked to me about a tattoo for you. She told me that in Egypt and other countries orchids were considered a love potion and aphrodisiac. At the very least, orchid tattoos are associated with sexuality and procreation. I'm thinking that suits you very well."

"Not that you've done research or anything?"

"Not as much as I intend to do. Hands on. With you."

"Bring it on, Kahoa."

Then she couldn't resist patting him lightly and lovingly on his tattoo as they went down the stairs side by side.

EPILOGUE

She and Dante sat on the tailgate of his truck at an overlook on the western side of the island. It had been a clear day, perfect conditions with no clouds and no haze, and Dante was determined that this was the sunset where she would see a green flash. The sun was fast sinking into the Pacific. She looked away from it, keeping its setting motion in her peripheral vision until the last moment, just as he had told her to do.

Things had calmed down a little for them. They had put out feelers to local jewelry artists about their olivine and hired an agent to sell Pele's Tears on their behalf, determined to put the gems "away from loved ones" totally, completely, and finally.

Their sale would certainly help Lehua survive. Their diamond had been described as a flawless D or E Colorless; their sapphire was a Cashmere, a pure, intensive blue with a velvety sheen; and their ruby was a Burmese red and quite rare in its size.

And their relationship was thriving as they discovered more and more about each other as adult male and female. She now wore a solitaire diamond set in a plumeria band on her left hand. They had fully intended to take it slow. But one soft tropical night, they leapfrogged over the getting-to-know-you stage right to the engaged stage — and all it entailed. Memories of that magical night and those that continued to follow made her weak in the knees and red in the face. She grew lightheaded when she recalled the look on his face and in his eyes when he told her he had something special planned for the meditation platform at the overlook.

"So Rosemary would be happy about us?" she asked, not looking away from the place in the sky he'd told her to look.

"About us and for us. She said something to me a few days before she died that left me speechless for a good ten minutes."

Speechless herself for a moment, she was excited and fearful at the same time. "What was it?"

"She said, 'I wonder when you two will get around to admitting you're meant for each other. You've always had a special bond between you, and I've prayed it would blossom into something more. The only caution

I'd give you is that you give yourselves time — and keep your heads while you shift from friendship to love *and* friendship. It won't be easy.' And she rounded it off by giving me one of her looks, the one that said 'Don't disappoint me!' And I don't think we have."

"Oh, Dante! She gave us her blessing."

"She certainly did. Now get ready," Dante said, squeezing her hand and guiding her attention back to the horizon. "Look now," he whispered.

The very top of the sun's disk was slipping below the horizon. A millisecond splash of intense emerald light was there and gone in the blink of an eye. Before she could even react, she was doubly blessed. The green flash was followed by a blue flash afterglow.

Then she gasped as she felt tears on her cheeks and buried her head against Dante's shoulder.

"My first blue flash in all my years of watching!" He gave a delighted whoop.

When she could speak, she shared something with him that she remembered the moment after she saw the flashes. "Rosemary quoted something to me years ago when I'd missed yet another green flash. Jules Verne described the green flash in

1882 like this. '. . . If there is a green in Paradise, it cannot be but of this shade, which most surely is the true green of Hope.' I told her at the time that he must have been talking about Lehua."

"And she probably agreed because I know I do," he said and wrapped her in his arms.

ABOUT THE AUTHOR

Sharon K. Garner, who enjoys writing stories about love and danger set in exotic locations, says she writes so she can grab all the great comebacks that sometimes elude her in real life, although she claims she snags her fair share. A former library cataloguer and newspaper proofreader, she keeps her hand in through freelance copyediting and proofreading for other writers. In her free time, she reads English mysteries and regularly prances around her living room doing walk aerobics.

The employees of Thorndike Press hope you have enjoyed this Large Print book. All our Thorndike, Wheeler, and Kennebec Large Print titles are designed for easy reading, and all our books are made to last. Other Thorndike Press Large Print books are available at your library, through selected bookstores, or directly from us.

For information about titles, please call:
(800) 223-1244

or visit our Web site at:
http://gale.cengage.com/thorndike

To share your comments, please write:
Publisher
Thorndike Press
10 Water St., Suite 310
Waterville, ME 04901